'TIL
GRIM'S
LIGHT

A GRIM AWAKENING NOVEL
BOOK TWO
MICHELLE GROSS

'TIL GRIM'S LIGHT

Melanie met the monster she feared most and survived—but at a cost.

A life was lost. And one became two.

Now that Killian was no longer Grim Reaper; he was back to being an incubus demon. And if waiting for demons to attack weren't enough on a girl, being around him while his pheromones were slipping—planting dirty thoughts inside her head—was enough to make anyone question their sanity.

But her dirty mind and trying to stay alive weren't the only thing she had to worry about. The Vessel had awakened inside her. She needed to figure out what it was and why there was suddenly a voice inside her head.

Soon, Melanie was questioning everything, wondering… all the while spiraling down a path toward Grim and Killian, discovering her own feelings.

Then came the question: What if they were wrong about the Vessel?

Dear Readers,

When I first started writing Melanie's story, I always knew I wanted it to be dark, touch base with some things that might make people feel uncomfortable. I even considered writing it differently, but that thought lasted all of one second. So, I wrote it exactly how I wanted to.

Which is why I'm writing this short letter to you all.

For the most part, I don't think this story is dark—at times, yeah. I liked to think it's filled with adventure and epic love (in the making), while adding all the cheesy and swoon worthy weirdness that I love.

I wanted Melanie to be real. I wanted her to question things—herself and make mistakes and continue to do so because let's face it: We all made stupid choices at some point in our lives and I'm pretty sure I still do on a regular basis.

Let's just say the story is different—unique, while having all the qualities we love: action, romance, horrible bad guys, and sexy hunks that want to keep you safe.

Read this book with an open mind—again, this is not everyone's cup of tea.

It's best to leave that pesky thing we call reality somewhere else and dive on in.

Thanks for reading,

Michelle Gross

PROLOGUE

Almost three thousand years ago in the depths of the Underworld...

I rubbed my hands together, anticipation coating my forehead. What the bloody hell was going on? The moment I stepped through the portal and entered the City of the Dead I knew something big was happening. The place was a giant ball of excitement. The streets were crowded and jammed, demons traveled the streets of every kind. My own emotions were tapping into everyone's, making me skittish. Someone—or thing bumped and slapped into my back. I whirled around to see what it was.

Banshee.

Lovely creature, she was. My demon traits kicked in the moment my eyes found the exposed top of her cleavage. Her green eyes caught me staring and an appreciated smile swept over her face. I tipped my head back with a smirk. My body drummed with excitement—the need my body required seemed to flare to life as my gaze dropped down to the curve of her hips leading to her backside.

"Incubus demon." Her eyes studied me with curiosity. It was no surprise. All females knew of incubus demons. Some loved us, some hated us. It was all according on how an incubus used their power of seduction.

"What gave it away?" I didn't have to see my face to know that my eyes had turned liquid black. I leaned closer, the busy street rustled around us, but my instinct was now focused on her. Desire rushed through my veins, the need to fuck her, not know her became my priority. I couldn't even remember the reason I came to the city. She bumped into me by mistake, but now she knew just as well as I, we were leaving together.

"Oh, I'm not sure." She pretended to be thinking, tilting her neck to the side. "You mean the fact that the enticing scent of sex you carry on your skin isn't enough to prove what you are? All incubi are easy to spot, just look for the most sexually charged men in the city that are handsome and built like a sex god." She gave me an appreciative glance from head to toe before she grabbed my belt buckle and looped a finger into my jeans. I gave her a sinful smile. She knew she was playing with fire but she didn't care. She wanted what only an incubus demon could give. Wicked, hot sex.

"Say, incubus, are you going to appear in my dreams tonight?" she purred, sounding hopeful. Incubus demons could do either one of two things. Slip into a person's dreams and steal

10

from their pleasure there or go about it the ole' natural way. Fucking. I was always for the second, to me, it always felt wrong to invade someone's dreams.

"I don't do the dream world, banshee. I like to be hands on." She liked my answer from the slight increase of her breathing. A sick knot twisted in my stomach as a wave of need flared in my loins. The battle of not wanting to do something and needing to crashed into me. I hated what I was.

Every day I lived as a sex demon was a curse.

Being a sex junkie wasn't all it was cracked up to be. It was fun at first, don't get me wrong. The release was always good but after a while, it just wasn't anymore. When I realized I stopped doing something because I wanted to, and instead did it because of my genetics, took the fun right out of it.

Even now, as the wave of both pleasure and need hit me, I only felt numb... but it wasn't something I could ignore.

No.

Incubi craved—needed the pleasure of sex. Hence, why I called us sex junkies. It was impossible to ignore a female. It was a torment, a sick, conflicting emotion that I would never be able to control. Incubi could never fall in love. It was impossible to be with just one female. Our train of thought would never let us focus on just one.

Thirty years of life and I was starting to accept the fact that I would always be alone. Never alone in bed but that wasn't the alone I meant. The loneliness that crept into my chest. That empty ache that would stay there because no one would ever be able to get close enough to reach it.

"He's here!" Voices echoed through the streets, demons pushed and shoved. I was being bumped and smacked into more than I could stand. I was too big for anyone to move me in their hurry, but my eyes still flared every time I was touched.

"What the hell is going on?" I muttered as I raked my hand through my hair in aggravation. I watched as everyone scattered toward the middle of the city.

"Oh, you don't know?" the banshee asked, surprised. I gave her an impatient glare for her to give me an explanation when she just stood there. "Some powerful entity entered the city. Rumors say he has come to find a demon to merge with."

I turned myself around to where the demons gathered and waited. An entity? Powerful beings, each made for a certain purpose. I moved forward, going with the crowd, suddenly interested. Compelled to get a look for myself. I had never seen one before and most of the time, you didn't want to come across one. But, if one was searching for another half to make him whole… that was worth checking out.

I pushed through demons of all sorts, it was shoulder to

12

shoulder—or tentacle—or worse, it was all according to what I bumped into. Before I reached the opened, circular part of the street to see what all the fuss was about, the city went silent. Everyone stopped and looked ahead in amazement. Murmurs, gasps, and awe's exploded around me.

Then it was like being hit with a heart attack, my heart screamed. My body surged head to toe with untamed energy, sparking a pulse of something knowing and new in me. I stood still for a second in the busy street. A pull, one that had me pushing and shoving through the demons—not caring that I was knocking some down. A tight squeeze clamped over my entire being. I clawed at my chest for air, the need I felt now was stronger than the need for sex.

I didn't even know why; I just knew I needed to be where everyone was staring. For the first time in my useless life, I felt a connection. Something was waiting for me. I felt it. I sensed it all throughout my body.

And finally, the opening came into view. I stepped on into where no one else would go. I stopped and simply looked at the entity several feet in front of me. Blue light, that of life, hummed around his tall skeleton frame. A black cloak wrapped around him and a hood rested over his skull. His clothes were even dark underneath the cloak. I liked his style. It felt like a reflection of my own dark soul, except I never wore a cloak.

Grim Reaper's eyeless sockets met mine as if he recognized me. That sense of knowing came to life in my chest, as if I somehow knew him too. I stared like the rest of the demons. His eyes never left mine.

I was struck with amazement. That was a normal reaction when seeing an entity such as Grim. He was known as the balancer. He balanced life and death. Good and bad. He was the symbol of death. He was *Death.* He stood as the most powerful besides that of God and Satan. He wasn't conceived; he was *made.*

He was an entity made by God. The other three entities were made by Satan.

And he was searching for a demon to merge with? It didn't seem possible. Demons spoke of him enough for me to know that he never merged with anyone. He had once tried in the past and never went through with it.

He stepped closer. My body hummed with excitement and power all over again. I took a step forward to meet him. Someway, somehow, I realized what had been wrong all my life. I was never born whole, but I finally would be. I relaxed some more and took another step. I never trembled in his presence—I welcomed it. I only felt like I was standing in the presence of myself that had been missing long before my birth.

"Grim Reaper," I called to him, knowing that I too would

go by that name.

His hand extended out between us, causing a ripple of shock through the demons.

"He's chosen someone to merge with!"

"And it's an incubus demon of all demons."

"I can't believe it!"

I heard the demons around us, but I ignored them all. I brought my hand out to his.

"Wait, Killian!" I recognized that voice and turned my head around to see Marcus running toward us.

"Marcus?" I squinted, confused. My thoughts were foggy with the need to become Grim.

"Don't do it," he pleaded. His blond hair fell out of his ponytail as he ran. Then as soon as his eyes left mine they went to Grim. "Merge with me instead. I am a far better choice. Killian doesn't have what it takes." I looked at my friend for more than ten years and glared. What the hell was he doing?

Marcus's hand latched onto Grim's already extended one. He gripped Grim's hand anxiously as he looked at him. Grim's skull swiveled around to look at Marcus. Something twisted in my gut, a nasty horrible feeling. Marcus was an incubus demon like I was. Would he choose him instead of me?

The thought didn't last.

Grim was here for me. I just knew.

Grim jerked his hand away from Marcus's. "Move demon, you're interrupting me." His eyeless expression went back to me. I stared back and knew everything about him felt right. This was right. Suddenly the chance to be something other than an incubus demon was possible. I would never be controlled by desire.

I moved my hand between us and Grim took it. "Two shall become one," he spoke. To me. To Marcus. To everyone.

Then cries erupted around us. I caught sight of another entity appearing next to us. The entity was frightening as he stepped in front of Marcus who was on his knees, crumbled up in anger. His face was red with rage.

But I could no longer focus on the two. My vision blurred when Grim tightened his hand. I felt his thoughts drifting into mine as my view of Marcus and the entity came back into focus.

I looked at the entity knowing exactly who he was.

Fear.

Grim's thoughts continued to echo into mine.

Enemy.

I was glaring at the entity before I even knew I was. Hatred rose up in my chest as I watched him. Fear offered his hand to Marcus. Something flickered in the depths of Marcus's eyes. A second later, he grabbed the clawed hand Fear offered.

I looked back to Grim who was waiting for me. He nodded as if to let me know what was happening.

Pain tore through my chest, slowly stretching out all over my body. I clenched my teeth but was unable to move my body or yell out in pain. We stood locked together by our hand as wave after wave of agony tore through my body.

After what felt like an endless torture, my body became slack and something told me that I needed to move into Grim. I listened to that instinct and stepped into Grim just as he did me.

Power like nothing I could have imagined before licked over my skin and teased me of what we—I now wielded.

I flexed my fingers and hands before straightening my shoulders and standing tall. A cocky smile played out on my face as I watched the demons' eyes travel over me. They had all witnessed the merge. My body left Grim's state and became flesh. I gave my hands another look of amazement. My smile only grew.

I was Killian: The Grim Reaper.

CHAPTER ONE

The cold blast of wind ruffled my hair out of place. A sign that fall was finally here. I let the wind chill me to the bone because I felt numb anyway. Next to me, Tess held my hand and squeezed tight, her eyes red and wet with tears. I gave her hand a gentle tug to let her know we still had each other. Not that it could help us right now. My own tears were dried out after three days of endless crying.

Today, I could barely feel a thing.

I glanced down at my black shirt and dress pants, the only thing I owned that seemed fitting to wear to a funeral. My eyes were on the preacher. I saw his mouth move, but I couldn't hear a thing he was saying. There was more crying next to me. It was Tess or her mom. Or both. I didn't know. I wouldn't look.

I could only stare at the closed coffin. If only I could talk to him one more time... I would tell him how much he always meant to me before things got crazy.

The preacher must have finished up because people began

to walk up to the coffin. They would place a single rose or flower of some sort on his coffin. Some would say something comforting and others would rub their hands across the coffin as if they were touching his body for the last time.

Tess released my hand and walked forth, her face crumbled with grief as she lay a single white rose on the coffin. She gazed down at the coffin. A smile crept against her lips for a moment like she was suddenly remembering something happy before it turned to tears.

I looked away, it was too much. I felt my own emotions threatening to come to life.

I never walked up to the coffin. I just kept telling myself it didn't matter now. He was already dead. What I thought now didn't matter because he would never know.

It wasn't until the coffin lowered and Ryan's body sunk to the ground that I fully grasped the loss of losing him. I grabbed my neck, unable to breathe as all the emotions came back full force. I inhaled and the tears fell like a waterfall.

Ryan was dead. It wasn't real. *Yes, it was.*

And it was all my fault.

All because I was Melanie Rose. I saw ghosts because Fear—a powerful entity—marked me as a child so that my soul would belong to him when I died. All because I carried the Vessel inside of me. A power I still knew nothing about. Then there was Killian. Grim freaking Reaper who stormed into my life claiming to protect me and turned my whole world upside down. Now because of Fear, Killian and Grim were no longer one person but two. My brain was still trying to wrap around that one.

I hadn't seen or heard from either of them since the night Grim dropped me off, which was four nights ago. I showered that night and went to bed beaten and bruised with four hideous claw marks slashed across my chest.

Only when I woke, the marks were gone. So were the rest of my aches and pains. Which meant Grim had come back some time that night to heal me while I was sleeping. A part of me had hoped it was Killian that healed me but that wasn't possible. He was barely breathing when we left him.

But, I didn't get a chance to wonder about those two before I woke to a phone call that would change everything. Ryan Jones. My best friend—secret crush since the day Fear attacked me when I was nine, died.

I never said a word at his funeral. Even now, on the drive home, I was speechless. Even Alex chose not to speak. Mom was the one that finally broke the silence. "He's in a better place now." And wasn't that what they all say? I clenched my fists. I stared out of the window as the trees and mountains went by in a blur. The green of summer was gone, replaced with the many shades of fall.

20

He was supposed to be alive. I should have been the one they buried today. Bitterness rose up in my chest at how horrible everything turned out. Life wasn't fair and it was continuing to show me just how unfair it could be.

The day was slow. Mom forced me to eat soup she made. It was tasteless. I knew it had nothing to do with her cooking and everything to do with my emotions. I spent the day locked away in my bedroom unless I had to go to the bathroom. When I had nothing else, I slid out the small trunk underneath the bed. It held all my photos.

If I was going to depress myself even more, I might as well do it the right way. And that was to stare at every goofy grin I had of him in my albums. There was a lot. Many of the three of us together—I stuck to Tess and Ryan like glue. Some of just me and him. Tess and him. I had a lot of just him caught off guard or smiling at me through the lens. I had some of him at the football field and one from Deb's diner.

I sighed. He was the sweetest, most fun-loving person I had ever met.

He was one of those guys that couldn't be ignored. His playful attitude may have been the only thing that has kept me going all these years. I sniffed and watched as a single tear fell on the photo I was holding. I wiped my face and stood up, leaving the photos a mess on the floor.

A whistle rang out in the room. I moved my head around to search the room but there was nothing. I grabbed my ears and shook my head.

I took a shower and when I came out, I was even more tired than I was before I went in. It was never easy for me to fall asleep, but I was already begging sleep to take me as I shut my bedroom door behind me. My body literally felt like it was shutting down, I was so exhausted.

I opened my towel and let it fall to the floor. I slipped into my black t-shirt and pink pajama pants. It took a lot of effort to pull down the cover and crawl into the warmth of my bed.

Ah. It felt good, though. I just knew I was going to get some sleep tonight. I couldn't even hold my eyes open.

Or so I thought...*Sleep, Melanie!*

My body had a way of doing the opposite it was supposed to. I was stupid for thinking my exhaustion was enough to keep my brain from thinking. It had that insane ability to keep itself awake no matter what. It wasn't until my feet hit the floor that my body would remind itself of all the sleep it never got.

I opened my eyes and sighed. I hated laying down at night. When the lights went off, the house grew quiet, nothing but the lamp on my nightstand on because I was too afraid to ever sleep in the dark. Or sleep, for that matter, but that hadn't been the case when Killian was around...

Since Grim tossed me on the bed the other night and left without a word, my thoughts always wandered back to Killian. No matter how much I tried not to. His face lit up like a picture in my mind. His smile—the one that wasn't his usual cocky or know-it-all smirk—played out the moment my eyes shut every night. Dark dreamy eyes and messy hair that made you want to run your hands through it... all the things that once made me afraid of him became my nightly visual.

My heart twisted in my chest as if it were breaking every time I thought of him dying while Grim left him there to take me to safety. The only thing that made it bearable was some part of me believed that he was okay.

I had to believe he was okay. And that scared me the most.

Which meant I was so screwed. Because a part of me, a huge part, couldn't get him out of my head. Even when I should be thinking of Ryan—grieving his loss—my mind would wander back to Killian. Which was absurd and crazy. Killian was something else entirely.

I shouldn't be thinking about the way his mouth moved and curved sinfully every time he spoke. I shouldn't be thinking about the way his eyes went all scary and a shade darker every time he got angry or excited. Or the way his body was a weapon itself and could break me in two. And the way he tensed when he was around me.

I thought back to the two weeks he came into my life. Somehow his presence changed me completely. All the things I once thought were so terrifying about him when we first met were what kept me up all night. That and extreme guilt. Because no matter how much Ryan meant to me and what happened to him— it still couldn't keep me from thinking of him.

And that made me so angry. Killian was clouded with mystery. Vengeance tore at my feelings when he told me that Killian was after the Vessel. It didn't make sense, though. Why wouldn't he take it sooner if that was his plan?

And it had been four nights and three days—not that I was keeping count for that reason, and he had yet to magically appear like he always did before. I was still in danger. The Vessel was still a part of me. Which meant demons would still come for me.

What did it mean for me now that Grim and Killian were no longer one person? Heck, I was still confused by it. Would Killian no longer protect me? Would Grim? It scared me when I thought back to the way Fear provoked Grim using me. I didn't really understand it, but Grim seemed upset with me when he left me the other night.

Fear would come for me again. It was only a matter of time.

A shiver ran through me at the thought of him. Not just fear of him, but disgust.

24

"Wow, Melanie. You have a lot of pictures of me with my shirt off. I didn't know you secretly liked to see my chest. Well, I kind of did. That's why I took it off so much."

I raised up on the bed, twisting my head around to the direction of the voice. Shock. Joy. Relief. All these emotions hit me so hard I felt dizzy.

"Ryan?" I whispered his name in amazement.

CHAPTER TWO

I blinked several times to make sure I was seeing right. It was dark, but I knew my eyes couldn't be wrong. Ryan was next to my bed. There was a playful tug at his smile that warmed my chest for the first time in days. "Didn't think you would be seeing me again?"

Did he not realize he was making a casual comment about his own death?

The worst part was seeing him like this… I glanced down at the blue hospital gown he wore. Metal rods hung out of both of his legs, attached to his bones from his surgery before he died. They were twisted at an odd angle, almost dangly-like. My throat tightened.

I couldn't believe he was here.

I felt my eyes prick with tears—tears of happiness as I jumped out of the bed to hug him. I practically leaped, which was the bad part because instead of happily embracing him with a hug, I went straight through him. I managed to catch myself before I smacked into my window, or worse, went through it.

Then came the crushing realization that I already knew but never thought of its actual meaning until now. Ryan was a ghost.

"That felt...*weird.*" He turned around to face me, rubbing his chest. I moved away from the window.

The feel-goods of seeing him were gone as guilt struck me. "Ryan." I shook my head, not brave enough to meet his eyes. "This is all my fault." I clenched and unclenched my fists.

"What is?" he asked, taking a step forward. His foot floated along with him awkwardly, but he had no limp.

"You're a ghost," I pointed out.

"Yeah, I kind of figured that out on my own, Melanie." I just stared at him confused. Why wasn't he angry or upset?

"Don't you think you're taking this rather well for someone that died and became a ghost?" I moved closer, staring down every inch of him. His face was paler. He had visible dark circles under his eyes now—that all ghosts had. I reached my hand to touch his that rested on his chest, like before, I went straight through.

"Will you stop touching me?" he grunted and even moved away from me. I dropped my hand and he added, "You are awfully touchy for someone that's supposed to be afraid of ghosts."

"Well," I sighed. "I never had someone I care about die

and come back as one either." His lips tilted upward slightly into a smile—a sad one. "This should have never happened to you," I whispered. My voice was slightly warped with the tears I wouldn't let spill. It didn't matter how much I tried to hold in my tears, the crybaby in me always managed to get out. I cleared my throat before asking, "When you wrecked…how did it happen? Do you remember?"

He squinted his eyes as he sighed and dropped his hand from his chest. "I was rushing to your house when I saw a young girl in the road. I swerved my truck to miss her, but the thing was… it was like she wasn't there to begin with. At that point, everything went to hell, my truck wouldn't let me do anything. My brakes stopped working, the gas sped up, my wheel wouldn't turn any direction. I knew I was fucked, but it was like watching a horror movie unfold. Only it was my ending and I could only stare the few seconds it took for me to hit the cliff."

I didn't know why I asked now. I already knew it had been Fear's work but after hearing what he went through… I felt sick. "It was Fear." I hurried the words out quickly to let the truth be known.

"I didn't think nothing of it when it happened. Kind of didn't get the chance, but I figured that much out…" His words faded for a second before he added, "There was never anyone in the road and the way my truck," he shook his head, "yeah, I think it had something to do with the demons after you."

I went past him, heading toward the bed. Only as I did, he followed my movement by circling around as I did. I gave him a funny look. "What are you doing?"

He placed his hands behind him, a weird gesture that had me arching my eyebrow at him before he grinned. "I'm in a hospital gown, Melanie. I think it's safe to say my white ass is hanging out. I was only saving you the trouble of getting embarrassed or having the displeasure of seeing."

I couldn't help it, I laughed. His sense of humor was still intact even as a ghost. It eased some of the tension I was feeling. I was still smiling when I realized this wouldn't last forever. That smile slowly vanished. "Ryan." The heavy way I spoke his name caused him to stiffen. "I never thought I would see you again. I'm glad, but you being here as a ghost isn't good for you. I don't want you to be like all the other ghosts I see. Did you run from Grim?" I asked, softly.

He gave me a confused look. "What are you talking about?" he asked. He puffed his chest as he spoke the rest, "I never saw him, and I wouldn't have run if I had." His eyes slanted in anger.

His anger didn't faze me, though the fact that Grim never came for him did. "When you died, Grim or another Reaper should have been there to ascend you to Heaven." I didn't say—

29

or descend you to hell because I knew Ryan didn't belong there.

He gave me a wide-eyed look. "No. I was standing in the hospital earlier, and it didn't take me long to realize I was a ghost. So, the first person I thought to go to was you."

That wasn't possible. I knew I probably looked surprised to him. "What do you mean? Ryan… you died three mornings ago."

He tilted his head at me, almost like he found it hard to believe me. He placed his hand on his head before saying, "Are you sure?"

I nodded. "You were buried today! It was the worst day of my life. It's not something I can forget." I couldn't help that I was slightly yelling.

How did he not know he died until now? Something didn't make sense… or more like, where had he been the past three days for him to only pop up now?

"Easy there." He placed his hand in front of him, in surrender. "I'm sorry. I can only imagine what it must have been like for you and Tess." He dropped his hands and looked down. "If… I would have lost one of you guys this way," he sighed and closed his eyes. "I couldn't imagine."

I rubbed my forehead and nodded. "Try to think, Ryan, where have you been the last three days?" I asked.

He closed his eyes, reopened them, and looked around as if he were thinking before he finally let out a frustrated groan. "Nothing. I remember the wreck and when I came to as a ghost, I was just standing in the hallway at the hospital."

"That doesn't make any sense," I told him, rubbing my forehead to ease the headache that was approaching. "Maybe, some ghosts forget or just come to be a ghost differently." I sounded hopeful.

He shrugged his shoulders like he didn't really care. I pinched the bridge of my nose and sighed. Same ole' Ryan even after death. I couldn't ignore the fact that I felt happy he was here. I never thought I'd get the chance to speak to him again.

"What are you going to do?" I asked him.

"What do you mean?"

"I mean." I made an open gesture with my arms then pointed at him. "You're a ghost, Ryan. You're not supposed to be here."

His gaze traveled over me slowly, surely before he replied. "I'm not going anywhere until I know that you're safe."

I gave him a ridiculous look to let him know how crazy he sounded. "You lost your life and you still worry about me?" I crossed my arms and arched my eyebrows at him. "You're a ghost now. What do you plan to do that's going to help me?" My words

31

held a teasing note in them, but I was still serious all the same.

He moved beside my nightstand and brought his hand to the alarm clock. When he tried to pick it up, his hand went through it. He squinted his eyes at the clock and tried again. Again. And again. He looked to me with determination in his eyes. "I'm new at this. Give me some time and I'll be a pro at the whole ghost thing." To make his point, he kept trying over and over until finally, the clock moved barely an inch. No, not even that but his eyes lit up anyway. "Yes!" He pumped his fist in the air excitedly.

I groaned before slapping my hand over my face. "You're killing me."

"So." Ryan dropped his hand. "Where is Grim Reaper anyway?" His playful tone disappeared and became serious.

"I don't know. I willingly went to Fear and Grim rescued me, but I haven't seen him since." I replied and his eyes grew wide.

"Excuse me, *willingly?*" His voice dropped even lower, and I realized I shouldn't have told him that part. His face that was once shocked when I told him, looked at me in horror. "Melanie, why   the—"

I cut him off. "My mom was going to be in the same situation you were in if I didn't make that choice. So, whatever crap you are about to give me, don't. I made my choice and I

32

would do it again." I felt sure of myself as I said it. I really would make the same decision if I had to.

After a few seconds, he finally dropped his shoulders and sighed. "I'm sorry. So, what happened?"

How in the world was I supposed to explain to him what happened there and what I saw? I rubbed my palm over my face. "It's hard to explain. Fear is an entity like Grim and he's the one that's been sending all these other demons after me. If it weren't for Killian—" I paused— "or, Grim, who knows what would have happened to me. They saved me."

Ryan's eyebrows went together. "They?" he said.

That was the confusing part. "Yeah, Killian and Grim split. They are now two people. As in, no longer the same person." He must of knew I was about to continue when he brought his hands up to stop me.

"Stop, I get it." He shook his head and sighed. There was a lot sighing going on in this bedroom tonight. "Wait, not really sure I do. He split?" I would have found it hard to believe myself if I hadn't seen it happen.

I moved on my bed and opened the drawer of my nightstand pulling out a notebook. I flipped it open quickly and ripped out a page. I held up the paper in the air in front of me and looked to Ryan. "Yes. As in, Killian and Grim who were one person, aren't anymore." I ripped the paper in half. "Killian is one person." I wiggled one of the ripped papers. "Grim is another." I, then, wiggled the other one.

He rolled his eyes. "I understood the first time. I didn't need the demonstration." There was another sigh before he added, "Demons are so messed up." I simply nodded, not entirely sure what I thought of it either.

"I should try to get some sleep." I wasn't sure how long I could sleep but I needed to at least try.

At the mention of sleep, he wondered, "Hmm, do ghosts still sleep?" I didn't know if he was asking me or himself, so I didn't reply.

"Where are you going?" I asked.

He shrugged his shoulders. "I guess I'll stay here."

"I don't think so," I added quickly.

That made him grin. "Why? Are you afraid I might do something to you in your sleep?"

This time, I was the one that wore the bigger grin. "Go ahead and try."

Needless to say, I thought I won that round of verbal battle.

CHAPTER THREE

It took a moment to remember everything that happened the night before when I first woke. My mind was still foggy with what little sleep I did get. My alarm clock was blaring, which meant it was a weekday... that meant school. I hadn't been there since Vengeance paraded around the cafeteria with his puppets and fought with Grim. Now that it was time to go back, I was nervous. Grim had taken us out of the cafeteria that day, meaning, we just disappeared in front of everyone. Even though they couldn't have seen him, they still saw me. Had anyone witnessed me vanishing out of nowhere?

That was the worry.

I hoped that whatever Vengeance had done to them hadn't left them time to notice. Tess never noticed and I had been with her the past three days... so, I felt calmer the more I thought about it. I grumbled and tossed the covers on the floor as I dropped my feet down, starting my morning routine.

First things first, I needed to pee so I waddled to the bathroom. I turned on the light switch and shut the door behind me. I pulled down my pants and my butt was starting its hover over the toilet when I heard him say, "the lid's still down." My eyes flew open at Ryan's voice, and I gave a girly squeal before I lifted my butt up in a hurry and pulled my pants back up. I glared at him.

I no longer felt sleepy now.

"Ryan!" I hissed.

His head was the only thing visible through the closed door, and he blinked his eyes a few times innocently like he could do no wrong. I swear I could strangle him if he wasn't dead already. "Yes?" he said, oh so pleasantly.

"Get your head out of the door, it's weird!" I yelled before shaking my head. No, that wasn't all that was wrong with this situation. "And don't come in the bathroom when I'm using it."

"But you were about to go all over the toilet lid." His hands went through the door so that he could point. I looked down at the toilet. The lid was down. I bit my bottom lip in aggravation before I groaned. I wanted to smack him, but I couldn't help that I was braindead in the mornings. Lack of sleep and ghosts—demons—this thing called my life, did that do a girl.

36

Now I had Ryan as a ghost to make matters worse who was peeking at me through a door.

"I see that." I stopped being snooty and frowned. "Seriously, Ryan, what are you doing? Shouldn't you go see your family and check on them? Not peek at me?"

That stupid grin of his that I adored so much, disappeared. I hated to see it fade at the mention of his family. "I did."

Silence filled the room. I was surprised, I guess he didn't stay here all night after all. "Oh?" was all I managed to say.

"Yeah." Then that frown disappeared and he perked up quickly, but it was unnatural and forced. "I'll step outside so you can do your business." And his head disappeared back through the other side of the door. "Raise the lid, okay?" I could hear the grin in his voice when he spoke through the door.

I smiled for a moment until I remembered his expression. What had he seen at his house that made his smile disappear?

––––––––

It was weird seeing Tess drive her white Mustang to school. She would always drive with her brother in his truck, another example of how close the two of them were. It was already parked when I arrived, and I felt that awful lump form in my throat at how different everything would be from now on. She never drove it much but now she would have to.

Ryan was always her protective big brother—by only a few minutes. He always looked out for her. Now that he was gone… who would be there for her as she sat alone in that empty house? That made me wonder if her parents were still home or were things already back to normal. Was she already being left alone?

I parked my Ford Focus, stepped out, and walked up the path to the school entrance. I stopped and had to do a double-take at the tree by the school. My heart went out of rhythm, a few feet away from the apple tree was a table, and at the table sat Fred. I just stared at him a moment. That moment lasted too long and he caught me looking, but I couldn't get myself to care like I always did before.

What did that mean? Grim really wasn't around…Fred wouldn't be here if he were, right?

He finally stopped staring at me and hopped off the table. He began to chase around girls. Things were back to normal.

I felt a nervous trickle moving into my stomach. I was feeling scared. What if he wasn't going to protect me anymore? What if he decided I wasn't worth the trouble? Or some other reason. My stomach bottomed out.

Oh, God.

I secretly hoped that he was still around protecting me, just not showing himself. Now I knew he wasn't. What was I more upset about? The fact that he stopped protecting me or the fact that I might not see Killian again? My thoughts were in turmoil. I grabbed my head and willed myself to calm down.

But my thoughts grew darker. What if Killian didn't survive like I hoped? No normal person could have survived that kind of chest wound.

Or, maybe it wasn't even that. Maybe it was because I so easily pushed him away when Vengeance's puppets had gotten inside my head. Or how I pushed him away even before that, when I stopped whatever was happening between us when Ryan got hurt. I didn't know anything, but I kept wanting to believe there was something between us. Something amazing. But I stopped it from happening and I doubted him over and over again.

"So, that's Fred." Ryan appeared beside me, and I jumped out of my thoughts, startled. He was getting good at the whole ghost thing. I rubbed my chest to calm my heart. I saw the disgusted look on Ryan's face as Fred stood in front of a girl, staring down her shirt. He shook his head. "What a creep." I nodded in agreement.

I saw him move in the corner of my eye and turned to face him. "Also, Tess had a rough night. I think she's been arguing with Mike."

I held my hand up before he could say anymore. I already knew what he was trying to say and I smiled. "Don't worry, I will

39

talk to her." He gave me a lopsided smile in return. Then I realized people were staring at me as they walked inside. I was openly talking to him out in the open, of course, I was going to get a few curious glances. I hid my face and stepped away from him, only to stop when I figured that was just as odd. I raised my head. "Now stop talking to me," I whispered.

I tried my best to act casual and normal as best as I could. I hurried up the steps and went inside.

It was almost time for the first bell to ring so I quickly looked for Tess in the hallway. It didn't take me long. I found her right in the open, standing in front of the bulletin board outside of the principal's office. I slowed my steps as I walked toward her and eyed the board on the wall she was so focused on. The entire board was made for Ryan. It was a memorial of him.

There were all kinds of pictures of him with friends, the football team, teachers—with everyone, doing anything and everything. He was just that outgoing. Encouraging words were written above the pictures. 'In Memory of Ryan Jones', there were words of missing him, going on about how amazing he was, and how much everyone would miss him, which was the truth. I wasn't the only one that adored him. The whole school had loved him—the entire town was grieving. That was the way it was in a small town, everyone knew everyone and everything about you, but in return, they cared just the same.

I stopped when I was next to her. Her face was stiff, eyes red from crying. I bumped my shoulder into hers, so she knew I was there. She looked up and smiled, it was sad but still a smile. It just showed how much courage and strength it took for her to come to school today, knowing that all of this would be waiting for her.

"Hey, Tess." Jim, a guy on the football team grabbed Tess's shoulder as he walked by. "I'm sorry about your brother. He was a great guy. I'm going to miss playing with him on the field." And he trailed on down the hall. She barely nodded, holding her lips together tightly.

On my other side, there was Ryan who just stepped up to see the board. I turned just enough so that I can see him. He looked conflicted with so many emotions—just what was he thinking? He tilted his head at me. He brought his mouth up into a smile, but I could see that it was forced. Then he saw his sister.

Another person came to Tess at that time, it was Stephanie, someone Ryan used to date. She was already crying when she went to Tess. She hiccupped before saying, "I can't believe he's gone." Tess looked down, around, and wouldn't meet her eyes.

It only got worse, people steadily approached her about Ryan. Girls were crying *everywhere,* literally. Ryan had that way about him and as the girls approached the board, they would tear up but wouldn't approach Tess. A lot of them didn't like Tess and she didn't care for them either.

She needed away from the board, people kept coming and I could see that Tess was at her breaking point. I heard Ryan swear before he said, "Just tell her I'm here." I turned around and gave him a horrid look. Was he crazy? Tess knew I could see ghosts, but it was one of those things where I didn't know if she actually believed me or just went along with it.

"Let's go." I grabbed Tess's arm just as the bell rung. I heard her sigh in relief, and we went to class.

Ryan had been right. Something was still off between Tess and Mike. At lunch, we sat alone. I watched as she stared at her tray for a long time before she finally tore off a piece of cornbread and placed it in her mouth. I made myself eat as well. I looked at the football players until I found Mike. I caught him glancing our way until he saw that I was staring and looked away.

"Do you want to talk about it?" I knew she would know what I talking about when I asked.

She sighed. "What's to talk about? He cheated on my ass with Haley." My eyes found Haley sitting with the cheerleaders. She was laughing about something, all cutesy as she tossed her hair over her shoulder. How did some girls look beautiful while doing everything? "Stupid whore," Tess muttered as she glared in her direction. I didn't care for her either. Haley had made it her

42

lifelong mission to point out how different I was from everyone else over the years.

I took a bite of my food. "How do you know?"

She looked into the distance several seconds before finally shrugging her shoulders. "He never denied it," she said casually as if it didn't bother her, but I knew better.

I placed my fork down and took a deep breath. "Maybe there's more to it than that." I sounded hopeful. I knew it wasn't the right thing to say when she gave me a moronic look. I frowned looking down at my plate. If Mike had cheated on Tess, then that meant the puppets were telling the truth. Which meant what they were saying about Killian…

I shook the thoughts away immediately, afraid of them.

"He hasn't talked to me since our fight. If he wasn't guilty, why does he keep avoiding me?" she said, looking his way. Wasn't that something all couples did, though? No one wanted to be the one that caved first.

———

After school, I picked up Alex and we went home. Mom was—as usual—crawling out of bed when we walked through the front door. She yawned as she slid her feet across the floor still half asleep and gave us a smile as we entered. She made her way to the window beside the front door and looked outside. Her hair was a tangled mess as she scratched her head and slid the curtain open. She stepped away from it a moment later, rubbing her arms. "Seems like fall is finally here."

"Yeah," I answered as I climbed the stairs to disappear into my bedroom. Alex went toward the kitchen.

Once I was at the top, she asked, "Do you guys want to eat out tonight?" I knew it was her way of trying to comfort all of us after Ryan passing away, but I didn't have it in me to go anywhere. I just wanted to disappear into my room. I shrugged my shoulders and hurried to my room.

———

The next day, I was amazed that everything felt so *normal* despite the fact that Ryan had just died. The ghosts were back. Fred was as charming as *never.* The prom couple was back to making out at everyone's lockers. There weren't any signs of demons. It had been six days. I didn't know whether to be glad or worried.

If Ryan wasn't standing next to me—as a ghost— everything would have been like before my eighteenth birthday.

"What is it?" Ryan asked as he walked with me as I left fourth period.

I shrugged my shoulders. I checked to make sure no one was looking my way before I spoke to him. "It's just, everything's so…normal. I don't understand. I thought for sure Fear would already have them after me by now." I opened my locker and switched out my books.

"Maybe he's left you alone. Don't worry about it so much. It's a good thing, Melanie." His words were meant to comfort me, I know… I just didn't share his positive outlook. After meeting Fear, I knew he wasn't someone to just give up on something that he desperately wanted. He was planning something and I was afraid to know what. "What about Grim Reaper? Still no sign of him?" he asked.

I shook my head with a sigh. "No, and it's almost been a week now," I replied.

"Melanie?" Tess's questioning voice drifted behind us and I jumped. How long had she been behind me? Had she caught me talking to myself—err, not actually… but to her and everyone else that was always what it looked like. When I turned around she was giving me a funny look.

"Tess," I squeaked, "I didn't hear you behind me."

She arched her eyebrow at me. "Melanie, are you talking to them now?"

I laughed hysterically. "Ha, what? No." It was very apparent I didn't know how to lie when under pressure.

Ryan tossed his head back and groaned. "Melanie, will

you just tell her! It will make things so much easier."

I ignored him and turned back around to shut my locker. "Hey, are you okay?" she asked, opening her locker next to mine.

"Yeah, I'm fine. Just having a conversation with myself, everyone thinks I'm crazy anyway." I tried to laugh the whole thing off but I was doing a crap job.

She shut her locker after grabbing her book. "We still have each other, ya know?" She paused. "Even without my brother, I mean, I still have my best friend." She smiled.

I smiled back and grabbed her hand. "I know. I know." I felt a pang of guilt as the words fell from my lips. I still had her brother, for now.

———

Something was causing a ruckus in front of the school after my last period. Tess and I exchanged curious glances before following the others outside to see what was going on. I could feel the cold air as we got closer to the door and pulled my thin cardigan around me tighter as I pushed open the door. The frigid wind slapped me in the face as we stepped out.

The girls on the steps were giggling and whispering, pointing toward the road. My eyes followed—wanting to know what they were acting so girly about. But as I did, my heart did that crazy flip—fluttering in the stomach, and *oh-crap I'm being a girl* like the rest of them when I saw what the big deal was. No wonder he was catching everyone's attention; there he was propped up against a shiny and new black Corvette looking perfect and uninjured.

CHAPTER FOUR

Killian had his arms resting over his muscular chest. He leaned against the car—that looked tiny in comparison to him. He still had that alarming amount of danger emanating from him. I didn't know what it was that made it look so... lethal. Was it the dark eyebrows and how they furrowed together even when his expression was relaxed? It didn't seem to matter with the girls, they devoured him with their eyes as he waited... but his dark eyes found mine instantly and gave me a sexy-as-sin smile that left me grabbing my neck and trying hard not to blush.

Everyone seemed to turn at once to see who the mystery person was smiling at. I wished the eyes of others didn't make me want to disappear but it did. I only wanted to fade away under all these glances. "Isn't that the guy from the football game?" Tess asked.

I nodded. My nerves were dancing along my skin as I looked at him. A rush of relief, excitement, and happiness swept over me. He never made a move or gesture for me to come to him as he pushed himself off the car and turned around to open the passenger side door. He didn't even turn around to see if I was coming to him. He tapped his knuckles against the top of the car and waited as if he knew I would come.

"I see he's back." Ryan appeared next to me. I turned to see the scowl planted on his face as he looked at Killian. "Is he waiting for you?" he asked, but there was no way I could answer him with Tess standing next to me.

"I'm going to see what he wants," I told them both. I could see the shock on Tess's face before I started down the steps. I cut through the grass to get to him quicker. His leather jacket couldn't hide the muscles that defined his back. I stopped once I was standing behind him, his knuckles stopped tapping against the car, then a second later he was turning his body around to face me.

Crap.

I must have forgotten how good looking he was. Or maybe I just let myself ignore it, but my mind wasn't doing that anymore. His hair whipped back wildly from the wind—and matched the dark magic of his eyes. He was still the same guy. He was freakishly tall and *just* big—and imposing. I knew how thick those arms were underneath his jacket and that he had to be packing six or eight pack abs underneath that skintight, black t-shirt. His jaw line was sharp and chiseled to perfection. I shook my head. Why was I only noticing these things now? Or more like, why in general, was I letting myself swoon over him the moment he appeared in my life again?

But I couldn't ignore the way my body was appreciating every bit of him like he was setting a torch inside me. He was truly marvelous. I had every reason to be afraid of him when I first met him, but what should I feel now? I don't know, but I wasn't stupid. I knew that he was just as dangerous as he had always been, but those feelings were only doing the opposite to me now. A fire was starting in my stomach, dipping between my thighs the more I stood here letting myself stare at him.

A slow grin was spreading across his face as I finally lifted my eyes to meet his. He knew what I was doing, the grin said it all. I stopped drooling long enough to cross my arms over my chest. I was wearing one of my baggy t-shirts but even still, Killian's eyes drifted to my breasts as if I pushed them up for him to see. His gaze felt charged with heat or maybe it was just me, I didn't know. He just stared and I felt so out of character.

He wasn't hiding the way his eyes ran over me. They drifted down to my hips, thighs—over my long legs before finally going back up to my eyes. Something weird was happening here. My breath caught as his smoldering gaze drilled into me. He wasn't smiling. He wasn't even being playful…no, his face was warped with desire. I might be new to this, but I was standing in front of him, so that look was being directed at me.

My face was on fire and I knew my flaming cheeks were probably on full display. I looked away from him, not sure what was going on. Killian had a way of making me feel what no one else could, but this... this was different. I couldn't figure out why I was burning on the inside. I wanted him. The sexual tension had my brain foggy. He was my only focus.

What was wrong with me? I tried to concentrate on what I should say to him. I wasn't like this before, or at least I wasn't this way before I met him, was I? "I see you're still alive." I was glad my voice didn't seem to give away what was going on with my body in his presence.

"Ah." He tipped his head up. "I see you care so much," he replied to my harsh words. I hadn't meant for them to sound so care-*less*, but I was only trying to hide what I was feeling.

"What are you doing here? It's almost been a week and nothing's happened." I tried to play it off like I didn't need him anymore.

He glanced behind him as a car pulled out of the parking lot. A few people were still hanging around the school building. Some of them were still watching us. He turned back to me. "I came for you." There went the fluttering of my heart at those four simple words. "Come on, we can't talk here."

He grabbed my arm and hurried me into the opened passenger door. I looked up to him as my butt fell in the expensive leather seats. "My car, Killian," I tried to tell him.

"Leave it." He picked my legs up and placed them in the car before I could lift them up myself. He slammed the door shut and walked over to his side and got in. And there it was, my life was under his command. Or so it felt when he did everything for me.

I studied the inside of the car. I didn't even want to know how much it cost. "Where did you get this car?" I asked.

"I bought it." He started the engine.

I stared at him, confused. "You bought it?" I said flatly.

"Yeah, you know, with money, Melanie." He smirked at me.

"You never bothered with a car before," I mentioned.

"That was when I didn't need one. Thanks to Fear, now it comes in handy to have one." His fingers tightened around the steering wheel as he pulled out of the parking lot.

I didn't want to bring up what happened to him since it was sort of my fault—okay, entirely my fault, so I hesitated, "Are you and Grim…"

"Still separated? Yeah. That's why the car comes in handy, I can no longer fade out of time and port myself where I need to be." His eyes focused on the road as he spoke.

"Fade out of time?" My face squinted up. "Are you referring to that thing you do…" And if only I realized how lame that sounded before I said it.

His eyes light up with his smile. "Yes, that thing I do is fading." He was looking me in the eyes as he smirked. "And it means exactly how it sounds. When I—Grim teleports himself wherever he wants to be—he's fading out of time, literally. Time doesn't exist there. He's stepping out of existence—life, away from the human world and the Underworld. Do you remember what it looked like when you last went through it?"

I nodded immediately. It wasn't something I could ever forget. "Yeah, it was always the same. The dark came first, followed by the light." It wasn't exactly bright; it was just a light falling over the darkness.

He nodded, watching the road as he drove. "Exactly. The light is what lets you know you are entering back into a time flow. But I can't do that anymore… Right now, I'm just Killian—with no Grim." Something about the way his smile slipped and revealed his sadness…

"Is that why it took you so long to come back?" I asked and regretted the words as soon as they left my mouth. It sounded like I had been waiting…it sounded like I had been worried. Like I missed him. Check yes, check yes, check yes! Which was exactly what I didn't want him knowing.

His eyes left the road again and met mine, a curious gleam cast my way. I looked ahead quickly, focusing on the yellow line on the road instead of the intense feeling he was giving me. "Yeah, it took a while for my wound to heal completely. Once I healed, it took time to find a portal chip to enter the human world without Grim there." Soon we were passing the tiny town of Denver by as he drove us away. Just where was he taking us? "I'm sorry…," he said. I looked back at him and gave him a funny look and he added, "For taking so long to get back."

I didn't know how to answer, so I changed the subject entirely. "Where are you taking us?"

"Taking you to my home," was all he offered.

I gave him another confused look. "You have a home here now too?" I asked, surprised.

He smiled. "I had it already. I actually bought it when I first started protecting you…just never had a reason for it until now." His smile faded as he said the last part. What was it like for him? To no longer be Grim?

"There goes the neighborhood," I muttered cheekily and he grinned. But why were we going to his home? My mind, as usual, went straight into the gutter. Dirty images flooded my mind of all the lewd and possible positions he could put me in. I slapped my palms over my eyes and shook my head to erase the images. He tilted his head slightly as he drove as if to question

54

my behavior. His eyebrows went up as he looked at me.

I had some serious problems…

"Why are we going to your house?" I asked in an attempt to ignore the nervous jitters I had all through my body. It wasn't like I was expecting anything to happen. He wasn't my boyfriend… but then I remembered the kiss we shared in the rain last week and squeezed my thighs together.

"I think you should stay with me." I turned my head slightly. Back to this, were we?

I leaned my head away and couldn't hide my startled voice. "W-what," I stammered.

Before he answered, his eyes left the road and drifted toward my legs which were covered in a layer of jeans. His right hand left the stick shift and found its way to my thigh where it stayed. I stiffened. I could feel the heat of his palm through the fabric of my jeans. "It's not safe. I can't fade now. If something were to happen, I would never get to you in time. We should stay as close as possible." Just how *close* was he talking? I was finally able to focus enough to swat his hand away from my leg. He simply grinned and turned his attention back to the road. I was right, something was definitely different. Killian was oozing sexual energy and all of it was being directed at me. How was a girl supposed to react?

I shifted uncomfortable in my seat. "Like I'd be any safer with you?" I huffed, looking out the window.

"I want nothing more than to keep you safe—" He cut himself off unexpectedly and I could feel his eyes on me again, but I didn't dare let my eyes leave the window. He had a hypnotic pull about him right now. I tried my best to ignore the heat of his glare against me and focused on the trees going by outside the window. I saw that he was taking a left turn ahead and looked toward the front. We were coming to a stop. I glanced over to him in time for his penetrating gaze to lock me in place. "I want you, Melanie."

Oh, God.

My mind went blank. I stumbled around with my hands before finally deciding to rub my sweaty palms against my knees. "You want my power," I corrected him, saying it more like a whisper spoken far too shyly.

He turned off the car before leaning between the seats. His face loomed closer, so close that I could feel his breath against my cheek. "Oh, Love, what do you use those beautiful blue eyes for if you cannot see what you do to me?" he asked. His voice was dark and hoarse. I found myself leaning toward him without realizing. "Do you still doubt me?" He looked sincere and even afraid. I fought myself with all the willpower I had in me not to claim his lips like he had mine so easily before.

"I don't know," I mumbled. At this point we were nose to nose and the words started falling from my mouth with all their honesty. "You're hard to understand. You've never once told me what you're thinking." A gasp escaped my lips when he grazed his teeth across my chin in a teasing way. I took a deep breath and whispered, "You were the one that made it clear when we first met that you hated the idea of protecting me… how am I supposed to know what's what when…" I couldn't remember where I was going with this conversation.

I felt his chest vibrate as he laughed deep and husky in my ear. I shivered and leaned away so that I could see his face. His expression was gentle, tender. "Because I knew I was in trouble the moment I laid eyes on you. It was," his smile faded, "Grim's way of protecting me—us—him, from you."

I leaned forward. "What do you mean?"

He sighed. "I haven't figured that part out yet." He brought his hand to my chin and tilted my head side to side. "I don't know what is it about you that makes being close to you feel, so…" I waited for him to go on with anticipation

But my phone started ringing in my pocket. I leaned away from him so that I could get the phone from my jeans pocket and answered. "Hello?"

"Melanie, where are you?" It was Mom.

"I'm out with… Tess. She wanted me to keep her company." I lied. I didn't feel good about it, but Mom wouldn't agree with me being with Killian.

I could hear her relief over the phone. "That's good, I'm glad. You girls have fun," she told me.

"We will." I ended the phone call with a sigh. I leaned back into my seat feeling guilty. Then I noticed we were parked in a driveway of a white, two-story house. I raised back up to admire the house. It was an older home but something about older homes always drew me in. Of course, I didn't like going to places with history because I was always afraid of seeing ghosts. But now, ghosts were so pale in comparison to demons.

"So, this is your place?" I asked.

He nodded, opening his door and climbing out. I noticed how he barely fit in his car and it made me wonder why he even bought it. I stepped out and followed him to the porch. The porch stretched around the house with bannisters. The blue paint that probably had once been beautiful was now chipped, giving a timely feel to the home.

I found myself smiling as I slid my hand over the bannister, following him toward the door. I heard the click of him unlocking the door and in no time I was stepping into the house. He flipped the light on.

"Nice place you got." I practically jumped out of my skin

58

at Ryan's voice.

My eyes traveled to where I heard his voice. He was sitting in the middle of the stairway, still ghostly and broken like the state he died in. The stairs were centered in the wide hallway. "Ryan, you scared me." My heart was still racing.

"You're dead?" Killian looked completely shocked and alarmed to see him.

Ryan stood and started walking down the stairs. "Give him a cookie, he's smarter than I originally thought."

I saw Killian's shoulders tense up, the tightening of muscles pressed against his jacket. "What the bloody hell are you doing in this house?" he asked Ryan.

Ryan brought his arms across his chest. "Making sure Melanie is safe." They stood at a stand-off with each other. I scooted to the side and gave them both a questioning look.

Killian arched his eyebrow before shaking his head at him. "Why be an idiot and stay in this world as a ghost?" he asked him.

Ryan dropped his hands and sighed. "I'm not sure what you're getting at, but when I came to, I was already standing in the middle of the hallway at the hospital like this." He brought his arms out and moved them over his hospital gown to make his point. "I never asked to wake up like this."

59

Killian frowned, clearly puzzled. "That doesn't make sense."

There was a crashing sound toward the back of the house.

Everyone tensed at once, growing alarmed. We all seemed to look toward the back at the same time. Killian wasted no time and hurried down the hallway to the kitchen. I followed behind him. Once he was at the backdoor in the kitchen, he swung it open. I heard something being knocked over, followed by a hissing sound. I leaned my head by the door just in time to see a black tail scattering away. Killian sighed and shut the door. "It was just a cat messing around on the porch."

I sighed in relief. "What is it, demon, have you lost your ability to detect danger?" I turned to see the smirk on Ryan's face as he taunted Killian.

And his words had hit the right spot. A vein ticked from Killian's neck as he glared at Ryan. "Yeah, you're right, I have and it's not a good thing. That puts Melanie in a lot of danger. There's Grim and I know he will protect her, but his mind isn't at a good place right now. And neither is mine." His eyes seemed to travel over me as he said it. He raked his hand through his hair, his stress filling up the kitchen. "It's all fucked up."

Ryan's smug looked vanished and the fine lines of worry replaced it. I dropped my head and stared at the floor. "If I'm healed, that means Fear is too. I don't know what he's up to but it

60

won't be good and once Vengeance learns that Fear didn't succeed in taking the Vessel from you, he will come back for you." I looked up. Killian's eyes were on me. I didn't like how serious he looked or if I looked hard enough, I could see even worry. "Right now, it's waiting on one of them to come after you."

I smiled, halfheartedly. "Tell me something I don't already know."

———

Killian brought me back to the school parking lot to get my car. I had to leave Killian's not long after arriving because Ryan had refused to leave until I did too. I got out of his car and walked around as he rolled down his window. I bent down toward the window, leaning into it. "I'll follow you home to make sure you get there safe." The smile was instant and I realized this part of my life almost felt normal. Of course, Killian was the one giving me these experiences when he was a demon! That wasn't normal at all.

I snorted. "I've been fine on my own this whole week without you, I think I can manage on my own," I told him.

"You were never alone, Melanie." His expression was soft as he spoke.

"Oh?" I mumbled, confused.

61

He leaned closer and smiled. "I don't doubt that Grim's been right here keeping you safe."

"I doubt it."

"Don't." I gave him a strange look. He was so sure of Grim.

That made me remember what he said. "What did you mean about what you said about you and Grim?" I knew I didn't have to explain further when he sighed and leaned back into his seat.

He closed his eyes and shook his head. "We have our own fears, Melanie. There are some things that even Grim and I are terrified of losing or knowing." He opened his eyes and I suddenly felt that nervous excitement again. "Go on, Love. Before I change my mind and take you back home." My skin tingled at his words and I leaned up quickly hiding my blushed cheeks. I heard him laugh as he rolled the window up.

I knew he was waiting on me before he left, so I hurried to my car and started it up. I drove home and once I pulled into my hollow, he sped off.

CHAPTER FIVE

I went to school the next day with Ryan following every step of the way. If I thought he had been overprotective when he was alive, he was ten times worse as a ghost. I glared at him sitting in the passenger seat and he grinned too widely. I got out of the car and slammed the door shut behind me as I made my way to the school building.

"Someone's moody," Ryan chirped somewhere behind me and I suppressed a groan.

"If you would stop following me around…" I said through clenched teeth, trying hard not to look like an idiot who talked to herself.

I turned my head slightly and saw that he was scratching his forehead and sighed. "What else am I supposed to do? You're the only one that can see me." He did have a point. Deep breath! I continued up the steps as he tagged along behind me. It was still strange seeing him with a hospital gown on, a bruised body, and broken, twisted-looking legs.

"Say." He caught up next to me. "You and the Grim Reaper, what's going on with you two?" he asked, something I didn't know how to answer.

I studied his expression for a moment before looking ahead quickly. This had been the conversation I had been dreading. "He's not Grim anymore." I dodged the question.

"You know who I meant," he went on and tried to grab my shoulder but he went through it.

I grabbed my shoulder, the cold spread across where he touched. I stopped walking. "He's protecting me," I answered.

He snorted behind me. "The way he looks at you doesn't seem like he wants to protect you."

I ignored him and hurried up the steps to the entrance. I made sure not to speak to him as we went inside. "Answer me," he started again. He stepped in front of me and I sidestepped from him, almost bumping into someone in the process. When he did it again, I went straight through him and he let out a frustrated sigh.

I couldn't stop the grin as I tried my best to ignore him. "Ah, man. This being a ghost really sucks dick." My grin only grew when I realized I had the upper hand. "Oh, oh, oh, no, Melanie. You did not just smile." He moved beside me as he spoke, and I was trying so hard not to laugh. "Are you raging a war? You know what this means, I can't have you making fun of me like this," he went on and I shook my head. I looked at him

64

like he was a moron—he was a moron. But I was smiling nonetheless.

Josh literally popped out of nowhere in front of me and I stopped dead in my tracks so that I wouldn't collide into him. His lingering dead ancestor stood behind him, glaring at me. Great. "Hey, Melanie." He smiled.

I tried my best to give him a smile back. "Oh, hi, Josh." I tried not to look at his ancestor as she tipped her nose up at me in disgust and poked her lips out in a snarl.

"Yeah, I see what you mean now." Ryan brought his hand up to his chin and rubbed it. "She is a hateful looking ole' cow." My eyes widened at him.

The ancestor gave him a murderous look. "What did you just say, boy?" She stepped around Josh and moved toward Ryan. I brought my head down and bit my bottom lip to suppress my laugh. It was all too funny and weird watching Ryan make her mad.

"I knew you were close to Ryan, so I figured…" I was trying to listen to Josh, but his words were drowned out when his dead ancestor lunged for Ryan. Ryan's goofy smile dropped when her brittle fingers grabbed both his shoulders.

Ryan brought his hands down over her shoulders as she held him in the air. He was a lot bigger than she was, but she held him up like he was nothing but air. He patted her shoulders. "I think we may have got off on the wrong foot here…" he tried to tell her.

She ignored him and with strength I didn't know a ghost could have, she slung him across the hallway. I saw Ryan's white butt through the back of his gown as he flew in the air in front of me. He slammed into some lockers. "Ryan!" I screamed out of panic, placing my hand over my mouth. The lockers even opened from the impact with books and papers scattering to the floor. I thought ghosts couldn't do those things?

Only I didn't have time to think of that. People jumped and stopped in the hallway from the shock. The sound had caught everyone's attention. Without thinking, I ran and bent down next to Ryan where he lay on the floor. I was about to ask if he was okay when I got that chill against my back and knew people were staring at me. I heard their chatter all around me and suddenly I was afraid to do anything.

I tilted my head around slowly and looked at everyone as they gazed down at me. What did they see? What did I look like to these people? I looked behind me to see Josh giving me a very strange and worried look.

The ancestor stood beside him and she curled her lip up at Ryan laying on the floor. "You're a new ghost. I can tell." She spat the words out. "Weakling."

Ryan rose and looked around. "You're drawing too much attention, Melanie. Everyone's looking at you." He didn't have to tell me what I already knew. I stood up, all the while I could still hear the hushed voices around me. I was that girl again that everyone thought was weird... crazy.

"I'm fine." Ryan shooed me with his hands to hurry and go. As I turned another chill ran up my spine. Tess was there watching me with a questioning look on her face.

I abandoned the hallway in a hurry and ran to the girls' bathroom. I wanted away from all those judgmental looks. I took a deep breath and turned on the faucet. I began to repeatedly splash my face with cold water before finally looking at my reflection in the mirror.

You're okay, Melanie.

I no longer had to worry if I was crazy. I wasn't. Ghosts were real. Demons were real. Grim Reaper was real. Heaven and Hell and everything in-between existed. The Vessel made me a target, but Fear made me this way.

I was a normal girl caught up in some not so normal things.

I heard footsteps entering the bathroom and I looked over to see Tess coming toward me. I looked back into the mirror and I saw her come into view in the mirror. She crossed her arms and her perfectly round face looked at me for an answer. "What's going on with you?" she asked.

I shrugged my shoulders. "Ghosts," I told her, but I knew it wouldn't be enough for her. That was the truth, but the big truth was her ghost brother was just slung into the lockers by another ghost.

Yeah…no, I couldn't tell her that.

"Something else is going on lately." She sighed, dropping her arms to her sides. I turned away from her reflection in the mirror so that I could face her. "Talk to me, Melanie? Something's happening, I know it. You're acting different." She grabbed her forehead and leaned her hip against the sink. "And that guy from yesterday, you clearly didn't like him at Ryan's football game a while back." She paused. "What changed?"

I grabbed my head. She was bombarding me with questions I didn't want to answer. "He's not as bad as I originally thought," I told her. It was the truth. That was when I knew nothing about Killian. Which he never made it easy to trust him. And I still didn't really know him.

She puffed her cheeks out. "What are you saying?" she asked, slowly.

I gave her a silly look. "I'm just saying he's not a bad guy." For the most part anyway.

68

Her eyes squinted in anger. "What about my brother." Tess was angry. I could only stare at her confused. "You're so quick to date the moment he's gone!" I blinked, momentarily stunned. "He tried so hard to be with you." I hated how broken she sounded.

I could see that she was on the verge of crying and I reached out to touch her, but she jerked away from me. "Tess, it's not like that." But my voice didn't sound as convincing as it should be because I knew it wasn't exactly the truth. Killian was growing on me like wildfire.

"It's time for class." She wiped her eyes and slipped out of the bathroom. My butt fell against one of the sinks, and I took a deep shaky breath.

Lunch was extremely awkward. We still sat together at lunch because when it came down to it, we only had one another at school. I didn't know what to say to make things better between us, but lying about my feelings wouldn't be one of them. It didn't help the situation that Ryan sat at the table with us as we ate in silence.

His eyes went back and forth between us. "What's with you two?" he asked, and I shook my head.

I glanced back to Tess and saw that she was giving me another strange look. I looked back down at my plate. "What's his name?" she asked, finally breaking the silence between us.

"What?" I looked back up.

"The guy, Melanie." She sighed and took a bit from her burger. "Ya know, the one with the smokin' hot ride." Her words were muffled with the food in her mouth.

"Killian."

Ryan's eyes shot over to his sister. "What? Is she interested in the Reaper?" he asked, shoulders slumped.

I shook my head to answer him. A loud smack landed on the table and Ryan and I both jumped. We looked to see Tess glaring at me as her palm rested on the table from where she smacked it. "Okay, that's it. I know you're talking to one of them."

"Uh," was all I could think to say.

"See, you're admitting it." She brought her hand out toward me and I was trying to figure out how saying 'uh' meant I was admitting to anything. "You've never tried talking to them before." She dropped her hand back down. She leaned in closer to the table. "I heard you scream my brother's name in the hallway when those lockers opened on their own." I think Tess caught on to more than I realized. Did she already suspect…?

"Just tell her, you can tell she already knows." Ryan sighed as he looked at Tess.

I glared at him before I turned my attention back to her. "Your brother is a ghost." There. I said it.

Her eyes widened. "You're kidding me." Oh, so now she wasn't going to believe me?

"No, Tess. He's right here." I pointed at the seat he was in. She was already looking in that direction before I pointed as if she had seen me look in that direction enough times to know where he was.

"Are you trying to make me feel better by lying about him being a ghost? If you are, that would be super messed up—"

"No, God, Tess, I would never joke about something like this."

"Tell her I said to stop looking at her phone every night and just call Mike and find out the truth. You won't be able to move on until you figure out what it is that you want to know." He was looking at her as he spoke.

"He told me to tell you to stop staring at your phone at night already and just call Mike. You won't know what you need to unless you do." Her mouth gaped open at my words. She looked to where he sat with tears in her eyes.

"Ryan, God, I miss you so bad." My own eyes were

watering because of Tess, I had to look away from her for a second. I looked around to make sure we weren't drawing any attention.

He smiled at her. "Yeah, I miss you too, Sis."

"I miss you too, Sis." I mimicked his words back to her and her smile was so big. It made me wonder why I didn't tell her sooner. I hadn't seen a smile like that from her since before his accident.

———

I was walking out to the parking lot after the last bell when I got a text. It was an unknown number but once I read what it said, I knew exactly who it was:

Come over.

Two simple words and I was blushing at my cell phone screen. I stored Killian's number into my contacts before slipping my phone back into my pocket.

"Melanie!" Tess called my name from somewhere behind me. I turned just as she stopped beside me. She was smiling. "Is my brother here right now?" she asked, hopeful.

"No, I haven't seen him since lunch." I hated to disappoint her and watch as her smile dropped. "But, I will let you know when I see him again. He's always popping up somewhere, believe me, he has the whole ghost thing down pat." I smiled.

72

"Okay." She nodded.

I had to pick up Alex from his elementary school. He ran out the front doors as soon as he saw my car pull up outside. I smiled as he raced around the car and hurried into the passenger seat. He slammed the door shut. "Hey," I said.

"Hey," he replied. He looked at me as I pulled out of the parking lot and back onto the road. "You're in a good mood." I tipped my top lip up slightly. Apparently, I must be grumpy most of the time.

But I understood what he meant. I gave him a small smile before focusing back on the road. "Yeah, I think things are going to get better for Tess now." That was enough to make me happy.

"Oh?" He tried not to sound too happy about it, but I knew he was. "That's good." He shrugged his shoulders.

"Say," I looked over at him, "do you want to go grab a bite to eat at Deb's?" I asked.

He turned around and said 'yeah' so quickly that I was glad I asked.

I grinned. "Okay, I'll call and let Mom know." He nodded.

Twenty minutes later, Alex and I were sitting at a back booth at Deb's. We were looking at the menus when the waitress came to our table. "Hey, I'm Sally, I'll be your waitress for the evening." She was friendly. Alex lowered his menu as he looked

73

at her. "What would you guys like to drink?" she asked.

"I'll take a root beer." He closed his menu and laid it on the table. I arched my eyebrow. Was he trying to make himself look mature?

I grinned at him. Look at him, acting all grown up. "I'll take a Dr. Pepper."

"Do you guys need a minute or do y'all already know what you want?" she asked as she pulled out her pen and a small pad.

"I'll take a steak and fries," he answered. "Well done."

"Cheeseburger and fries, please," I added.

She looked up after she was finish writing down our order and smiled. "All righty, I'll be right back with your drinks." Alex was drilling holes in her as she walked away.

"She's so hot." He was staring at her butt as he said the words. I snorted.

He raised a blond eyebrow, so much like mine. "Unlike you, I'm mature for my age. I love girls." He made sure to point out. I hadn't cared about boys at his age and by the time I did, ghosts were already a part of my life. Now I knew, though, I was coming out of that shell. Well, when Killian happened to be around, that is. But that wasn't entirely true... Ryan had made me wish I was someone different my whole life... but everything was different now.

Sally brought our drinks out and not even five minutes later she was bringing out our food. Another reason why I loved Deb's. They were fast about getting your food to you, despite always being busy. All the workers were friendly.

There was only silence while we ate, we only knew how to stuff our faces with delicious food. We were being pigs at the moment—I meant that in every way possible, ketchup all over my shirt and Alex looked no better. Mom taught us good table manners but they never really stuck. Sally came back to our table shortly after and placed two hot fudge cakes in front of us. I looked up from my plate and frowned at her. "Um, we didn't order dessert," I told her.

There was a twinkle in her eyes as she grinned at me. "This is from the man sitting over there." She leaned back and pointed toward the bar. My gaze followed to who she was pointing at and I recognized the leather jacket—that broad, sexy back. I'd recognize Killian anywhere—any which way. He sat on a stool at the bar, elbows propped up against the bar as he leaned forward. As if he knew I was staring, he turned and met my eyes with a confident smirk.

I leaned back, hiding behind Sally as best I could. Which made me look extremely goofy since Sally was as thin as paper. "He already paid your bill and anything else y'all want," she added.

"Who is that?" Alex scrunched up his nose at Killian. Sally walked off and Killian stood and headed toward our table.

"A friend," I replied quickly when I knew he was coming this way. Without a word, he slid in the booth next to me, forcing me to scoot over so that he could fit. But he ended up just kind of cramming himself in there, leaving his long legs out and in every waiter's way.

"Melanie," Killian drawled, his arm rubbing into my shoulder.

"What are you doing here?" I asked him.

"You didn't come over like I asked you to." I elbowed him in the stomach, but he didn't even flinch. I motioned my head and gave him a look that said my-brother-is-right-there and that he needed to shut up.

"Yeah, I didn't want to," I said quickly, although it was a lie. I did and didn't want to see him, I was very confused right now. "Now, how did you know I was here?" I asked because I didn't think he could find me as easily now that he wasn't Grim.

He lowered his mouth to my ear and his nose brushed against my hair. Pinpricks broke out over my skin. "You can't escape me, Melanie, now that I know your scent. Just like I can't escape you." His words shouldn't turn me to liquid like they do, but everything he whispered in my ear seemed to scorch me. I leaned away from his mouth and grabbed my ear, remembering that Alex was right there watching us. What did he mean? Scent?

"Sis." Alex was giving me a strange look.

I coughed, straightening out my voice before I spoke. "Alex, this is Killian." I motioned toward the both of them. "Killian, this is my brother Alex." I introduced the two of them because I had no clue what else I should do.

"Hey, kid." Killian moved his arm across my shoulder and leaned back. I had no choice, but to lean back with him since he was too strong to get away from.

Alex crossed his arms over his shoulder and glared at him. "Who is this tool, Sis? How do you know him? Isn't he the one that came by the house a while back?" My eyes widened at the third degree my seven-year-old brother was giving me.

Killian only laughed. "Did you just call me a tool? I like you already." I eyed the hot fudge brownie in front of me. The ice cream was starting to melt. I leaned up to grab a drink of my pop. I was sipping through the straw when Killian said, "I'm your sister's boyfriend." I spit what pop was in my mouth all over the table. I grabbed my chest as I coughed and looked at Killian like he had lost his mind.

Stop fluttering heart, darn you. Or it could be the fact that

77

I was strangling, not that I was happy or anything. Definitively not.

Alex looked to me. "Is that true?" he asked.

I shrugged Killian's arm away that kept lingering close despite the fact that I was leaned away from him. I gave him a heated glare. "No, he's just a friend." I was still looking at Killian when I spoke. "A very big, annoying one that I'm going to unfriend if he keeps it up."

Killian's eyes matched his smile, dark and dangerous. He brought his hand up to my ponytail and began to twist it around. "You hurt me with your words." I rolled my eyes and grabbed some napkins on the table to clean up the pop I had spit everywhere.

Killian leaned forward, still twirling my hair as he scooted the hot fudge cake in front of him with his other hand. He started eating it and I kept wondering why I was letting him play with my hair. Another minute went by before Alex said, "Wow, I didn't think anyone besides Ryan would ever like my sister." Alex took a sip of his pop after he spoke before looking back at us. Killian's hand stopped twirling my ponytail before he dropped his hand away completely. "I always thought Ryan would be my brother-in-law one day, I was so sure..." Alex's voice trailed off as he took a bite of his steak. I looked at Killian and saw that his smile was gone and Alex's words had tensed him up entirely.

Killian brought his hands up against the table as he looked at Alex. "I think there's someone out there that suits your sister better. Someone that can make her happy and mean more to her than Ryan ever could." His hand closest to me snaked out and grabbed mine. The warmth I felt was instant and spread across my fingertips. A small gasp escaped my lips as he brought our hands—linked together—and placed them over his leg underneath the table. I simply looked at him in awe. I continued to be amazed at how much I felt every time he touched me. Was that normal? His thumb lazily stroked over mine and it felt intimate.

"When two people are meant to be together, I think there's no stopping it—or escaping it." He then looked me in the eyes like it was some sort of promise. His eyes seemed to dance under the dim lights of the diner. "I think they call it fate." I felt like he just gave away a big secret. Something that I was constantly running from.

I was quiet as Killian walked us to my car. Alex walked ahead of us at a distance and I found myself walking even slower like I was in no hurry to part with him. I hadn't said a word to him since he had said those things in the diner, but then his hand was reaching out to mine—twining his fingers with mine as we continued at a slow pace. I looked down at our hands and the way they looked when together. My mind was in chaos and things were going to get crazy again, it was only a matter of time—but my heart recognized something through it all. This felt *right*.

I squeezed his hand and looked up at him so that I could see the expression he wore. There was something sweet and precious in those dark eyes, but it could never mask the burning desire rippling around him—around us.

I don't want this feeling to go away…

"Are you sure you want to part?" he whispered softly. Alex was already getting in the car. I smiled because I had been thinking the same thing.

We stopped once we were in front of the car and I shook my head with a stupid grin on my face. "What are we doing?" I tugged at my hand trying to pull them apart, but he was reluctant to let go.

"Well, right now…" I loved that sexy grin he wore. "We're holding hands and I'm trying really hard not to kiss you in front of your brother." His voice wasn't sweet, it was deep and husky—full of dark fantasies and promises that were sure to come alive in my dreams—and when I looked into his eyes again they were solid black. The color of black licorice candy, only more liquefied. Enchanting and almost scary.

"Come home with me." His words had a mesmerizing effect on me. I felt my mind and body go lax, and I knew I wouldn't turn him down. I would do whatever he wanted.

I grabbed his t-shirt and pulled myself into him. "Killian…your eyes…" My voice was like a hum. And then his smile faded and turned to anger. He pushed me away so abruptly and hid his eyes under his hand. I actually pouted. When he looked at me again, they were back to normal. I shook my head at my reaction, it felt almost like I was being enchanted by him

Once the feeling was gone, I looked back up to him. "You should go," he said harshly.

"Killian?" I said his name suddenly afraid. I didn't like the distance between us when we had been so close moments before. What just happened?

"Take your brother home." He sounded closed off—distant. He was shutting me out. Alex chose that moment to honk the horn. I glanced at Alex in the car for a moment and when I turned back to Killian, he was already walking down the street. His broad back disappearing underneath the streetlight.

CHAPTER SIX

Girlfriend?

That was what he said at Deb's yesterday evening. I didn't know if he was messing with Alex or me. I couldn't get over the weird way he acted before he left... I walked through the hallway hugging my books against my chest. I brought my pen up toward my cheek, clicking it against my skin as I thought of him. A warm fuzzy feeling floated around in my chest. I sighed just as I bumped shoulders with someone walking the opposite direction, knocking my pen from my hand. I bent down to get it and pointed heels stepped toward me. I glanced up to see who they belonged to.

Haley.

I groaned on the inside as I stood up. "Sorry, I didn't—"

"As if I have time to deal with the freak of the school." She snarled at me. "Move over." She pushed me aside. What was her problem with me? I didn't understand what I ever did to make her so mean to me. I felt my anger fizzling to the point of bursting.

I swear she needed an attitude check.

Something ignited inside me. I had no idea where it came from. The tingling started at my chest as it traveled through my arms into the tips of my fingers. Then before I could wonder what was happening to me, a voice filtered through my head.

Don't let her treat you that way.

I gripped my hands and sniggered silently to myself before obeying the voice. Without much thought to what I was doing, I pointed my finger at one of Haley's heels and flicked my wrist. The heel broke and her ankle came down too fast and too awkward, a sickening crack echoed as she fell to the floor with a painful scream. The crowd scattered away from her before they all noticed what happened and went to her. People were squatting down next to her, checking on her. Her hands were clutched around her already swollen ankle, tears falling down her cheeks, and I smiled.

My finger was still pointed and when I took notice and felt the twisted smile on my face, I let my hand fall to my side and stumbled back a step.

Oh, God. What just happened? What did I do?

Heart pounding, I brought my hand to my mouth and fled

in the other direction. I squeezed my palms that shook so hard and slipped in and out of my classes in a hazy rush. My heart was racing and my chest hurt. I couldn't believe I did that. I just knew I was the one that did it. I didn't know why or how; I just knew I was to blame.

"Hey, Melanie." I jumped when Tess spoke behind me. I turned around and rubbed my sweaty palms against my jeans. "You're jumpy today, and I thought you were finally getting over being so afraid." She shook her head smiling at me. "Ryan still hasn't shown up today?" she asked.

I was staring for a long time until I realized she had asked me a question. I shook my head. "No, I don't know what he's up to." I hadn't seen him since lunch yesterday. He hadn't come to the house last night.

"Oh." I could hear the disappointment.

"Don't worry, I'll let you know when he comes around," I promised.

She nodded then her eyes lit up like they did every time she was about to gossip. "Oh, did you hear about Haley breaking her ankle wearing these ugly giant heels?" Tess snorted, and I felt sick. "That's what she gets for messing with my man, but his stupid ass will sleep with anything, apparently." She was looking off to the side as she spoke.

"Have you taken your brother's advice and talked to him

84

yet?" She squirmed at my question and avoided my eyes. That would be a no. "Just talk to him, Tess. Don't just assume anything." I tried a different approach, a smarter one that I should have said sooner. "Who was the one that even told you that?" I knew she wouldn't be able to answer that question because Vengeance's puppets had planted the doubt in her head.

She squinted her eyes and tilted her head to the side, clearly confused. "Huh, I don't know. I don't recall…"

A strange coldness swept through the hallway out of nowhere. I felt the unease run down my spine. I looked around, back and forth in the hallway. The only thing I saw was people hurrying to get to class, getting in and out of their lockers while laughter and chatter flooded the hall.

What was that feeling just now? I sighed.

A breeze blew right by me. I watched as the breeze lifted my hair as it blew by. It was cold. How… "Jesus, where the crap is that cold air coming from?" Tess grabbed her arms and looked like she was shivering. I placed my hand over my hair where it had been lifted.

I watched the hallway for the longest time after that. Sure that something was going to happen, I waited, gripping my book. The bell sounded but I stayed in place. Tess gave me a strange look before finally saying, "Are you going to just stand there or are you going to go to class?" She laughed, giving me another what's-with-you look. I gave the hallway one final glance before following Tess to class.

I had a feeling my quiet days were over.

———————

I pulled my phone out of my pocket as soon as my last class was over hoping there was a text from Killian. There wasn't. I frowned and tucked it back in my butt pocket and placed my books in my locker before heading to my car. Maybe it was a good thing. I wasn't sure how I was supposed to act around him after yesterday anyway. He was hot and cold—but I was equally hot and cold.

One minute he was placing his hand in mine and giving me butterflies, the next he was pulling away from me. He had been somewhat charming at the table until we walked outside… and then what? I couldn't figure him out. I was getting goosebumps just thinking about him lately. Just what the crap was wrong with me?

Something new, something dangerous was settling between my thighs lately—a lot more than usual—and I knew it had something to do with him. I wasn't stupid, I knew what I was feeling. I had a sexual attraction to Killian.

Maybe he was awakening something else inside of me? I remembered the moment the Vessel awakened, it was the dream with Killian. Did that have something to do with what I was feeling? There were too many things I still didn't know.

As I walked outside of the school building, I wrapped my jacket around me and hurried to my car. I was already missing summer. Once I was in the car, I started it up and cranked up the heat. It would take a second to warm up so I took my hands to my mouth and blew hot air on them. Then I placed my hands on the wheel and took a deep breath. *Should I go see him?* My stupid stomach was already fluttering at the thought. Crap, I was getting nervous too.

Relax.

I guess even I knew how to be a girl.

My life was in danger and all I could think about was Killian. What was up with that? I was changing. I didn't even feel afraid like I should be. There was so much to worry about.

Yet…I pulled out of the parking lot and headed toward Killian's. I turned on the radio and listened to music so I wouldn't have time to think about what I was doing. I gripped the steering wheel and smiled. I had no clue what I was doing. I just wanted to do something I normally wouldn't.

Pop!

The wheels started turning toward the left side. I leaned forward and saw that the front of the car was lower on the left. The car was jumping on that side. "Crap," I muttered. I had a flat tire in the front. I pulled off to the side of the road at the nearest opening that put me out of the road. I just had to get a flat tire in the creepy part of town. Well, not exactly town, this two-lane road was called Willer and it was on the way to town. No houses were on this road or anything for that matter. A creek ran where I pulled off. Across the creek was a steep hill covered in trees. On the left side of the road was an open field that usually kept horses, only there were none running now.

I stepped out of the car and saw the flat tire was on the front left side. The tire had blew-out, I could see the huge gash in the tire. No wonder my car had jerked like it had. I didn't know how to change a tire. The situation I was in made me think of Dad and how this would have been something I could have called him to help me with. I didn't know if I missed him or the idea of a dad. I spent a lot of years on bad terms with him before deciding to pretend for my parent's sake—they desperately wanted a normal child. Of course, he was there for me after that.

Then there was another pain in the chest when I thought of Ryan. I knew I could have called him but now I couldn't. The one person I could rely on was dead. A ghost. A constant reminder that I was the blame for his death.

I sighed and bent down to grab my phone on the passenger side seat. Should I call Killian? I wasn't sure I could call him over a flat tire. I wasn't exactly sure about anything when it came to him. Mom couldn't help me and she would probably call my aunt Brenda's husband to come out and help me. Which would be weird since I didn't know him.

The wind picked up and I got that same chill up my spine like I had in the hallway at school earlier. My skin rippled, I held my phone and was trying to decide if I really wanted to lean up out of the car or not. That horrible tingle was running up my back. The one you got when someone was standing behind you.

The X set me on fire. I gritted my teeth and ignored the need to grab my chest. I raised up from the car and turned quickly.

My quiet days were indeed over. Demons were back.

This one was creepy looking. His skin was black, chiseled and burnt looking. The only part of him that wasn't charred looking was his red lips. His eyes were bright and stood out from the rest of his body and when his lips opened as he growled, his teeth were white and human.

I sidestepped away from him and began to run. I felt his hand sliding through my hair almost catching me, but he didn't and I was already hurrying to the other side of the car. Bad mistake. He only jumped onto the hood of the car, and it bent with his weight. He hissed at me.

I took off in a dead run trying to get as much distance

between us as possible. I remembered the cell phone that was in my hand. I immediately started searching for Killian's number. My hands were far too shaky as I ran and twice I hit the wrong contact. "Oh, God!" I panicked. I went back to the contacts and finally succeeded in pressing the right name. I pressed the call button and saw that it connected before raising it to my ear.

He made a growling sound behind me just as his arm grabbed me around the waist, hauling me backwards. The phone went flying from my hand and smacked against the blacktop. The battery flew out and landed next to it.

The demon twirled me around to face him. His solid white eyes were frightening against the burnt skin. He growled like an animal. I tried to jerk my arms free. I desperately tried. I had to do something instead of panicking.

Fight.

The voice told me. My body went still as he held me by the arms. I stopped thrashing against the demon. His face loomed over mine, breathing his nasty odor down into my nose and mouth. When I thought he would least expect it, I jerked my arms downward and slipped out of his grip. I stepped back when he reached for me. Running on instinct and the voice, my body leaned to the side and I swung my leg out and kicked him in the chest. He stumbled back a few steps.

As soon as he caught his balance, he headed toward me

again. I stood and looked around, not sure what I should do. I tried to think. Crap! I had no clue. When his hands reached out for me, I closed my eyes and held my hands in front of me. I wouldn't let him hurt me or take me.

The same tingling energy surged through me like before, only stronger. The power lit up my skin and made it glow. I felt the power resting at my fingertips. Something sparked out of my palms. The demon was flown backwards as he screamed in pain. He lay there a few seconds before raising back up. A huge hole was in his chest and he held his hand over it. It was nasty and torn right open.

I looked down at my hands. What did I just do?

I didn't have any more time to think about it because the demon was standing up and moving after me. And the deadly look on his face probably meant that I had made him mad. I was screwed.

I stumbled around like a moron and the demon lunged for me, but he never reached me. Someone collided into the demon and sent him sailing through the air. The demon landed on the hill on the other side of the creek, knocking into several trees on the way down. I looked in front of me where the demon had been. Grim stood before me, his blue essence moving inside his cloak and his hood rested over his skull.

Surprise and relief hit me all at once. "Grim," I called his name.

His blue essence flowed around him from what I could see through the opening of his cloak. My heart raced under his eyeless gaze. He was intimating as always. A roar came from the demon and we both whipped our heads around to see him jumping across the creek. He landed on the blacktop and went after Grim.

Grim straightened his stance, readying himself for the demon. When the demon went to grab him, Grim flung him over his shoulder like he was nothing. The demon was already up and went for Grim's waist. Grim stumbled back a step and gripped the demon, slinging him back to the ground. As the demon was trying to scramble back up, Grim brought his boot over his shoulder and pinned him down. The demon lashed out at his leg but couldn't reach it. Grim brought out his hand and his scythe materialized in his hand. Something I was getting used to.

I knew what would happen next. I saw him do it enough times before. The demon twisted his head enough to see the scythe as Grim brought it over his head. His eyes widened like he knew what it was—what it meant for him. The demon growled through his clenched teeth at Grim. Then he simply vanished just as Grim swung the blade. His boot that had been resting on the demon's shoulder hit the blacktop along with his blade. Grim circled around looking for the demon.

I looked along with him. I kept glancing back and forth on the road, toward the creek and trees, and the open field. The demon was gone. I finally looked back at Grim.

His eyeless sockets were already watching me, and I sucked in a breath. Had he been watching me this whole time? Something echoed in the distance. I looked behind him, straining my eyes and ears to do their job. As the sound grew closer, it became more recognizable. I knew it was a vehicle coming. It was going too fast. As it grew louder, a black Corvette came into view from a curve in the road.

I smiled as the Corvette came to a stop next to my car where Grim and I stood. Luckily, this road was never busy or it would be hard to explain to anyone that I had been running from a demon. The driver's side door swung open and Killian stepped out.

Grim never once turned as Killian approached, and I had the feeling he felt him coming long before I did. Grim turned around slowly to face him. He twirled the scythe around a few times—I didn't understand how it was possible with its length being taller than me—before it disappeared. Killian's eyes landed on Grim first before he looked at me. His shoulders dropped and a sigh fell from his mouth. He was relieved that I was still alive. Or maybe because Grim had protected me.

I walked toward him, and I watched him nod at Grim

before running to me. I didn't have time to protest, or think before he was wrapping his arms around me and pressing me against his hard chest. My feet left the ground as he held me and a surprised squeal left my mouth. I grabbed onto his shoulders.

And then his exotic scent was taking over my senses. It made me not care that we were in broad daylight. I just knew he smelled great, manly and powerful. Sexy. My body recognized these things because it was what it wanted. While I had been cold from the autumn air moments earlier, I now only felt heat pressed against him.

He held me tighter, it felt like I would snap in half. I tapped his shoulder to let him know that I wanted down. It took several seconds, but he finally let me go, placing my feet back on the ground. I didn't even know why he was grabbing me like he did. But when he looked down at me, I could see he was worried. He slowly began to relax as he brought his hand up to my hair. "You scared the fuck out of me."

"I'm fine." He brought his hand over to my cheek. I placed my hand over his and smiled. His other hand found my waist and pulled me close. He liked touching me, good thing I was starting to like it just as much.

"I knew something was wrong. I could feel it and when you called and hung up before I answered…" He was staring at my lips. I bit my bottom lip, nervously, not even doing it on purpose, just instinct. His grip tightened around my waist and his eyes were liquefying to black. My pulse sped up and I inhaled sharply.

"Enough, Killian. Hands off." Grim's voice, a replica of Kilian's, only laced with all his power and demand. It was like his voice carried all the death he had seen over the years, all the knowledge he possessed, all the suffering and pain he witnessed; it was all there in the sound of his voice.

"No." Killian took the hand that was on my cheek and raked it through his hair. His other still held me possessively at the waist. Killian didn't seem bothered that Grim was turning his creepy shade of black like he did every time he was angry. He leaned his head back, almost in a bored-like manner and said to Grim, "Why should I?"

I heard the crack of Grim's fingers popping and saw the darkening of his essence grow around him. "Time to go," he said to Killian or me, I wasn't sure.

But Killian was the one to answer. "You go. I'm going to make sure Melanie gets home safe."

Grim swore, tossing his head back and in the process, knocking his hood off his skull. He brought his skeletal hand over his skull as he shook his head, annoyed. I tilted my head and eyed his movement with a smile. Killian did the exact same thing when he was aggravated, it was funny to see something so similar about

95

them.

Right after I took notice, Killian went and did it right after Grim. He blew an aggravated breath as he scowled at Grim. What was crazy was how alike it looked between them, I was suddenly intrigued.

"You are the danger, *incubus.*" Grim's voice rumbled, and I didn't miss the way the word 'incubus' dropped from his mouth like the word itself was dangerous. I pulled away from Killian and stared down at my feet… incubus… incubus, I was pretty sure Killian had told me what that meant.

"What does that mean?" Killian's voice rose, and I looked back up. I felt ignored as I stared back and forth between them. Grim moved toward Killian and shoved him. He stumbled backwards.

Oh, boy… the look on Killian's face was not a good one.

"You know exactly what I mean, you don't even realize you are doing it." Killian looked surprised then worried, and I watched as Grim's eyeless gaze drifted down to Killian's jeans…? I arched my eyebrow. "Control your… *problems.*"

Grim turned toward me and I went stiff as a board. Then the next thing I knew, his arm caught me by the waist, pulled me closer before hauling me over his shoulder. I squealed out of surprise and grabbed ahold of his back to keep from falling. But

Grim was the same height as Killian and lying across his shoulder still made it seem like I was falling.

"What are you doing?" I screamed.

Killian groaned somewhere close by, but I couldn't see anything as Grim started walking with me. "Will you put her down and stop acting like a Neanderthal. Girls are not into that." Grim stopped walking and I felt him turn slightly to look behind him. I then felt his hand travel over my back. He jerked his whole body and I went bouncing over his shoulder for a second, a girly peep came out of me as I landed back on his shoulder.

"OMIGOD!" I yelled.

His hand grabbed a hold of my butt and readjusted me over his shoulder. There was a moment of relief before I turned my head toward his back and glared at him. Did he just grope me? He started chuckling and it vibrated his whole body. I let my head hang and tried hard not to blush. He seemed to be enjoying himself.

Killian was right, he was a Neanderthal. I smacked his back and it only caused his hood to fall in my face. I smacked it away and cursed. "Really, what's with the cloak and hood anyway? It's totally lame." Yeah, I liked to start arguments when I was either embarrassed or mad. Although, that had been a lie, nothing about Grim was lame. It just made him look like the badass he was, and that much scarier.

"No, it's not." They both said at the same time. I pushed my arms against Grim's back and raised myself up enough that I could see Killian walking behind us. When I met his eyes with a snort, he looked away. Was he embarrassed? I smiled.

"Whatever you say." I dropped my arms down and fell against his back. Grim stopped beside my car. I felt his arms reach around my stomach as he placed me on my feet. His hands left my sides and I looked up at him. It was strange, letting myself be around Grim when he looked the way he did. Powerful and nothing at all human. I must be getting used to the way he looked because I didn't cower as much at him anymore.

He went to open my door and his cold skeletal hand pressed against my back as he forced me inside. I huffed and tried to maneuver myself in the seat the correct way instead of the way Grim was shoving me in there. Once I was sitting, I leaned back and moved my blonde strands out of my face. I looked over at him with a scowl. "Stop acting like a caveman, I know how to get inside a car."

His eyeless expression peered down at me as he shrugged his shoulders and slammed the door in my face. He had no manners… I started the car and rolled down the window.

Killian was standing beside Grim by my car door. "What about my flat?" I asked.

"Grim's already taken care of it," Killian told me. When

98

did he get the chance to fix it? While he was carrying me over his shoulder?

"Is my hood okay?" I hadn't thought to look at it.

"It's fine." He nodded leaning into the window. He smiled at me and there I was going all girly on the inside again. "Go home and don't worry. Don't even think about anything." I sucked in my cheeks at his words, I knew I couldn't not do those things. "You're safe as long as I'm here." Grim snorted behind him so he added, "As long as *we* are here." He corrected himself, and I grinned.

"You can come to my place if you want." That got him yanked out of the window by Grim and punched in the gut. Killian bent over, holding his stomach as he glared at Grim. "Will you cut it out!"

"Actually, I was going to his house before the demon—" I spoke up only to be cut off by Grim.

"Not anymore." Er, what?

"Why should I listen to you?" I pointed out. His hand went to the window, and I watched as his blue essence darkened enough to know he was getting serious. His grip tightened.

"You can't be left alone with Killian. Have you forgotten what he is? He's an incubus demon." I turned my head to the steering wheel and felt my face go ten shades of red. "He's a sex demon," Grim said what I finally remembered.

When I looked up, Grim was watching me—staring at everything I wanted to hide. Nothing left me more exposed than him, he was always reading me like I was an open book. Did he see my flaws? My weaknesses? I bet he saw all my wants and the desire growing inside me. My face just kept getting hotter and I knew there was no hiding the blush.

Killian raised up and was staring at me now too.

"Now I remember." My voice was tiny, and I gripped the steering wheel. That explained so much. Why my mind always seemed to be in the gutter lately. But I was already attracted to him before. He meant something to me before he was only an incubus demon. I couldn't stop thinking about him after he got hurt… I was so confused. Were my feelings real or not?

"That doesn't mean anything," Killian argued. He started moving closer.

I only looked at him long enough to look back away. I took a deep breath. Funny how something as simple as remembering he was an incubus demon left me feeling foolish. Because what I was feeling around him might not even be me to begin with. I started rolling up the window. "I'm going home."

I was buckling up when Grim tapped on the window and I rolled it down slightly. "I only meant that the more he's around you, the harder it will be for him." I nodded, not sure what he

100

meant.

Without a word, not even looking at Killian, I turned my car around in the middle of the road and drove home.

I looked back to see both of them standing in the rearview mirror as I drove away.

CHAPTER SEVEN

I was surprised and glad to see Ryan lying on my bed as I walked in the room. Or more like hovering above it. Ghosts were strange, they never really seemed to touch anything, only float. After seeing what Josh's ancestor did to Ryan yesterday, I knew they could at least touch each other. I shut the door behind me. "Where have you been?" I asked him.

He glanced away from the ceiling and smiled at me. "Right here waiting for you to get home." He looked right back toward the ceiling when he asked, "You took a while… did you go to see Killian?" I pretended not to notice the disappointment on his face or the fact that he wasn't meeting my eyes as he spoke.

I walked to my desk and flopped down in the chair placing my book I brought home on the desk. I had homework but that didn't seem as important as everything else that was going on. I circled myself around in the chair for a moment before scooting it toward the bed. "No," I told him because I never made it to his house. I wasn't sure I should tell him about the demon that attacked me. Look what happened to him when he found out the first time... although, he couldn't get any worse than a ghost, right?

Then I remembered the strange light that came out of my palms and how it hurt the demon. I forgot to mention it to Killian or Grim. Although, if it had something to do with the Vessel, would they have any idea themselves. They didn't seem to know too much about it either.

I sighed. "I had a flat tire. That's why it took so long."

"Can ghosts get headaches?" Ryan propped himself up, floating Indian style above my bed with a hospital gown on. No, that wasn't awkward at all. I watched as he grabbed his forehead. "I swear it feels like my head's going to explode."

"Your guess is as good as mine," I answered and blinked a few times when I thought of something. "Maybe it's something that happens when you stay in the human world as a ghost? Might need to ask another ghost..." I couldn't believe I just told him to ask another ghost a question. I didn't want him getting too comfortable as one.

"Yeah, I think Josh's ancestor has weened me from talking about or to any other ghosts," he muttered.

I agreed. "Oh, your sister wanted me to let her know when I saw you again."

He squinted his eyes at me. "Yeah?"

"Yeah, I'll call her before I start on my homework." I leaned my weight onto the chair arm and reached into my pocket to grab my cell phone. I blinked, my cell phone wasn't on me. I stood up and checked the other side. Then I swore. I forgot to pick it up off the road. It was probably road kill by now and I was probably the one who ran it over... I covered my face with my hands and groaned.

"What is it?" he asked as I dropped back down onto the chair.

There was a knock on the door downstairs. I heard someone running to the door and knew it had to be Alex. Mom wouldn't run. I listened with Ryan, I couldn't hear anything until footsteps started echoing up the stairs. Alex threw open my door with a scowl on his face. "You have a visitor." I raised one eyebrow and got up from the chair.

"Who is it?" I asked.

"Killian."

Ryan practically leaped off the bed at the mention of Killian. Alex walked out of the room, and I pointed a finger at him. "Stay here. What if Grim's with him?" He stood still but frowned at me. I hurried downstairs.

When I reached the bottom of the stairs, I saw Killian

standing outside the door. He had his hands in his pockets. He tried to smile as he saw me—a failed attempt at normal. He wasn't good at not looking dangerous. Mom stood next to him, on the other side of the door, arms crossed as she scowled at him with the same look Alex had given me. Where were their manners when it came to Killian? He was on the losing side when it came to them.

And that sort of ticked me off. I meant, sure, I had been afraid of him too and might have possibly treated him the same way, but now… it was frustrating to see someone like Mom, who was normally a nice person, treat him like he was *nothing*. I made sure she saw my angry look when she turned toward me.

I was supposed to be figuring out how much of my feelings for Killian were real, but as soon as I met his eyes again, I didn't want to hide my smile. "Hey." I didn't want to smile at him too much, though since Mom was watching, and I didn't want him thinking I was putty in his hands or something… because I definitely wasn't!

There was just something I liked about myself when he was around. Almost like I was breaking free and letting myself be the girl that had been hiding for far too long…

"Can I speak to you a moment?" Mom was mad, I could hear it in her voice. I followed her into the kitchen, and I didn't miss the nervous look on Killian's face as I walked away.

The moment Mom was at the sink, she twirled around to face me with an aggravated look on her face. "What is he doing here again?" she asked.

"He's a friend, Mom."

With knowing eyes, she looked into mine and planted one hand on her hip. "Melanie, it's almost nine. Why would a guy that's just a friend be over this late?"

"I'm not sure why he's here, you haven't even given me the chance to find out, but he's not a bad guy." I crossed my arms and looked at her disappointed. "It's not like you to be so rude to someone."

She huffed, looking down before shifting her weight to the other hip and looking back to me. "Melanie, I know nothing about this guy. You say he's a friend of Ryan's, but I find that hard to believe. He looks a lot older than you guys, and why does he keep coming here?"

"He is older," I admitted.

"How old is he?" she asked.

I looked away. How was I supposed to answer that? "I'm not sure." Her mouth dropped, and I knew I needed to change my words. "Twenty-four, maybe?" I offered quickly, feeling the lie heat my face. I couldn't tell her he was three-thousand-years old—in demon/Underworld years, now could I?

"Do you even know anything about him?" She searched my face for clues. She always yelled at me for not getting out enough and doing things. Why was she acting this way now that I finally felt normal more than ever before?

I spent years hiding myself for her and Dad. I never did anything wrong in my life besides being able to see ghosts. I even hid that for them to make them happy. Every time I saw one and was scared to death, I panicked—all alone. I was afraid all the time—on my own. I felt angry as I looked at her. My life was in danger, hers too, but she would never believe me even if I tried to tell her.

And I won't let myself be alone anymore.

"I know him," I said. "Well, I will eventually know him." Wouldn't I?

"Melanie!" she went on.

"Mom," I said calmly. "I'm going to go see what he wants, and you can yell at me when he can't hear you." I hurried out of the kitchen before she could say anything else.

When I walked into the hallway, Killian still waited outside the door, face tight with worry. Just like that, I knew I needed him. I liked that he cared enough to look at me like that when something was wrong. My anger dissipated and I smiled as I walked toward him.

I slipped on my shoes at the door and stepped outside on the porch with him, shutting the door behind me. I rubbed my arms trying to keep the coldness away.

"Is everything okay?" I asked, not sure what other reason he could be here. God, it was really cold. I kept rubbing my arms.

I heard movement on the right side of the porch. I was surprised to see that Grim was here as well. I closed my mouth shut to hide my shock. He sat atop the bannister, one foot propped up on the bannister with him and the other tapping on the porch. I looked back to Killian. "What are you two doing here?" I muttered and went to Grim. His head was turned away from me, looking somewhere in the distance. I couldn't see anything beyond the porch light.

"He wouldn't let me come alone," Killian answered behind me.

"You can't be out here," I said to Grim. "What if Mom was to look out and see you. I hope you have yourself hidden so that people can't see you! She would freak—"

I shoved his legs and didn't realize he wasn't hanging onto anything. His head swiveled around to face me just as his whole body started toppling over. The leg next to me flew in the air, almost hitting my head—and he fell off the porch. I heard the thud and covered my mouth with my hands. "I didn't mean that," I said immediately, scared to death with worry and fearful of his wrath.

Oh, God. I just pushed Grim Reaper off the porch. He was going to give me an early grave.

"I thought you were hanging on." I bent my head over the bannister, sounding a little too desperate to make him understand. Only he wasn't there.

I looked around until I heard Killian laugh behind me. "She pushed you off the porch." He was still laughing when I turned around and came face to face with Grim. Well, more like I was looking at his chest, but when I looked up I was staring at his face. Killian laughter died out behind him. "Let's not forget why we came here."

Grim ignored him and grabbed my wrist. "Only you." I didn't know what he meant.

Then the weirdest thing happened, his hand left my wrist and moved toward my face. I thought for sure he was going to touch my cheek until he hesitated and decided against it. I stared at his back as he hurried away from me.

What was that? *Stop racing*, stupid heart, he wasn't going to hurt you. But why did I have the strangest feeling that wasn't what was happening at all.

Killian came toward me as Grim left. He held something in his hand and brought it up so that I could see it. It was my cell phone. "This was why we stopped by. I would have let Grim bring it to your room if I knew I would upset your mother..." I ignored the comment about my mom and made sure the phone still worked. It a took a few seconds for it to come back up but it worked. There was a small crack on the screen but otherwise— she lived.

"Thanks," I whispered with a smile.

I noticed Grim was looking up randomly. I looked at the porch roof where he was staring, wondering why in the world he was staring at that spot so intensely, but then I realized that if the roof wasn't over the porch, he would be able to see straight into my window. My stomach knotted, did he know Ryan was in my room?

Of course he did. He was Grim Reaper. He told me he had that sense about ghosts and death and all that weird crap; I watched him nervously. I knew Ryan needed to move on from this world, but I wasn't ready for that.

Killian turned toward Grim when I wouldn't stop looking his way. "What is it?" It didn't take him long to figure out what was happing. When he looked back, his handsome face was warped with anger. "Has he been staying here?" he asked slowly.

He wasn't worried about what Grim might do to Ryan like I was. No, he sounded like a man angry to find out another man was in his woman's room. That scorching heat slid up my neck

110

and face as I looked anywhere else than at him. I wasn't feeling guilty or embarrassed that Ryan was in my room. I was just afraid of what he might do to Ryan and... secretly pleased that he was jealous.

"Yeah, he stays here a lot, although, I'm not sure where he goes when he's not here," I told him quietly. That got Grim's attention and he finally looked away from the roof. There was a thick amount of tension coming from them both as they gazed at me. I rubbed my neck awkwardly.

"He needs to ascend." Grim lifted his hand and his scythe materialized. I stepped in front of him.

"No, Grim." I gave him a shove as he stepped forward but, of course, it had no effect. His essence darkened. "Not yet,' I whispered.

"Ghosts are only lost souls, Melanie. He doesn't belong in this world anymore." I nodded, understanding completely, but I couldn't accept that for Ryan just yet.

I pressed my hands against his chest just in case he might disappear on me and go to Ryan. "I know, but have you forgotten that I'm the reason he's dead?" Grim went still underneath my touch, and I kept my hands in place as I went on, "It can't happen, not yet. Not until he tells me he's ready. Not until his sister gets to tell him everything she needs to," I paused for a heartbeat, "Not until I learn how to say goodbye." They had to

111

know I wasn't ready for that.

Grim placed his cold skeletal fingers against mine on his chest and his essence changed back to its normal shade of blue. "When he's ready." *When you're ready,* was what it sounded like he actually meant.

"Thanks." I managed to smile.

The front door opened and Grim and I were standing in front of it. My eyes widened just as Grim disappeared underneath my fingertips. Without the support of his chest, I lost what I was leaning my weight against, and began to tumble forward. Killian managed to grab me before I fell, only it was awkward. I ended up twirling around in the process and smacking into his chest.

When I looked up, he was grinning at me. Glad he thought it was funny. I leaned away and turned toward the doorway. Alex was there. "Mom wanted me to see when you were coming back in?" Which meant she was telling me to come back in. I hated how little she trusted me or how the moment I started doing the things she always wanted me to, she was against it.

I sighed. "What are you guys doing?" Alex finally asked.

Killian grinned. "I was showing your sister a few moves."

"Moves?" Alex's nose scrunched up and I was oddly worried where this conversation was going myself.

"Dance moves," Killian answered, looking down at me.

"But she's really bad."

I glared and Alex snorted. "I could have told you that." I noticed that my brother was trying to suppress a smile. That made me happy, anything to make him and Mom like him—I desperately wanted them to. Then I blinked a few times when I realized what I had just admitted to myself.

"Alright, I should go inside already." He slipped his hands in and out of mine so quickly, it wasn't nearly enough contact.

"If you must…" he said reluctantly.

I smiled over my shoulder at him as I stepped inside. I shut the door and was still grinning when Alex said, "You guys really are dating."

"No, we're not." I walked through the hallway.

"Doesn't look that way," Alex muttered next to me, and I wished I never looked to the top of the stairs. My smile vanished as I saw Ryan staring down at me, his expression filled with hurt. His eyes reflected his sadness and I started up the stairs. He didn't move from where he stood, not even when I reached the top and needed him to move to get by—or I would have to go through him. I finally let myself look into his eyes again.

"You're falling for Grim," he stated, sounding so unlike himself. Ryan never sounded closed-off, especially toward me.

"Ryan," I whispered so low that even I could barely hear myself.

He moved aside and I hurried into my room and shut the door. It didn't take him long to follow me, I took a deep breath and released it as I turned around to face him.

"I'm right," he said, sounding more sure of himself this time.

I didn't know how to answer him, and I didn't want to lie. I grabbed my ponytail and pulled it loose, my blonde hair fell over my shoulders. I felt the headache coming and knew it would be better to have it down.

Grim and Killian were separated now, so I wasn't sure how to answer him. He still called Killian, Grim. Around Grim, I either felt safe or afraid but was even that changing? Killian made me feel things no one ever had before. He lit me up head to toe, it was dangerous and mind-consuming because it was all I could think about anymore. Something was happening, something was changing between us all. I just didn't know what that was.

I didn't even know if any of it was even real.

But Killian was still a demon. Grim didn't even have tendons and flesh. Whatever I kept thinking, couldn't be possible… Killian's incubus voodoo was only doing a number on my body and brain.

So, it was nothing at all. I closed my eyes and dropped my hands from my hair before reopening them. "Grim doesn't even have flesh, he's an entity, Ryan. And Killian's a demon. I don't have any kind of feelings toward him." Then why did it feel like I was lying?

Ryan had that look of longing as he gazed at me. I looked down, a heavy feeling rested over my heart. I knew how he felt about me. I knew how I had once felt about him. And because of those feelings he had for me, he was a ghost. What must it feel like to ask the girl you died for if she was falling in love with someone that wasn't even human? "Ryan." My throat tightened and something pressed against my chest. An awful, horrid feeling that threatened to eat me alive.

He broke. "Don't look at me like that. Don't look so perfect that it breaks my soul to look at you because my soul is the only thing I have left." My hand moved out between us, I wanted to reach out to him and touch him but remembered I couldn't. My hand only hovered midway as if it was proof of his ill fate. "You know I can feel the Grim Reaper now as a ghost. I knew he was close; I could feel the danger he meant toward me now, clawing at my chest to either run or go to him. I know I'm not supposed to be here, and he won't hesitate to send me wherever I should be."

"No," I said, shaking my head. "He promised he wouldn't make you until…" It was hard to say. "Until you are ready to go."

"He promised you that?" he asked in disbelief. He rubbed his head and walked toward me. "This is going to sound stupid and lame, but I need to say it." I could only look at him confused, afraid of what he was going to say next. His jawline hardened as he continued to look in my eyes. I knew whatever he meant to say was serious for him. "Melanie, I've always known how afraid you are. How that fear has kept you sheltered and stuck in your own little world—afraid of what you might see next." His deep, sorrowful eyes wouldn't let me look away as he continued. "I always thought—hoped—I would be the one that brought you out of that shell." He took a deep breath and closed his eyes, then reopened them.

"I thought that someday you'd look at me and see that I was enough." He turned away from me and went toward the other side of the room. "But, I wasn't and now

I'm watching you become the woman I always knew you were."

"Ryan," I whispered. I felt myself shrinking inside my own skin. I heard his words, felt them against every part of me but...

He looked at me from across the room, shaking his head. "You don't even realize how much you've changed, do you? You're not afraid of ghosts anymore, Melanie. I remember when you didn't even like to go to new places because you were so afraid of seeing new ghosts."

I thought about it. I wasn't afraid of them anymore. "No, but that's because ghosts seem so pale in comparison to demons."

"Yeah, exactly, listen to what you're saying. You should be more afraid now. Your life is all kinds of crazy but look at you..." He looked at me with a hint of admiration. "You're more alive than I've ever seen you."

He was right. I knew it. I felt it and I have been asking myself why I wasn't more afraid like I used to be; like I was when I first learned about the demons. I was in just as much danger now as I was three weeks ago. Had I changed that much within such a small amount of time? I was clueless growing up, not knowing what happened to me in that classroom, now that I knew, did that make it easier?

"I had to change, I had no choice in the matter," I told him what I thought I knew.

He shook his head at me again. "No, it's more than that. You also know, whether you admit it or deny it, the moment he entered your life, you've been happy…different. It has something to do with Grim."

"Grim has nothing to do with—"

"He does. Killian and him are the same. They might not be the same person now but somehow they just are." He looked like he didn't understand it himself. "They protect you, and somehow it's changing you." I searched his face, unsure what to say. What did he want me to say? "You're stronger… you're getting braver. You're probably still afraid but that doesn't stop you from sleeping at night." I blinked a few times when I realized he was right. "What? You haven't noticed? —Or you didn't think I would notice how good you sleep now that he's back in town?"

My heart beat wildly; he had just peeled back a layer I hadn't bothered to notice. I was sleeping good and I never slept good.

"I feel safe," I admitted.

"You do," he agreed.

"What is it you're trying to say?" I asked nervously.

Was his expression what heartbreak looked like? "Just wanted you to know…that I wanted to be that person for you." He disappeared from my room. I didn't remember going to my bed and curling up in my cover. I only remembered the sick and twisted feeling of guilt.

CHAPTER EIGHT

I spent Saturday morning with Alex at home. He played a video game in his room while I read in the living room. So, maybe I wasn't really spending time with Alex, but we were under the same roof. That had to count for something.

Ryan never came back last night. Which was probably a good thing, I wasn't sure what I was supposed to say to make things better between us.

I didn't sleep as well last night as I had been since Killian showed back up. I tossed and turned, everything Ryan said the night before was on repeat inside my head. He was right about a lot. I was different now. Whether he was right about Killian and Grim being part of that reason, I wasn't sure. I did know they meant something. Maybe I was just afraid of admitting what that might be.

And if Ryan hadn't gotten into that accident, my feelings might have never paused. My guilt had stopped me from going anywhere with what I felt. I shared something special with him that night before Ryan had wrecked… maybe it was only a matter of time before the feelings spilled over. I no longer worried about what Vengeance's puppets had said, although, I had easily let them manipulate my thoughts in that moment…

It should have been clear from the beginning. Killian hadn't even wanted to protect me at first, he was never curious about the Vessel. If he had wanted the Vessel, he could have taken it the first night instead of saving me.

I truly believed his only interest was me.

He stuck around and continued to save me… I never made it easy for him… I willingly went to Fear and he even saved me… again. Again. I wondered how many more times he would have to sweep in to save me before I would ever get the chance to do something in return?

All these emotions were hitting me at once. My freaking heart felt like it was going to explode. It was making my heart swell up.

I clamped my fist over my chest and took a deep breath, *I can't ignore it anymore.*

I had to see him.

I would continue to hurt Ryan, but I forced myself to shove all my thoughts of him to the side just so that I could do what I wanted. And right now, I wanted to see Killian.

Like a woman possessed, I threw my book on the couch and hurried upstairs. I found my cell phone sitting on the nightstand and quickly sent him a text:

I'm coming over.

I meant to ask if he cared if I came over, but my brain wasn't working right. It didn't take a minute and he replied:

I'm waiting outside.

I tilted my head at the phone. Huh? There was no way he had gotten here so fast; he must have been outside before I even sent the text. I went to the window and peeked outside. His Corvette was parked in our graveled driveway. I watched him step out. He glanced up at my window. My heart beat out of rhythm.

I didn't understand this nervous excitement I felt, but I wanted to follow along with it. I placed the curtain back and ran to my closet. I wished I had something cute to wear. I didn't have much besides t-shirts and jeans. I puffed out my cheeks and continued looking.

I didn't want to make him wait too long and I was in a hurry to get to him so I grabbed a white top. I tossed my shirt I had been wearing somewhere and slid off my pajama pants. I slipped the tight shirt over my head. It revealed my cleavage and I thought, why not. I wanted his eyes on me. I grabbed a pair of jeans. I pulled out the brown leather jacket I got from Tess one year for Christmas that I never did wear.

I yanked off the tag as I moved in front of the mirror. I brushed my tangles out of my hair before tossing my head over and ruffling it back up to give it some volume. Why was I so pale? I grabbed my cheeks and glanced in the mirror. I looked horrible. I grabbed some pink lipstick and began to put it on when Mom stepped in.

I stared at her through the mirror. "You're putting on lipstick?" she asked, but she didn't sound angry or accusing, it was more curiosity.

"Yeah, Killian's waiting for me outside." I found a tube of mascara and started applying. I poked my eye in the process and swore, I wasn't good at makeup.

"Yeah, I saw that he was outside." She walked into my room and sat down on the bed. "Do you know what time you will be back?"

I shook my head, still looking at myself in the mirror. "I'm not sure. I don't even know what our plans are—" I cut myself off, meeting my own eyes in the mirror. "I just want to be with him right now."

I saw her nod at me through the mirror as she sat on the bed behind me. "Then spend time with him. I hope you enjoy yourself."

I frowned as I turned around to face her. What was with

her? Why was she suddenly okay with me being around Killian? "Don't stare at me like that," she huffed and stood up. "I'm your mother, Melanie. I worry about you, but I remembered something about my daughter. She's smart and beautiful." She moved forward and placed her palm against my cheek with a bright smile. "I've tried and tried the last few years to get you to go out and try new things. Do new things. Meet new people and that totally backfired on me when Killian showed up at our doorstep the first time." She laughed. "I didn't realize how scary it would be when you finally did. But honey, I do want you to experience new things. Falling in love and everything in between is a part of growing up and it's something I won't keep you from doing."

"Okay...?" I grinned at her, feeling weird that Mom had just said that. But it was a happy kind of weird.

Killian knocked downstairs and Mom dropped her hand. "Looks like he's brave enough to come to the door again and face my fury." We both grinned as she walked toward the door. She stopped in the doorway and looked back. She hesitated, "Melanie...I know we've never had *that* talk..."

My cheeks heated. "Mom," I said quickly. "Believe me, I know. You don't have to tell me."

She sighed in relief. "Good, just be safe...okay? You don't hang out with guys like Killian and remain a virgin. It's just not possible." I groaned, covering my red face.

"Mom!"

"What?" She laughed. "He is good looking. Just older than I wanted for you, but that's how the first ones usually are." I was still staring at the doorway after she disappeared. I couldn't tell her how wrong she was. Ryan had been my first love, the love I kept hidden until it was too late. I never told him…and now it would never matter because Killian entered the picture.

I shook the thoughts away. *No thinking.* I didn't want to think myself out of what I was doing right now. No second guessing everything. I grabbed my jacket and hurried downstairs. The front door wasn't open and I grew worried that they weren't at the door. I grabbed my boots on the shoe rack next to the door when I noticed them in the living room. Mom, Alex, and Killian… Would he ever look normal inside our home? He just seemed too big and out of place for this world. I felt a pang in my chest when I remembered we were from different worlds.

Stop… thinking.

I zipped my boots up and moved behind him in the living room, sliding my hand across his back. He was smiling down at me as I made my way beside him. "There you are," he said. I smiled, and his eyes raked over my body just enough to set me on fire before his gaze went back toward Mom.

"We should go," I whispered quickly, and I didn't miss the sly look in his eyes as they dropped over me.

125

"Call and check in, okay?" Mom said hesitantly. I saw that she was gripping her hands tightly and knew she was fighting against herself to let me go.

I embraced her in an unexpected hug, surprising her. Her breath fell over my shoulder as she gasped and finally hugged me back. "I will, Mom." When I pulled away, she had the biggest smile on her face. I never hugged her—we never showed any affection.

"Don't worry, your daughter is safe with me." Killian had chosen the exact wrong words to say to her. She gave him a yeah-right glare for a second before she disguised it with a smile.

"Have fun," she said before we walked out.

The moment we were next to his car, the biggest sigh fell from his lips. I gave him a look and he shrugged his shoulders. "What?" We got in the car and he started it up. "Your mom scares the fuck out of me, and I have never feared anyone, *ever*."

I laughed loudly, giving him a dumbfounded look. "Why?"

He backed out of the driveway. "Because." He stole a quick glance at me. "She's the woman that gave birth to you. And she also liked Ryan a lot…" His words faded and I arched an eyebrow.

"What's Ryan got to do with this?"

"Your mom has always liked Ryan, probably from the very beginning when she first met him." He sighed. "She's never once smiled at me until today and even that was forced."

"She just hasn't gotten to know you yet." I looked ahead at the houses and trees that went by.

"You sound so sure…"

"Killian, look at us." I tilted my body around to face him as much as my seatbelt would allow. "You couldn't stand the fact that you had to protect me, and I was afraid of you but now look."

He arched an eyebrow and his smile turned devilish—so mischievous that I knew I dug myself in a grave for what I might have admitted. "What about us?" I felt like a deer caught in headlights, and his tone dropped a level, sounding huskier. 'Is there anything different about us now?" There was a twinkle of no good in his eyes.

I turned forward and groaned. "You're impossible."

"Still waiting on what's different, Love." I looked out the window, trying to ignore the fluttering going on in my chest and stomach… calling me 'Love' was definitely a reason why we were different now. He knew it too, he just wanted to get me started.

"We get along just… fine," was all I offered him, choosing my words carefully. He must have thought I would admit

127

something because he looked disappointed. Only it didn't last as his eyes traveled down to my cleavage, which was mostly hidden by the seatbelt. There was still enough visible that his breathing changed—becoming more labored. There was a sudden shift in the air. I moved the seatbelt a bit so that it didn't press against my shirt so much. Now that I thought about it, wearing a pink bra underneath was very noticeable. But that was what I wanted when I left the house.

Only I couldn't think right now. I went to pull my jacket over me but almost never got my body to obey. The air was thick with his intoxicating scent, surrounding me. I felt his presence next to me like one felt the need to breathe and when I finally let myself look over at him, I wished I never did. My body was getting all tingly and all he was doing was looking ahead driving.

With a barely functional brain, I admired him. I really loved his hair. It was always out of place but in a way that looked great on him. I wanted to run my hands through it…and I realized my hands were reaching out toward him and I yanked them back.

Killian noticed and when I saw that his eyes were solid black, I knew it was his incubus voodoo working on me. He brought his hand up to his face and shook his eyes as if trying to throw off a bad feeling before looking back over at me. "Melanie, I…"

"Where are we going?" I asked purposely, avoiding what

128

he might have said. He didn't seem to like that he had no control over his seduction powers lately.

"My house." My mind went back to the R-rated in zero seconds flat without the need of his incubus nature helping me along. "I figured that's where you wanted to go. You said you were coming over in the text." Oh, yeah.

"But you were already at my house," I added.

"Yeah, it's easier to keep you safe if you're with me." That was the only reason?

"Oh," I managed to mumble. I never hid disappointment well.

"Was there another reason?" His voice held a tease, but I was already upset.

"Of course not," I said, crossing my legs and leaning against the door. "I hope you have books or movies or something so I don't die of boredom." Seemed I had a while to go before I got rid of my childishness, but he brought out the best and worst in me.

"Yeah, I grabbed a few things while you were at school yesterday, actually."

We rode in silence until we were pulling in his driveway. I unbuckled and got out, the wind slapping me in the face. He was already waiting for me at the bottom of the steps. Now I remembered why I never wore my hair down, my hair was constantly slapping across my face. I moved my head awkwardly, trying to get it out of my face.

He was walking in front of me and it was only natural that I noticed the way his jeans hugged his butt perfectly. *Very nice*, I thought. And that was when I also noticed, very embarrassingly, that I was bent forward as I checked him out... I blushed and quickly raised up. Too late. My gaze went up to meet two very teasing and knowing eyes. He gave me a smirk.

I looked away and straightened my voice, faking a cough. Playing it cool. Only we both knew what I had been doing. "What?" I mumbled innocently. I let the wind carry my hair into my face so that he couldn't see anything... like flaming red cheeks.

"Are you coming?" I moved my hair from my face to see that he was already walking in. I hurried to catch up. It was nice and warm when I slipped inside.

And, oh, God.

It smelled like him in here. I looked over the place again since I didn't get a chance to the first time with Ryan popping up. I ignored the pang I felt when I thought of Ryan and tucked it away for now. I could tell the home was older. The wallpaper even looked out of date, beige, and weird patterns, yet still beautiful. The stairs were wooden and so were the floors.

130

I followed the rustling of bags through the hallway past the stairs into the living room. Shopping bags were scattered over the couch and floor. The TV on its stand still had the plastic on it. I sighed, he hadn't been joking. It looked like he had only now bought anything. I started snooping through the bags as he came up beside me. "I wasn't sure what you liked."

He bought a ton of movies, books, and even a board game. I smirked, tossing it aside. "Movies and books were fine," I said.

He grabbed another bag and pulled out a Blu-ray DVD player and shoved it in my hands. "Here, you can hook this up."

I looked up and huffed at him. "But the TV isn't even hooked up."

He was already heading into the hallway. "Then you better get started."

"And what are you gonna do?" I grumbled, looking into the hallway where he disappeared.

"Make some grub." He yelled from somewhere in the house, possibly the kitchen. I arched my eyebrow in his direction before turning my attention back to the task at hand. I took the DVD player out of the box and placed the box and plastic into a bag to throw away later. By the time I was finished hooking up his TV and everything else, and even categorized his movies on his TV stand for him—I realized I was doing his housework. I rubbed my forehead and groaned.

It bothered me that I had nowhere to put the books he bought, and it equally bothered me that they were in bags so I placed them in a neat stack next to the TV stand. If he planned to stay here a while, he needed to get something to put them on. My mind could not tolerate the book abuse.

Whatever he was cooking, it made a scent trail through the house and smelled so delicious. I followed the amazing smell to the end of the hallway where the kitchen was. Killian was standing in front of the stove, something about seeing him in such a normal way had my pulse skyrocketing. I held the bag of trash I carried with me and asked, "Where is the trash can?"

He pointed to his left, not looking back. "In the closet." I walked around the table and tossed the trash away before closing the closet door back. I fiddled with my shirt, making sure my cleavage was still eye-catching as I walked next to him.

"What are you making?"

"Chili."

"Mm." I tiptoed next to him to peek at the food, but my chin wasn't even able to reach his shoulder. He leaned over enough so that I could see.

He was leaning over me, getting closer, so close that I could lick my tongue across his lips or chin if I wanted to. And I

132

shouldn't want to do something as weird as that but that was exactly how he made me.

"Say that again," he groaned in my ear, feathering it with a tickle-tingle sensation that made my skin ripple on that side. I shivered.

"Say what?" I wondered if this was what animals felt like when in heat?

"What you said before, say it again. In. My. Ear." His voice was husky as he punctuated the last three words. A sweet growing ache moved between my thighs, spreading into my stomach. I looked up at him. Really looked. His eyes were still the beautiful dark brown they always were, they weren't black right now so it meant this was *us* happening, nothing else.

His lips curved in a devious way. The more I let myself look at him, the more I wanted everything about him. I craved to know everything I didn't know about him. With each passing moment, my heart began to whisper things like *forever* with each beat.

"That smells good," I mumbled, sliding my hands across his muscular arm. Something similar to a growl tore from his chest.

"Before that." He leaned his body around to face me— away from the stove. I had better access to reach him and brought my hands over his amazing chest. Hard abs ran underneath my fingertips. His hands found my waist, pulling me in. Thank God because even this didn't feel close enough.

My softness met with his hard chest. "Mm," I moaned, giving him what he wanted to hear again.

His hand tightened around my hip as the other went to my hair, threading itself, and he bent my head back. "Oh." He was rough with me, but I found that I liked it. He tilted my head back further with my hair and I relaxed my neck so that he could. I watched his eyes swim with desire as his mouth came down over my neck. Goosebumps broke out over my flesh as he sucked along my collarbone. Heat ruptured inside me. "Oh—" I arched into him as his teeth grazed over me before it turned into feather-light kisses across my neck—then he would repeat it all again. I gripped his shoulders, positive that I would fall to the floor if I didn't.

He gripped me like a madman, his touch becoming less composed and more frantic. He pulled himself away from my neck long enough to grab ahold of my legs and hauled me up against him. He moved forward a few steps and tossed me over the table, it slid a few inches from the force of my weight. I gripped the table and panted, making sure the table was going to hold my weight. Killian didn't seem to worry, he pulled my thighs apart and moved his body in between them.

134

Everything about this situation was turning me on and when I watched the way his body moved to control mine, I knew I was freaking putty for his making.

There was a moment of panic when I felt the hard length of him pressing against my thigh. But it was also creating a pulse between my legs—making my stomach clench. My skin flushed with desire and I needed him touching me more.

It was a battle of nerves and desire. When his hard-on pressed against my sex, my nerves seemed to be winning and I stiffened. And all I had to do was look up and see the desire washed over his face and somehow, it won over my panic.

Nerves forgotten, I brought my arms around him forcing him to lean over me. He groaned in response as his hands roamed up my back. Then his hands stopped. I looked up to him—skin flushed and achy. Everything about this was new for me and exhilarating. There was a moment where we just looked at one another, devouring each other with only our eyes—taking everything in. One hand left my back and pressed a finger against my bottom lip. He brought it down, exposing the inside of my mouth before letting go.

"Will you stop staring already. I'd rather do the kissing part now," I urged him. His eyes liquefied into black, fading in and out between his brown and black. I could feel his scent spilling around me, coaxing me into the dark side but I was already there. Only now I felt more laid back and hazy.

"Don't tempt me, Love." *Love,* I freaking loved when he said that word.

He studied my lips as his thumb pressed into my collarbone. There was disappointment clear on my face when he still didn't kiss me. He pulled at my jacket, tossing it on the floor. His eyes fell over me and the disappointment started to dwindle. He yanked my shirt down from both shoulders. I could hear the fabric stretching as he pulled it down, exposing my pink bra. My breath quickened, the rise and fall of my chest was his only interest.

His mouth started along my neck again and I whimpered—feeling displaced and out of my mind. I clung to him, urging him further down by pushing his head. He bit my collarbone and cupped my boob through the bra. He slipped the strap off my shoulder, letting it hang over my arm as he pulled the cup down, exposing my pink nipple. I watched it disappear in his mouth and the pleasure was more than I could handle. The sensation was foreign and when he sucked roughly—gripping my breast even harder, my core clenched. I was afraid of exploding into a billion pieces from his mouth alone.

"Killian," I moaned. It felt amazing yet too much all at once. The ache between my thighs had me feeling wild—out of control. The ache was torturous yet… I didn't want it to go away.

136

I wanted to see where it would take me—take us.

He gave me a sly look with my nipple still in his mouth. I moaned in frustration and he bit my nipple with a grin. It was game over for me.

He had me. I was his and he knew it.

"Too much, Killian!" I pushed at his head, taking his mouth off my pebbled nipple. When I saw his eyes again, they were liquefied and so was my brain.

I pulled his face to mine—drunken with his scent wrapping around us and did what I wanted to do since the beginning. I kissed him, tearing my nails into his scalp and across his back. He growled and his tongue slid across my teeth. He pushed me down—I fell back against the table as my head smacked the wood with a loud thud. He stared down at me through half lidded black eyes. He was incredibly good looking.

I wondered what he saw when he looked down at me. My arms were bent out beside my head as I watched him above me. My shirt was still pulled down, revealing one boob. My mind was in a weird haze, but I knew what to do. I smiled and went to pull him close, but the black of his eyes faded back to brown and he leaned away from me so quickly that it was more of a jump. My smile dropped and I leaned up.

"Killian?"

He covered his face with his palm and panted. Now that I got a better look, he was sweating a lot. He brought his shaky hands to my bra and shirt, covering me up. "Go to the living room, I'll be there in a minute."

My feelings were all over the place. I was feeling embarrassed—mortified, but I was also worried. "Killian, what's wrong?"

"Melanie!" He smacked his hand down on the table causing me to jump. "This should have never happened," he paused, "not this way... He's going to fucking skin me alive!" He took a deep raggedy breath.

I slid off the table and hurried to the living room. My heart pounded in my ears. All I could think about was starting back where we left off. Did he mean Grim? Was he upset that his incubus nature was getting between us or did he regret what we did? Unease made its way into my stomach.

I waited impatiently in the living room. I didn't know how much time had passed but I put on a movie. He came in some time later carrying two bowls of chili. He handed me a bowl and placed his on the coffee table. "Is water okay?" I nodded and he disappeared and came back with two bottled waters and a pack of crackers.

We ate in awkward silence. I placed my empty bowl down on the coffee table. "It was good." He glanced over at me and I added, "The chili, I mean." Then blushed. Of course, he knew that... I really shouldn't let myself say anything sometimes. He grunted in response and nothing else was said. Thirty minutes further into the movie, I was feeling uncomfortable on the couch—and I might be fishing for some of his attention.

There was nothing else to do... so why not try again?

I splattered out on his couch, taking up every cushion besides the one he sat on. He went still next to me—I grinned on the inside. I waited a bit, stealing peeks at him as he watched the movie stiff as a board. I would catch him looking at me from the corner of his eye but when I turned to face him, he would turn away.

I wiggled around some more on the couch and his shoulders grew tighter—winding up with his rigid frame. It was getting harder for him to pretend he wasn't staring at my legs... the ones that were sliding closer to him every few seconds. I finally stretched them out across his legs. He sucked in a breath and I did too when I felt his erection with my foot.

He tossed my legs off him and stood up, facing in the opposite direction—as if to hide what was going on in his jeans. I sat up quickly. He adjusted himself in his jeans. He raked his hands through his hair with a frustrated groan. "This isn't working." He turned and grabbed my wrist. He was dragging me out of the living room. And I was feeling disappointment and fear—had I went too far? "I'll take you home."

I pulled out of his grip. "Why?"

"Because this was a bad idea to think that it would be okay to be around you when I'm like this."

I leaned my weight on one hip. Every move I made seemed to upset him—his eyes fell over me, nostrils flaring. "Killian, it's okay," I tried to tell him.

"No, it's not. I can't even fucking think straight right now," he argued and reached for me again but I wouldn't let him. "It's only this hard when you're around."

"What gets harder?" We both caught the unintended pun, and I glanced between his legs. He swore under his breath and grabbed my arm, pulling me toward the front door.

"Put on your shoes," he told me.

"No, Killian. You being an incubus demon doesn't bother me." I had already gotten over that bridge on my own.

He ignored me and started looking for something. "Where did you take your jacket off?"

"*You* took it off me in the kitchen." I took pleasure in the moment he let himself devour me with his eyes. "Killian!" I yelled but he was already in and out of the kitchen, shoving my jacket in my hands. "You're being a jerk," I huffed. "And making me feel embarrassed." And ashamed.

140

His jaw tightened and his eyebrows furrowed in anger as he glared over at me. "You're lucky I'm taking you home right now and not doing what I really want to do with you."

"And what's that?" I snapped back with anger.

"Fuck you." My anger all but faded into blushing cheeks. "Not the romantic shit you want—" he went on, "—No, I can't give you that when I'm in incubus demon." He brought his hand between us. "All I can think about is fucking you over and over, and since I've been back around you, I'm having these sick and twisted thoughts about taking you away—locking you up, keeping you there all to myself so that I could do what the fuck I needed to get you off my mind." I stood frozen like a statue as his eyes broke through me. "I'm guessing you want to go home now."

He grabbed the doorknob and swung the door open. I looked in horror at our uninvited guest on the other side. The charred demon growled, teeth exposed. I moved on instinct and took the doorknob from Killian's hand and slammed the door shut. I looked to him afterwards. "You really should reconsider who you invite over."

Killian's eyes stayed on the door. "Fuck!" he yelled just as the demon charged through the door—entering like a ghost and tackled him to the ground. The demon's claws went for Killian's chest, but he was able to grab his wrists before he could. He pushed the demon upward by the throat—using the other hand to punch his face before he kicked him off. Killian hurried to his feet as the demon scurried around like an animal before standing. The demon growled—claws outstretched, flexing in and out toward Killian.

Killian bent down and took a knife from his boot. He lunged for the demon, grabbing it by the arms. He threw a punch, the demon staggered back. Then he sunk the knife into the demon's skull. I automatically looked away—the blood and the sound of the blade piercing through the skull—all of it was brutal. The demon roared and it made me look back. How was he even still alive? I watched in disbelief as the demon pulled the knife from his skull. He tossed it on the floor.

"Killian, he's new. Try not to kill him, would ya?" I recognized Molly's small voice and whipped my head around to find her behind me. She was still the same—same ole' bored-like expression and body of the child she died as.

"Molly," I spat her name out.

"Yeah," she said. "It's been a while." She brought her hands up and rolled her shoulders once. "Sorry for the wait."

"Get away from her, Molly." Killian stepped in her direction, picking up his knife on the floor as he watched the charred demon.

Molly smirked. "Oh, Killian," she said his name with pity.

142

"How sad it must be to go from being a powerful entity back into a mere sex demon."

"You shouldn't have said that," he warned her.

"I don't fear you. There's nothing left to fear." She even mocked him by laughing.

He charged at her but she faded—as Killian called it, or was what she did something different? —and reappeared next to the demon who was already fully recovered from the knife wound. Blood still covered his eyes and face, but he looked angry.

"You think you know everything." Killian smiled but it wasn't friendly.

"What blubber are you trying to speak now?" Molly glared.

"Stay behind me." He tucked me behind him before answering her. "Like I said, you know nothing."

"Oh?" She grinned and glanced my way. "Kill her, take her—I don't care, do whatever you have to so that we can get that Vessel for Fear," she ordered the demon, and he nodded. His eyes landed on Killian, then me.

"Don't fucking dare," Killian warned him.

"I think you have other things to worry about, incubus,"

143

Molly said. Growls echoed through the house at her words. Lots and lots of growling in every direction of the house. Behind her, bright eyes came into view along with their giant bodies. Two behind her and the charred demon with more coming out of the kitchen. Some were standing on the second floor waiting to attack. Wolf demons. I didn't even hear them come in.

One jumped from the second floor and lunged for Killian. "Go!" he yelled as he wrestled the wolf demon to the ground.

"What about you?"

"Melanie!" he hissed, stabbing the wolf demon in the head with his knife as he pinned it to the ground. More were coming for him—us, only it was too late for me to do anything. The charred demon yanked me by the arm and I used the opportunity to kick him between the legs. It didn't hurt him. He grabbed me by the other arm and pushed me his way.

A wolf demon howled in pain, and I turned my head to see it dropping to the floor. Already dead. Only it hadn't been Killian that killed it. "Need help?" Grim's velvety voice dripped with power. Another one dropped as he impaled it with his sword. Relief washed over me knowing he was here.

The charred demon threw me at Molly's feet. I looked up to see her grin. Molly wasted no time now that Grim was here. She grabbed me by the hair and yanked me up. I was fueled by anger when I swung at her, but she laughed as my fist went

144

through her.

Hot with rage, that same energy I felt before vibrated through me—calling to me, letting me know it wanted to be released. I tingled with power and without the voice telling me to do it, I pointed my palm toward her and let go of the energy at my fingertips. The golden light shot out and knocked her in the chest. The impact on her small body was strong but instead of hitting the wall, she flew through it.

Grim saw it happen and just stood there staring at me. Something grabbed my shoulder and pulled me to my feet. I saw that it was the charred demon and glared as he continued to pull at my arm. Killian football-tackled him into the wall and the wall caved in from their weight.

Grim was already at my side, pulling me close. His cold-boned touch ran along my arm causing chills to break out over my skin. I glanced up to see two more wolf demons jumping down onto Grim. He let go of me and slung them off easily before killing them.

There was another crashing sound and I swung around to see the tables had turned between Killian and the charred demon. The demon had him pinned against the wall with a tight grip around his neck. I started running to him, not sure what I could do to help, but Kilian's leg shot out and kicked the demon backward before I was even there. Killian grabbed his neck and coughed.

145

"Just what the bloody hell are you?" he asked the demon as he came after him again.

"We need to get Melanie out of here," Grim told Killian impatiently. Three more wolf demons came into the halls. "Molly has a portal opened up for them to keep entering."

"You can't kill him, Killian," Molly laughed, stepping back through the wall. She rubbed her chest as she looked at me. "Oh, my. Fear will be most intrigued to learn that you can even use the power now."

"I won't let Fear have it," I hissed, not realizing that I was holding my chest possessively. Since when was I so protective of the Vessel?

"He already has it." I looked at her confused. "Did you forget that mark on your chest means you belong to Fear the moment you die?" She smiled when my eyes widened. "Ah, see... I think you understand what I mean now. The power is his because you're his as well."

"She doesn't belong to him." Grim's blue essence darkened.

"Kill her or something, we don't have all day!" Molly snapped at the charred demon. He pushed away from Killian, but Killian grabbed him from behind. "I told you, you can't kill him. Fear made him using a part of himself to do so," Molly said. I eyed the demon, no wonder he was so hard to deal with.

146

Grim took one stepped toward Molly and she faded. I wasn't surprised, she was good at running away. The house was crawling with wolf demons. "Open a portal and leave them!" Grim looked at Killian. "I'll take Melanie."

Killian nodded as he threw the charred demon to the ground. I felt Grim's cold fingers through my jeans as he scooped me up in his arms. I leaned into his chest and looked up. The blue essence danced around the inside of his hollowed eyes and he asked, "Ready?"

"Get her!" Molly reappeared just as the darkness swallowed us whole. And now I knew what this place was in between. It was actually no place at all… a place out of time, an in between our worlds—then the light came.

CHAPTER NINE

There was a look of utter amazement on my face when we reached our destination. "Where are we?" I asked as he eased my feet to the ground. I moved my hands from his chest and stepped to the side. With my mouth still opened ridiculously, I circled around to look at our surroundings. I had never seen anything so beautiful or strange. We stood high on a cliff looking over the woods. Grim pushed his hand into my back urging me closer to the edge. I leaned back, pinpricks of sweat and fear breaking out over my skin. I didn't want to get any closer to the edge.

The dirt was pink at my feet. Or maybe a light purple. "Home," he answered as I leaned against his chest. I took everything in with a smile. This place was magical. I knew this couldn't be any place in my world...

The sky wasn't blue but a reddish-yellow looking color. I saw no sun and although the sky seemed dull, the place was vibrant with colors. The trees in the woods were all variety of colors. There were pink and purples, blue and greens, orange, and reds. My mind couldn't fully grasp what it was seeing.

Although this place was beautiful, something still felt terrifying. Maybe it was because I wasn't in my world anymore. I was in his. I closed my eyes—letting this enchanted place control my every sense. It smelled pleasant here, almost fruity. Something stirred inside of me. A feeling of content.

Home.

The voice told me. I didn't know what it meant, but something about this place did feel… right.

Everything about this place made me think of Grim and Killian.

"This is where you live?" I asked with a smile, completely mesmerized. He nodded, and I took in another deep breath.

I could hear a waterfall somewhere in the distance. Birds chirped and I heard other strange animal sounds I couldn't recognize. There was a piercing roar above us and I shrieked, stumbling back into Grim. His hands fell over my shoulders and held me still. Dragons flew above us. I counted five…six…seven. Ten or more—and more seemed to fly over the mountains in the distance. Nothing was a normal color here. Pink dirt, bright trees, and odd, skyscraper-sized mountains.

"Dragons?" I asked fearfully. The first dragon I encountered tried to kill me…

He nodded. "You don't have to be afraid of them. Although, they are protective, deep down, they are very loving and gentle creatures."

"Not the first one I met." I eyed them with wary.

"They're a very different breed than the one you saw at Fear's." He brought his hand up to point at them. "Look how different—these are flying, Melanie. The one you saw was a lot bigger and had no wings." I nodded, noticing the difference. He dropped his hand. "My land has been their home for a thousand years, maybe more. A group of demons were wreaking havoc on their lands and hunting them down. When it was finally time for me to step in as Death and descend the demons hunting them, they were nearly extinct. What was left of them, I offered sanctuary here in exchange that they would protect these lands and everything in it."

I tilted my head back so I could look at him. The more I learned about Grim, the more unpredictable he was—proving how very wrong I was about him. I didn't know nearly enough about him or Killian. I was beginning to understand that I was never a burden to him—protecting was a part of his nature. He either didn't realize that about himself or liked to keep it hidden under a very cranky façade. It was incredible what he did for these dragons when he didn't have to. I smiled.

Looking up at the dragons, I studied how different they were than the one I encountered previously. Grim was also right, these dragons were big but nowhere near the size of the one with no wings. These dragons were still slightly terrifying with their bat-like wings, but I was also mesmerized by their mysterious beauty; they were all black with red scales underneath their wings. Long, slender necks—I couldn't make out any of their faces from this distance.

A piercing call echoed behind us and I twirled around to see what dragon it was. It was a beautiful white dragon. She flew over us, looking down at us with interest. She was every bit the same as the other dragons only she was solid white. Bright blue eyes met mine for several seconds before catching up to the others. It was sad to watch how they treated her. They would scatter apart when she got close like they were shunning her. One even swept behind and bit into her tail. She cried and flew away from them.

"What's going on?" I squinted my eyes.

"What do you think? She's different than them, they treat her different because of it." I felt unexpected sadness for the dragon. She was treated horribly because she was different. In a lot of ways, I was just like her... maybe that was why.

"That's horrible," I told him. I could feel the bubbling rage entering my chest—I despised the others for treating her differently.

He sighed, looking up at them. "She has to find her place." He whistled—I wasn't going to wonder how a skeleton could whistle and I had still couldn't, okay? One of the dragons jerked his flexible neck in our direction before heading toward us. When he swooped down, I saw how impressive his wings were up close. Sharp and edgy looking. I backed away as he landed at the edge of the cliff. His talons gripped into the ground. As he tucked his wings away, pink dirt flew in my face. I had to guard my face with my arm as I watched him curiously. At this distance, I was now one hundred percent positive the dragon was a male. He might even be a little bigger than the rest. Grim walked past me. "This is Rixen, their leader." Rixen hunkered down, lowering his head as Grim came close so that he could rub his head.

Deep, bright red eyes flickered up at me. I had a moment of panic when I thought of Fear's red eyes, but then I took a deep breath and told myself not to compare this beautiful creature to a monster. And Rixen was beautiful. There was a crunching sound in the dirt behind me, and I twisted around to see the white dragon was lowering her head at me.

No, not me. I realized her blue eyes watched Rixen with fear as she stepped closer to me. I could be wrong, but it seemed she wanted to come to me. But at the same time, she was afraid of her leader. She eased closer and Rixen noticed, jumping on his hind legs as he roared at her. Grim stepped back to give him space. He shook his head at the white dragon. She lowered her head and backed away. I took a step in her direction. "This is between the dragons," Grim reminded me, but I still went to her.

I shook my head, brushing my hair behind my ears with my fingers. "I think she just wanted to come to me. She wasn't trying to make her leader mad." Once she saw me coming, her head perked up and she helped shorten the distance between us. I brought my hand out and her head dipped underneath my palm, rubbing against it. Her scales felt oddly smooth and warm. I smiled while rubbing her head. With my other hand, I cupped her chin and pulled her to my face. Her blue eyes had a clouded look about them as they peered into mine. She was so beautiful. Why would they treat her so poorly? "See?" I turned to meet Grim face with a cocky smile.

Rixen nostrils flared in our direction. Grim shrugged his shoulders and patted him. "She's never came to anyone before," he told me.

"What's her name?" I asked.

"She doesn't have one. Not even in their language would they give her a name." That was cruel. Grim looked over to Rixen. "I gave him the name Rixen, but he has his own name in the dragon language that can't be pronounced."

So, if he named Rixen... I looked back to the white dragon, feeling a connection with her. That likeness we both seemed to share. "Do you want a name?" I asked her. She lifted her head from my palm and nudged me slightly with a shake of her head. I gave her a toothy grin. "Is that a yeah?" She made a

153

whimpering sound. "How about…Sky?" She tilted her head slightly, a dog-like manner that I found adorable. "Your eyes are the same color as the sky back where I live. Beautiful, bright, and blue. Not like this reddish-yellow sky here." She rubbed her head into my hand. I took that as a sign she liked the name.

Rixen made a huffing sound and I smirked. Someone didn't like that I was giving the outcast a name, or attention. "It's only a name," Grim told the leader, and I turned to see the dragon shaking his head in disagreement. Rixen looked away, not wanting to meet my eyes when he saw me staring.

Grim looked at me. "Shall we ride?"

My stomach bottomed out. "What?" Just the thought made me queasy.

"Rixen will take us to my castle." *Castle?*

"Why don't you just poof us there instead?" I suggested, and he laughed.

"I don't poof anywhere, Melanie, and this will be a lot more fun." I extremely doubted it. And if he didn't poof anywhere, what the heck did he call his disappearing skills. Oh, right… like *fading* was any better.

"You do poof," I mumbled to myself.

He heard me. "I fade out of time—or look at it this way— I have my own travel line that no one can use except me. I do not

154

poof," he swore. "Don't make me sound like a witch."

I tried not to laugh. He didn't know that Killian had already sort of filled me in. Sky bucked beside me and I turned to her. What was she doing? She kept spinning around, showing me her back as she nodded her head.

"I think she wants to take you there herself." Grim sounded surprised.

"I don't know, Sky… I'm not a fan of heights." I looked to the cliff and the flying dragons and literally swayed.

Sky nudged my shoulder and I tried to smile. Grim was already mounted on Rixen. He grabbed the small bit of hair lying over Rixen's back to hold on to. "Don't worry. Nothing will happen. Besides, I'm here if you were to fall."

I poked my lower lip out into a pout as Sky excitedly turned her body for me. "You better poof and get me if I fall or I swear—" He had the nerve to laugh at my serious anxiety.

I sighed. Now, how did I climb up? Sky lowered her stomach on the ground and pinned her wings to her sides. I used her mane—which was silvery-white like her—to pull myself up and over her. My nerves kicked in the moment she started raising up. My grip was probably hurting her hair as I momentarily freaked out. "Relax. All you have to do is hold on. She will do the rest," Grim assured me right before him and Rixen dove off the cliff.

It took a minute before I saw them again. I was looking around frantically for them. I was thinking that they had dropped to their death—then they were flying toward the sky. Grim was hunkered against Rixen as they flipped upside down into a circle. Feeling reassured, I smiled. Nervous excitement trickled up my spine. I didn't want to do a flip, but flying might be okay...

Sky was taking us toward the edge of the cliff—every step she gained more speed. I held my breath and we dived over the cliff just as they had. "Oh my God!" We fell alongside the mountain, traveling downward to the lake at the bottom. I gripped her tighter as the water grew nearer and nearer. Too close! I closed my eyes and screamed moments before she finally lifted her body just in time. We glided over the lake. Our legs dipped into the water and I released the breath I had been holding. She turned back, and I swear it sounded like she was snorting at me.

"Not okay, Sky!" I told her with a smile. She turned back, her round eyes watching me closely. I dropped my gaze to the water and saw our reflection racing by before she took off to the sky. I locked my knees against her and laughed as she took us up—we continued upward, she wasn't stopping. We passed the cliff with ease and soon we were in the sky with Grim and Rixen who were waiting.

I was starting to relax as she flew next to them. Rixen

didn't like her being close and shot forward with impressive speed. I felt Sky tighten as she whipped her wings back and easily caught back up with him. With a growl, Rixen took off faster. "I think he's trying to outshine you," I told her. She bucked her head in agreement. "Males. It doesn't matter the species," I said it like she could understand, and I was sure she did.

Grim looked back. "No wonder she's an outcast. She can barely keep up." Rixen looked back at Sky at his words.

Straightening her neck out, Sky dived underneath them. She caught me by surprise and I screamed. Her speed also caught me by surprise. She flew back up beside Rixen—as if to make sure he saw her, but she didn't stop there. She went on ahead.

We were in the front now. I looked back and stuck my tongue out childishly. Rixen flew faster—a desperate attempt to catch up, but Sky never let him after that. Her leader was no match for her speed when she didn't hold back. "Look at how fast we're going, Sky! Not even Rixen can keep up!" I had to yell over the roaring of the wind in my ear. She looked back and wiggled her tail at them.

My eyes widened when the castle came into view. I knew it was his home because there was nothing else—no other homes but the colorful land, mountains, and trees. The castle reminded me of something medieval, only everything else was so much more vivid and breathtaking than something I could imagine from the past. This place was a dream come true. A small laugh escaped my lips as Sky swooped us down toward the castle.

A wide-stoned pavement stretched half a mile out in front of the castle. She landed gracefully on the light-gray pavement. She kept her wings out as she walked several steps before finally stopping. I slipped off her side and she waited until I was off her completely before tucking her wings back. Rixen arrived with Grim, his landing less graceful than Sky's and more with an impact. Rixen looked like he might blow steam out of his nostrils, he was so angry.

When he landed, it caused my hair to fly out of control from the wind off his wings. Grim jumped off his back, rubbing one of Rixen's wings. Sky took off in a blur. I turned to watch her speed away. Rixen took off after her with a roar.

He caught up with her and she twirled away from him just as he snapped at her tail. He kept at her. "Is she going to be okay?" I asked Grim. I watched them with worry.

He shook his head. "No, it seems she may have found her place after all." There was an awe in his voice. I hoped he was right. I gave the dragons one last glance before I looked at the castle.

"Is that your home?"

"Yes." I knew he was watching me from the side. "Are you disappointed?"

158

"Why would I be?" I moved my hand out and grinned. "Although, I am curious as to why you would live in a castle. I bet it has a ton of rooms."

He didn't get a chance to answer when a tall, curvy redhead appeared out of nowhere between us. I felt my forehead wrinkle as I stared at her. "Grim," she purred his name and my skin crawled. Oh-no-she-didn't was the look I must be giving her. I had no idea why the sight of her made me feel so horrible.

"Penny," Grim acknowledged her.

"I've missed you," she pout-smiled at him.

I tensed, feeling sick with anger. I didn't like her already. She probably wasn't dangerous since she was someone Grim knew. I had no reason to feel so weird around her. He didn't look at all worried to see her, he was relaxed which meant she wasn't someone I should hate... Was I being jealous? No, this was Grim... he was a freaking skeleton!

And Killian's other half, I reminded myself.

"Who is she?" I tried not to sound grouchy.

"She's a Reaper." Penny's eyes shifted from him to me. Her green eyes scanning over my body right before she smirked. I dropped my hands down and glared at her. What was that smirk for?

I studied her appearance. She wore a tight black shirt and

159

pants that had her boobs wanting to burst out… Not to mention the black stiletto boots that made her taller than me. Did she think I looked like a child compared to her? Why was I being so negative? I sighed. Crap, she was attractive and that had me feeling depressed.

I shouldn't have time to worry about my appearance with everything happening in my life.

She crossed her arms. "You must be the Vessel." She made it sound distasteful.

"It's Melanie," I said through clenched teeth.

She shrugged her shoulders uninterested. "How much longer do you have to protect the Vessel? It's boring when you're not around much." I just knew my ugly giant vein—the one on my forehead had to be popping out as she referred to me as the 'Vessel' again. Or maybe it was the way she was giving Grim the googly eyes. She grabbed his arm, pressing those huge breasts of hers against him. "Killian, too. When will you guys merge again?" Grim looked over at me and shoved Penny away from his arm.

"Penny." There was a warning in her name. She whined and twirled away.

Another one appeared in front of him. This woman was petite and a blonde. I was happy to say I had the same amount of curves as her. She looked to Penny in disappointment. She

160

greeted Grim with a bow before meeting his eyes. "Grim, Killian is inside. He has several injuries that need to be tended but refuses to have any of them healed."

"Why?" Grim hissed. Petite's eyes drifted to me quickly and he sighed. "Follow me," he told me. I had to run a few feet to catch up to his pace as he hurried to the castle. It didn't take me long to see Killian stumbling out the huge castle doors looking worse than I remembered. I passed Grim and went up all the giant, gray steps to get to him. His eyes fell over me and a brilliant, lazy smile played out over his face. Even his face had bruises.

My heart stopped as I stared at him. I knew my feelings were leaping into dangerous territories. I slowed as I got closer knowing that there were the other two Reapers next to Grim who were watching everything I did.

"Come here." He jerked his wrist back and forth wanting me to hurry. He was limping so it was apparent he couldn't be the one that hurried. I grinned, but it disappeared when he bent over grabbing his chest. The charred demon must have done some more damage on him before he managed to get away.

I hurried the rest of the steps and grabbed him by the shoulders. "Killian, God." I looked at his wounds and winced myself—he had to be in a lot of pain. "You're pretty banged up."

Dark eyelashes fluttered open when he smiled. "I believe I have that part figured out, Love." He groaned in pain.

"You need Grim to heal you or a doctor—whatever you guys call them here," I panicked.

"I'm the healer here." A male voice drifted from the top of the steps. I looked over Killian's shoulder and my mouth dropped open—me and my stupid mouth. I tried not to, but it always seemed to want to open when creatures like him appeared before me.

"This is why I hate humans," the centaur—half man, half horse—grumbled. He trotted down the steps next to us. I closed my mouth. I had offended the female centaur at Fear's the same way. His dark eyes glared at Killian. "You can't take off right when I'm trying to heal you."

"Once I caught her scent—" Killian cut himself off and pulled me closer. "Anyway, Lincoln, where are your manners? We have a guest."

Lincoln looked the other way with a snort. "The only thing you're greeting is your womanizing ways, you leech." I didn't like any of what he just said.

"Lincoln." Killian's voice was like ice, the same as his expression as he glared at Lincoln.

Penny laughed behind us, she still stood next to Grim.

"Why are you being so offensive?" she asked Killian. "You can't deny your pervy genes. You love the ladies. You love—"

"Penny, do you not have any souls to guide?" Grim's tone was sharp. Her smile faded. "If not, then wait for me inside. I'll have a word with you before you go." I couldn't tell what he meant.

She smiled, swaying her hips to the side. "You got it." From the sound of her voice, she didn't sound worried.

He's mine!

The voice was back, giving me strange thoughts again. The same voice that made me break Haley's leg and also helped me with the charred demon and Molly. I didn't know if the voice was a good or bad thing. Killian winced and I lost my focus on the voice. My hands were gripping his side and I knew I was the one causing him the pain. I let go and he sighed in some relief. His shirt was covered in a lot of blood. Just how bad was he really hurt?

"Are you okay?" he asked. I smiled and nodded my head, amazed that he still felt the need to worry about me. But—my heart skyrocketed—didn't he always take care of me before himself?

I touched his shirt and he tensed up immediately. I squinted my eyes together. "Killian. Just how bad are your injuries?" He brought his hand over mine so that I couldn't pull up his shirt.

"I'm fine."

"He's not," Lincoln interrupted. "It looks like he has a lot of wounds that needs to be closed and probably some internal bleeding. And the way he's breathing…" Lincoln shook his head. "I need to get him inside."

Killian muttered with his head hanging. "It's not that bad. The pain doesn't bother me."

Uh-huh. *Keeping telling yourself that.* He had no one fooled.

"Let's go get you fixed up," I whispered trying to help him stand. I hated seeing him in pain. I looked to Grim with an expression that must have read 'help'.

"Melanie will go with him so that he will let you heal him." Killian eyes were closing, but I could tell that Grim's words put him at ease. "You may leave, Gin." Grim spoke to the petite Reaper still beside him. She nodded and disappeared. Did no one believe in walking around here? I was feeling very mundane around them all. "Just follow Lincoln—" Killian collapsed against me and there was no way I could hold the big guy up. I started falling with him until Grim pulled him off me.

"I knew his wounds were worse than he was letting on," Lincoln muttered.

164

Grim was looking at Killian as he held him upright against him. "This has nothing to do with his wounds." Lincoln's eyes widened in surprise as their gazes both fell on me. What?

"Don't tell me…" Lincoln's eyes went back to Grim and I had no idea what was going on. "Grim, all this time…he hasn't? That's simply unheard of!" Lincoln sounded downright disturbed—or maybe shocked by whatever it was.

"Escort Melanie inside, I'll take him in," Grim said fading with an unconscious Killian.

CHAPTER TEN

Grim's castle was even more stunning on the inside. Once I followed Lincoln through the giant double doors it was like stepping into a fairy tale. The doors were a dark gray on the outside like the rest of the castle, but on the inside of the door, gold and white spiraled together in unique patterns.

The door led right into a huge circular room that made me think of a ballroom, but I seriously doubted he invited anyone over to dance. The room was darkened from his choice of colors. The floor was a light gray and the walls were a deep purple. Chandeliers hung across the middle of the tall ceiling in a row. The chandeliers were big and had sharp points that hung beneath them. I avoided walking underneath them. I saw Lincoln looking over his horse-body at me, smirking at my behavior.

This place was beautiful, yet disturbing like its owner. There was also a piano in a far corner and I wondered if he played. Strangely, nothing else was in the room. At the other end of the room was two stairways that circled out from the walls to point toward one another. That was where Lincoln led me. The

166

stairs and bannisters were a dark marble color with specks of gold and white.

I kept a distance behind Lincoln as we went up the stairs. I guessed I was a bit paranoid when it came to being around horses and standing behind him was no different. I was afraid of getting kicked.

"Does his home fascinate you human?" Lincoln twisted his neck around. His long ponytail fell over his back as he studied me like a hawk watching his prey. I dropped my hand from the bannister. I had been running it across the smooth marble without even noticing.

"My name's Melanie." Which he knew that. "And yeah, this place reminds me of him."

He grinned turning his head back around. "Do you think much of the master of this place? Or no?" His question surprised me enough that I stopped walking up the stairs for a second.

I continued up the steps. "I suppose. I am alive because of him."

"So, he's nothing but a savior to you?" That was another odd question. I didn't like him asking something personal when we only just met. Before I could answer, he added, "That's for the best. Humans and demons—entities can never be. It's not allowed."

167

I tried not to let what he said get to me, but it split my brain open. I knew I would obsess over it now. I felt sick to my stomach and there was a tightening in my chest.

"This way." I hurried to catch up as he took us through a long hallway. I followed him into a door, and another—I honestly couldn't remember how many we went through, my mind wasn't letting me process anything correctly after what Lincoln said.

The next door was our last; we reached our destination. We were in a bright room, and I knew it must be some sort of room for situations like Killian's. A cabinet full of medical supplies rested on the other side of the room and it made me wonder why it was needed when Grim had the ability to heal. Killian lay on a tan bed looking worse. I hurried to his side. "He looks even paler than a couple minutes ago."

"Step aside," Lincoln ordered me. I did as he said and stepped away. He moved next to the bed, bending his front legs enough to even his body with the bed. Lincoln grabbed a knife from the table and cut Killian's shirt up the middle. I knew I shouldn't have been admiring an injured man's body, but this was the first time seeing any hint of what he hid underneath all the dark brooding colors he wore. Blood and bruises weren't enough to hide how breathtaking and perfect his chest was. So muscular, broad—just all out flawless, everything about him was powerful and manly and the trail of hair going down… I looked away with a blush. I had no shame, he was hurt and I couldn't stop noticing how freaking sexy he was.

"How bad is it?" I asked, forcing myself to remember how injured he was.

"Actually, it's not bad. The way he looked made me think he was in rough shape." He placed his hand over Killian's chest and light flew out of his palm onto Killian's chest. I didn't understand why Grim couldn't have healed him like he did me. His wounds closed instantly. The bruises faded away.

Only when I studied Killian's face, it was still wracked with pain. Sweat coated his skin. Lincoln moved his hand and stepped back with a sigh. "Why does he still look so bad?" I whispered, not bothering to conceal my worry.

Lincoln shook his head. "That's his own fault. You can ask him yourself." He trotted toward the door. "I will get Penny to wash him up." Something nasty bubbled up in me at the thought.

"I can do it," I said quickly. He was staring at me too hard, almost like he was trying to piece something together. I didn't like it. "It's my fault he's this way so I should be the one," I added carefully.

He dropped his head and sighed. "Melanie, this isn't my place to tell you, but you are aware he's an incubus demon, correct?" When I stood there quiet, he grew frustrated. "He needs sex to survive. He can never go without something that's so vital to his kind. Like food is the energy you and I need to stay alive and healthy; sex is his."

He continued, "Without it, they only grow weaker and weaker because they are denying what their body needs to survive. Hell, I've never even heard of one being able to deny themselves at all until now." He pointed toward Killian unconscious on the bed. "When he was separated from Grim, he lost the ability to live without the need of sex. And Killian was already badly injured by Fear when he became an incubus demon again and he's been all this time without it… his weaken state proves it." My face was hot and the thought of Killian being with someone other than me… I couldn't stomach it.

"I don't know what he's thinking," Lincoln muttered at the door. "I'll get Ralph to bring you something to wash him up with."

I didn't get a chance to ask him who that was. I turned back around to the bed and grabbed a chair on the other side of the room. I placed it next to the bed and sat down, scooting it as close as I could get to the bed. I placed my hands in my lap and just looked at him. He looked somewhat better, I guessed. His breathing was more even now… and at least his body was healed, but he was still too pale.

Humans and demons can't be?

I studied the shape of his nose. Straight and slightly pointed. A perfect nose to go with his sculptured chin. It made my chest hurt to look at him. Even his eyelashes were longer than mine…

He needs sex.

Something fell over my cheek. I brought my hand up and touched it. Tears.

I see.

It was so simple. The answer was always there. The one I always tried to hide. Only I couldn't any longer, it was spilling over. I wiped my eyes and laced my fingers into his.

What do I do? I was in love with this demon.

CHAPTER ELEVEN

An odd-looking butler walked into the room a few minutes later carrying a pail of water and a sponge. He nodded in greeting before setting it at my feet. His skin had brown spots all over. He looked normal for the most part until he turned and went back out the door and I saw his long feline tail swaying as he did.

I must be getting used to everything because nothing was phasing me anymore. I smiled at myself as I bent down and took the sponge. I squeezed the water out and began to wipe the blood from Killian's chest. I traveled the sponge across his ribs where most of the blood was and admired him in the process. I wrung the sponge out and repeated the process of cleaning him up. Cold chills broke out over his chest and I looked down to find something to dry him off with.

"He didn't bring anything to dry him off with," I mumbled to myself. I was deep in thought when I felt something touch my hand that rested over his chest. I jumped slightly but not enough to make me look silly. He was awake. "How do you feel?" I asked immediately, leaning forward.

He had that groggy look about him as he scanned the room. His hand slid over his damp skin and his eyebrows pinched together. Then he looked at me with a stunned expression. "Are you sponge bathing me?" His voice was thick, hoarse from sleep. I covered my mouth to hide my smile. The way his face lit up when he was caught off guard was surprisingly cute. He looked younger.

And oh, God, I was finding something to obsess over with every little thing he did.

"Yeah, I am." I dropped the sponge into the blood-colored water. "It only seems fair I do something in return, since I'm the reason you keep getting hurt."

"Well… this is rather odd." I arched my eyebrow up as he spoke. He raised up slowly. He was still a bit sluggish so I got up to help him. Once he was sitting up on the bed, his cut shirt caught his attention and he picked it up to examine it. A slow grin played out on his face. "You even ripped my shirt off. See, normally I'm the one—" He cut himself off.

I blushed and planted my butt back in my seat with a groan. "Oh, God, don't even start. Lincoln was the one that cut your shirt so he could heal you."

"Spoil a man's fantasy, you will." I looked around the room quickly to occupy my mind on something other than him. But there was nothing besides the cabinet of medicine.

173

He propped his knee up, placing his elbow over it as he ran his fingers through his hair. This might be the first time I had ever seen him look so relaxed. Was it because this was his home? I wanted to know everything I could about him.

I started fiddling with my hands in my lap. "You're nervous." He noticed. "Has something happened?" he asked with a hint of worry that was always there when it came to my safety. He was so pale…

He needs sex. The thought kept entering my mind and it wouldn't let me forget.

"No." I tried to think of something else. Something important. Like what were we going to do about Fear, but then Killian's well-being was important to me and he needed what he needed. Then I remembered something else. "I should probably get back home. Mom's probably really worried about me."

He moved his feet off the bed and stood with a shrug of his shoulders. "I told you before that time is different here. Weeks spent here is merely minutes in the human world." He swayed as he spoke.

I jumped up to steady him. "Are you okay?"

Sweet warmth started spreading inside me and my mind hit a fuzzy wall—one that left me hazy and without a care in the world. I molded myself against him like putty and slid my arms around him. His arms wrapped me in his embrace and I sighed

174

happily. Alarms were going off inside my head—this wasn't us anymore, it was his need taking over my senses, but my brain was far too lax. My body only cared about how good he felt against me—all these intense feelings rippled through me.

I could only focus on touching him. I wanted him. I was burning all over—a terrible ache rested between my thighs. "Killian," I moaned bringing my hands to his face. His eyes were liquid and trapping mine. His scent—something almost chocolatey and coffee-like—invaded me, it was dangerous and spiraling me further into his hold. "You smell good," I mumbled, breathing in every bit of him I could take.

In a frenzied rush, Killian threw me on the bed. I looked up at him all dreamy-eyed. Again, those alarms were knocking, telling me this wasn't right. He let his cut shirt fall off his arms and I took in the magnitude of him. Then he came down over me, his lips seeking mine.

Oh, God.

That was as far as it went. Someone was yanking Killian off me. Through the lust fog, I could see that it was Grim. Slowly, that haze began to fade and I could concentrate on the room. Lincoln stood in the doorway, a hand over his face.

"The whole Underworld will be feeling the effects of his lust." Lincoln sounded just as rough as I felt. "I'll leave you to deal with him. I have to go…fuck something." His words were enough for me to put everything in place. Killian had me under his incubus voodoo again and apparently I wasn't the only one affected by it. This was by far the strongest it had ever been.

"Was that your seducing thing just now... between us?" I asked him. I knew how ridiculous it sounded, but I didn't know what he called it. Grim held him steady as he leaned against him. Killian wouldn't even be standing if Grim wasn't holding him up.

Shame heated his face as met my eyes. "Shit, Melanie. I'm so sorry, that shouldn't have happened."

"You can't be around her anymore when you're like this," Grim told him, and his head fell. My heart dropped.

'This is happening all because he needs to have sex?" I asked.

Grim nodded. "He's refusing to give his body what it needs, so his body throws out these pheromones to make sure he gets what he needs to survive."

"I don't want to stay away from him just because of that." The words flew out of my mouth.

Grim sighed. "Just because of that?" he repeated my words sharply. "It's not okay. It won't be forever Melanie—"

"The sex..." What was I about to say? I already felt my cheeks on fire. "I can give it to you." I met Killian's eyes with all the seriousness I could muster onto my face. My voice wavered,

176

but I knew I was serious even when my heart was roaring in my ear from what I had just offered.

They looked at me for the longest moment before Grim finally brought his hand up to his face and took a deep breath. Killian was a block of stone as his gaze traveled to Grim. "Are you sure she's not the seducer because I swear it feels like I'm the one being seduced," Killian groaned.

"I see what you're saying," Grim agreed.

He pushed his weight off Grim and staggered toward me. He brought his hand out to hold mine once he was in front of me. My breath became a tangled mess in my throat when I saw the sincerity in his eyes. "Melanie, if we ever have sex, it will be because we both want to, not because I need it." Something sweet bloomed in my chest from his words. A sweet, bubbling sensation—I didn't realize how happy those words would make me. Suddenly, I was releasing the breath I hadn't realized I was holding. I didn't want it to be like that either

But then an ugly, nasty thought interrupted those feelings. I couldn't shut my mouth up even if it bothered my pride to ask. "Then are you going to have sex with someone else?"

"Never." That word held more than just a promise.

"But look at you—"

"Don't worry, you will be with Grim while I'm this way,"

he told me.

I sighed out of frustration. "I'm not talking about me!" I hissed. "Will you please worry about yourself for once instead of me?" He only smiled—one that left me speechless.

"Does that disappoint you?" I was caught by surprise with Grim's question. Things were changing, even the way I viewed the skeletal being standing behind Killian. He was nothing like Fear. He was my protector, and he deserved the chance for me to understand him. Because when it came down it, Grim and Killian were one and the same. I didn't get it, but somehow it just made more sense when I viewed them that way.

I nodded. "Yeah." Then I realized I messed up my answer by mistake. "I mean, no, it doesn't," I said quickly.

"See you soon," Killian said.

I had no idea what the plan was, but I tried to smile.

I told myself that Grim and Killian were one person and now it was making me feel awkward as we walked down the hallway together after leaving Killian alone. I didn't like that Killian was so weak, but I trusted that the two of them knew he would be okay. I brought my hands together nervously. I wanted to calm myself, but the silence that fell between Grim and I was making it impossible.

"You're fiddling." Of course, Grim would notice. I dropped my hands to my sides.

"Oh." We walked in more silence and I couldn't bear it any longer. "What happens now?"

"You stay here under my careful watch where I know you will be safe," was his answer.

"You could do that while I'm back home. I can't just leave my family alone, what if Fear tries to use them like he has before?"

"Already taken care of. Penny is watching your family." He opened a door and let me walk through it before following after me. I would get lost in this castle by myself.

"That doesn't make me feel better. It didn't seem like she was happy that you are protecting me," I muttered, feeling aggravated that he would send her to protect my family.

"She wouldn't disobey my order," he added as we walked down the stairs. The butler waited for us at the bottom.

I puffed my cheeks out in frustration. There were a million things I wanted to ask when it came to Penny, but they all seemed childish to say out loud. Grim's footsteps stopped and I leaned my body against the railing of the stairway and peered up at him. I frowned when he just stood there staring at me.

His essence lightened. "Does Penny bother you that much?" He cocked his head to the side amused.

I sighed. "No, why would it?" I couldn't believe how believable the lie sounded. I started back down the stairs and the words that followed were a sure fail to hide my jealousy. "She just seemed awful touchy and intimate with you… just what is she to you?" I found myself leaning back around to ask.

"In the past, we slept together a few times." I let his words sink in. "Whatever you're thinking, it's not like that." I felt the jealousy hot against my face, and I hurried to turn and it all happened too quickly. I lost my footing and began to fall. Grim was there to catch me. My back fell against his chest.

All I could think about was how weirdly right it felt… which was very *wrong*. Grim was no demon, no being with flesh, he was an entity. Grim was Death itself. He was a walking-talking pile of bones covered in leather. I shouldn't be getting the warm feel-goods from his cold touch.

What happened to him being terrifying to me?

"Are you okay?" he asked while I was still leaning against him.

I moved away from him and tried to control the flood of emotions I was suddenly feeling. "Is her room ready?" Grim asked the butler as we walked the rest of the stairs down.

"Yes, shall I take her to the room?" he answered Grim.

"No, I will show her. Just make sure to come and get her for dinner." The butler nodded. Grim stepped past me and I followed. The butler hurried off in a different direction.

We were heading in the direction of the piano and my eyebrows pinched together. There was nothing in the corner— except for the piano. I looked at his back. Was he going to play? "You play the piano?" I asked out of curiosity.

He nodded. "I do."

"How intriguing," I mumbled with a bit of disbelief.

He stopped, and his skull twisted around halfway. "How so?" he asked.

"Just… who would think the Grim Reaper played an instrument, let alone a piano."

"There's a lot you don't know about me, Melanie, but that will change in time." His words sounded intimate and it shut me right up. "Shall I play for you sometime?" When I didn't answer, he chuckled softly and walked behind the piano. I thought he was going to the piano at first until he pressed his hand against the wall—a door started to form in the wall. The door was wooden with black paneling and circular across the top.

Well, well. This place and him both were full of surprises. "Really?" I muttered, but he ignored me. I walked into the room without him telling me to and he followed. He shut the door behind us.

This was my bedroom? I smiled then frowned in disbelief. There was a huge bed centered against the wall in the back of the room—the bed itself was bigger than my actual room. The room was fully furnished. There was a nightstand, a full-length mirror, a dresser, and an open trunk overflowing with beautiful colored gowns at the foot of the bed. The bedding was black and gold with a black canopy falling around it.

What the crap? It seemed like a lot for a short stay... it was a short stay, wasn't it?

"Are you not happy with the room?" I could feel him watching me as I moved toward the bed, running my hands across the comforter. So soft.

"Is it really okay for me to use this room?" I asked, a bit skeptical.

"Everything in this room is yours," he replied. "If you want it." I felt like there was an innuendo in there.

"Yeah, I mean." I turned to face him with a smile. "Of course, I will try to make good use of everything while I'm here. Don't mistake me for one of these girls that refuses gifts to make themselves look good. I'm not that type, more like gimme, gimme, gimme." Or more like I had never been on the receiving end before. He laughed. "No take backs, okay?" I brought my

182

index finger to my mouth. "Hmm, I wonder with all that power at your disposal if we can somehow bring all this back home with me? Or better yet, let's take the whole room." The color of his essence lightened into almost a baby bluish-white color as he shook his head at me and laughed. I wondered what color that emotion was?

"You haven't seen the best part." He motioned me with his hands to the empty part of the room.

"I don't see how—" He snapped his fingers and the wall extended and stretched out to reveal a giant library. "Is this book heaven?" Books everywhere. Shelves and shelves—neatly lined up and categorized. Some books looked new while others looked worn. As I stepped into the extended part of the room, I realized the library had a second story.

"All yours," he told me.

I couldn't contain my girly squeal, although, I never even tried. I hurried through the beautiful library and started sliding my hands across the books like the crazy book fanatic I was. "Everything's been changed into the English language so that you can read them. These are books of the Underworld. It will have everything on demons and anything else you might be curious about. I made sure there were plenty of those erotic romance novels you read added to the library."

I gave him a curious look. "Are you making fun of me?"

"Not at all." Strangely, I believed him.

I went and stood back next to him. "Thanks."

He nodded and rubbed his head. I got the sense that he was feeling awkward or bashful about something. "I appreciate how much you're trying to make my stay here comfortable, but how long will I be here?"

"Until it's safe."

"Is that even a word that we can use in terms with my life?"

"I will always make sure you're safe, but I will make it so that Fear is no longer a danger to you."

"You already said he couldn't be killed. I'm not safe from him. *Ever.*"

"I can't kill him, but there's always another way." Which probably meant he still had no idea himself.

"Looks like I'm always relying on you," I told him. "So, I guess this is where I should tell you to take care of me?" His hand lingered toward my face, but stopped midway and fell back to his side. "Grim?"

"Yes..." Why did I keep expecting him to call me *Love* the way Killian always did?

"Why haven't you and Killian merged back together?" I

184

lingered next to one of the bookshelves, drawing lines with my finger over the books.

He turned around with a sigh. "We've already tried. Whatever spell Fear used to break the merge is also preventing us from piecing back together. It's like our bodies are rejecting the merge."

That made me slightly panicky. "So, you won't ever be one again?" An awful twist lingered in my gut with the thought. I could tell how much it bothered them to be separated.

"We are going to try again three nights from now on a Blood Moon. In the Underworld, it's a night of extreme power."

"Will it work?"

Nothing about the way he carried his shoulders was positive. "I don't know," he replied honestly. "What Fear did to us has never happened before. I don't know what the consequences will be. We were forcefully torn apart."

I couldn't even stomach the idea of what he was admitting. They were one and the same when I first met them, that would always be the way I saw them. What if... I shrugged the thought away before I let it consume me entirely.

Lost in thought, Grim touched my shoulder and I jumped. His hand retreated quickly. "Sorry, I was thinking," I told him, but I wasn't sure he believed me.

He put distance between us. He was retreating far away from me. His actions left me confused—did he think I jumped because I was afraid of him? "Don't worry about him, we will figure it out." He sounded closed off and oddly cold. Then he said something ridiculous, "If we don't merge, that would make you more comfortable, wouldn't it?"

"Grim," I said sharply. "Why would you say that?" But it was too late. He was already gone.

I stood alone in a beautiful room. I clamped my hands together and whispered, "You misunderstood me."

I didn't see him as a monster like I had called him before. I did at first but not anymore. He had every reason to think I didn't care for him. I never showed him otherwise and it was something I was only realizing myself. I didn't see him as a scary glowing skeleton anymore.

I saw him as my haven. My rescuer. My protector. But the most important one was that I saw him as Killian—just as when I saw Killian, I saw Grim.

Three more days until they were one again.

What happened if it didn't work?

That made me afraid. Very, very afraid.

CHAPTER TWELVE

The butler returned shortly after to lead me to dinner. I changed into one of the many dresses spilling out of the trunk. I chose a pretty light blue one. It was snug around my upper body and flared out starting at my hips down to my knees. Shimmers of glitter bounced off the dress as I walked underneath the chandeliers in the ballroom.

He took us through the double doors in between the stairways—the doors were also underneath the balcony of the second floor—and into the dining room. It was spacious and beautiful. This room was vibrant, full of color compared to all the rooms I had seen so far. A white, round table awaited me with a candle lit in the middle. A single chair was placed by the table.

"Is Grim not joining me?" I asked, turning on my heels to look at the butler.

"No, I'm afraid not. He said to enjoy your meal." He went to the chair and pulled it out for me. Once I was seated, he opened the tray in front of me. There was a moment of terror that washed over me when I remembered dining with Fear, and I fully expected the hand to come crawling toward me as he opened it. But that panic eased when he revealed a salad instead of my nightmare. I sighed, feeling a bit silly that Fear still had control over me—my life. "This may seem odd, but when you bring the meals out in the future...can you please not put any lids on them?"

"Yes." He nodded.

I ate the salad in silence with the butler standing by my side. When I was finished, he walked away and came back with another plate—no lid. It was steak and a baked potato. Thankfully, everything was normal and the food was delicious.

I was in a fairy-tale-like castle with beautiful dresses and a huge library, but it was all temporary. My life was a mess, that I knew but the idea that right now, I might even have the prince to go with it all seemed oddly tempting. Only he was broken. One-half of him thought I wanted nothing to do with him and the other... couldn't control his nature.

What was I going to do?

———

I spent the rest of the evening and late into the night skimming through the books in the library. There were so many, it was hard to choose something to read. A purplish book finally caught my eye called 'Monster's Seed'. Yeah, I knew I probably shouldn't have read something with a title like that but curiosity got the best of me.

It was about a human woman falling in love with a demon and it was very... detailed about their love making, and I will only say that the demon used his tail for all *sorts* of things. I couldn't stop reading it and ended up finishing it all in one sitting. It was a simple love story... they met, fell in love, had a child, but it was all forbidden. So, the two were torn apart and the baby was taken from the woman to the Underworld.

It was sad and now that I finished it, I regretted even reading it. Still... the tail had me wondering. The butler had a tail but it was furry and not at all like the one described in the book. Fear's long tail flashed through my mind, and I broke out in a cold sweat. I could only imagine the things he would do with his.

Now I regretted reading the book *again*. Anything that made me think of that monster wasn't worth reading.

I fell asleep at some point. I saw Ryan in my dreams. He was smiling and that made me happy. He was playing football and laughing with the other players then out of nowhere, the scenery changed. Ryan lay lifeless on the road. It was a familiar place to me, a road I traveled every day. I was standing over him, his blood coating my fingers. Panic gripped my chest, but I couldn't do anything. The charred demon appeared beside him.

He smiled at me. Not a smile you would ever want to see. It was the kind that gave a person nightmares. It was laced with something evil, wicked—like a disease. He bent down at Ryan's feet and started dragging him away from me. Just as I reached out for him, I woke up gasping for air, desperation crawling through me to get air in my lungs. My hand was extended out above me like I had been doing in the dream.

I raised up and the book that rested at my side fell off the bed. I wiped the dampness from my forehead and tried to understand the way I was feeling. What was that dream? Ryan was probably worried sick about me, and maybe that was why he was creeping into my dreams since I wouldn't let him in my thoughts when I was awake.

Still... it was a weird feeling. Like something bad might have happened or a premonition. Ryan was a ghost; I didn't think he would be in danger… I just had to make sure. I scooted out of bed and ran barefoot to the door wearing a small pink nightgown. The door automatically started opening for me and as soon as it did, I started staggering. I reached for the closest thing which was the door and leaned against it.

An enticing scent filled the entire castle warping all my senses, even my ability to walk. The scent felt like a tight cocoon wrapping around my body. All I could think about was the ache pressed between my thighs and it didn't help that I now had shaky

190

legs. Sex was all I could think about and I knew it had to be Killian. His incubus seduction was freaking out of control!

I wasn't directing my body anywhere—I could hardly move—but it seemed to know where it wanted to be. At this point, I knew I was trying to get to Killian but when my hands left the doorway, I crumbled to my knees in a mess. I panted—I was on fire. I closed my eyes. I felt exhausted, depleted, yet turned on at the same time.

I felt the cool touch of Grim's boned fingers lifting me up in his arms. My body went completely slack as he cradled me in his arms. With his touch, I could escape the insanity of the castle. Slowly, the lust fog began to evaporate from my body as well as my mind.

"This is why I sealed your room off from the castle. He can't control himself anymore, his body knows what it needs and is determined to get it to survive. Even though your room is sealed, he stills knows you're here… so he's seeking you out." I took a deep breath against his chest. I heard moans coming from somewhere in the castle and looked up to Grim in wonder. "It's affecting everyone in the castle. It should pass through the night," he told me. Just how many demons were here?

"What about you?" I asked.

"I'm no demon, human, or man. I exist for one reason, Melanie. I am Death, such desires do not become me." That

191

sounded so lonely. And sad.

But I got the feeling that wasn't all true. "Oh? I find that strange. If you had no desire for intimacy, then why did you merge with an incubus demon? You could have chosen any demon, right?" His essence lightened around him and I smirked. I thought right, I believed.

"You're right, I do have desires. Would it make you happy to know how much I longed for the touch of a woman? The idea of them thrilled me when it shouldn't have. I'm an entity, I wasn't made for any sort of desire, just a purpose, but I developed feelings over time." I bunched his shirt up in my hand as he spoke. He was sharing something of his past with me. It excited me and made me nervous. "But that wasn't why I merged with Killian. I was pulled toward him. I felt him one day and knew he was me. It wouldn't make sense to you, only Killian and I, we just got that feeling and knew. We were meant to be one," he sighed. "Not even Heaven understood."

"Actually, the two of you apart doesn't make sense to me so I think I do understand," I admitted. "And, I don't think your purpose is a bad one. You showed me what it is you do; I think it's beautiful. The fact that there's something beautiful in death is amazing. And the fact that you rid the world of the bad guys is—" I shut up, realizing I sounded too desperate to make him feel good about what he was.

His eyeless gaze stayed locked with mine for the longest time. "Did I ever say I disliked what I was?" There was a hint of amusement in his strong voice.

I blushed—still in his arms—and looked the other way. "I didn't say that you disliked it." I puffed my cheeks out.

"Did you need something?" he asked softly. This should be weird that we were having an entire conversation while I was in his arms but it wasn't. I still nudged myself out of his arms, though for what I was about to ask him. He placed me on my feet and when his touch left mine, the scent of Killian came back. I swayed and Grim reached out to grab my shoulder. "Either we go to your room or your stuck with me touching you. That's the only way I can keep you from experiencing the effects."

"I don't mind," I said quickly. There was a hesitant nod on his part but I told myself that was fine. I would one day prove to him that he didn't scare me anymore. That I wasn't afraid of him. That I cared for him as I did Killian.

"It's about Ryan. I just got a strange feeling, and I need to go home to check on him."

"He's not there." My stomach churned.

"What do you mean?"

"I don't sense him anymore. Well, I do occasionally. His light keeps flickering in and out of the human world when I search for him."

"Grim, I don't know what that means." I gave him a look of horror and frustration mixed.

"He might be possessing someone's body. A lot of ghosts do it in order to hide from me. I can't sense their presence that way," he added, but still couldn't shake the bad feeling I got when I thought of Ryan.

"Can they really do that?" He nodded, placing all his weight on his right side. "I just can't see Ryan doing that." I shook my head. There was no way.

"Melanie, I wouldn't worry. Fear can't take a ghost to the Underworld unless they want to go or he marked them while they were alive." The missing puzzle piece finally came together. I couldn't escape what grew at the pit of my stomach—nausea and fear. My head to spun with the horrid truth.

"No," I whispered, the word kept falling from my mouth until Grim tightened his hand that was on my shoulder and I looked up to him. I could feel his concern but it also revealed itself through the change of his essence.

"Melanie." I knew he was waiting on me to tell him what I realized, but I was ashamed. Ashamed that he had the mark as long as I have, and I never once thought to worry about his life. Why did Ryan encounter someone like me?

"The day Fear marked me… Ryan was the one that found me afterwards. While the mark was still imprinting itself onto my skin, he touched it and somehow it transferred onto his hand." Grim's essence darkened and I knew it probably wasn't a good sign. "He died because of me… How much more will he go through because of me?"

My nerves were tearing me to pieces. "I just need to figure out what has happened," he told me.

"I can't even imagine what might have happened to him or what he could be going through." I started to panic, and Grim placed his other hand on my shoulder trying to reassure me. "Not only is he dead, he may be experiencing something far worse because of me." I could hear the fear in my voice. "I didn't even think to remember Ryan had the mark this entire time as well! Now he already belongs to Fear, doesn't he?"

"His soul belongs to Fear if he has his mark." I was stunned, caught off guard by his honesty. I already knew that, but Grim was Grim. He was powerful… surely he knew a way we could save him.

"There has to be a way we can save him. You're powerful and know a lot… isn't there some way?"

"Melanie, stop…"

"Grim, there has to be a way!"

"Enough! Melanie." His voice echoed the ballroom. It was frightening and reminded me of all the times I was afraid of him before. I took a step back. I wasn't afraid of him now, just overwhelmed with panic and guilt—not just because of Ryan but Grim. The fact that I was begging for his help to save Ryan when I had decided to show him how I really felt. "There's nothing that I can do to save him. The mark is law in the Underworld, it's binding."

"No…"

"Why do you think they sent me to protect you? To keep you safe and alive? Because the moment you die, you belong to Fear. It's permanent after death. Dying is what seals the deal, Melanie. The same applied for Ryan."

"Grim," I whispered softly tugging at his cloak. The tears started to fall down my cheeks. "Don't say that, please!" I cried. "I can't stand it. Don't tell me that I killed him and sent him to an eternity trapped in a nightmare at the hands of Fear! Don't tell me that this is what he gets for being my best friend!"

He pushed my hands away from him but kept a hand over my shoulder despite his growing dark essence. "Didn't I warn you to keep a distance from your friends? Their life was clouded in darkness and hard to read when you were around them. Especially Ryan's." His words were harsh. "But I don't think it would have made a difference for Ryan or not. His fate was

196

already sealed the day he met you." His words cut me like a knife. I couldn't handle it. I thought he would be my comfort, not the thing that made me feel worse.

"I didn't ask the Vessel to be inside me." I fisted my hands until my nails were digging into my palms. "I didn't want this kind of life or to put everyone I loved in danger." The reality came crashing down over me. I couldn't play pretend in this dark enchanted place. It wasn't real. The sad truth of my pathetic life was nothing but fear and death. "This stupid power." I brought my fist against my chest where the X was exposed because of the tiny nightgown. "Just take the Vessel from me. Go on and take it or whatever—I don't care! So, I can be done with it. I don't want to feel like this anymore." I even brought his hand to my chest, I was so serious. He went rigid, but I didn't care.

I continued in anger, "Do whatever you have to. I want it gone. I'll give it to you. Whatever. Just let me live out my miserable life until it's time to die and belong to Fear. At least I can make it right with Ryan that way. I'll make sure he doesn't suffer alone."

"Quiet!" His voice was like thunder inside the castle. Every noise in the castle died out, including the random lovemaking that was still going on somewhere in the castle. I stood there trying to collect my thoughts, but that was impossible. I was broken—shattered. "You're driving my patience for the last

197

time, *human*." The word was spoken the same way Killian spat it out when we first met. With hatred. I hated how easily it hurt me. I hated how easily I fell for Killian. I hated myself for thinking I could love something that wasn't covered in flesh! "The Vessel has already awakened inside you."

"So it's back to calling me human again?" I glared, and I sensed that he was equally frustrated. If the mass of black starting to swarm him was any indication. It was a bit scary.

No need to be afraid of him.

The voice told me and I always listened to it. I stood straight. "I saw you use it more than once. I was waiting on you to bring it up, yet you haven't." He sounded upset.

I always meant to tell one of them, but always got sidetracked by something else. I shook my head. "I meant to tell you, but I keep forgetting with everything else going on."

"You're saying you forgot how you broke someone's ankle?" I didn't like his accusing tone, but I still managed to feel ashamed when he brought up what I had done to Haley.

"You were watching?" I asked, voice dripping with venom. And he hadn't mentioned it either.

"It's my job," he said equally angry.

"I wasn't sure if I was the one that caused her heel to break."

"Then why do you look guilty?" He knew exactly how to press my buttons. "But the Vessel is already a part of you. And with every time you've used it, even more so."

"I don't understand." I just wanted to curl up and hide from all my troubles but there was no point. I would drive myself mad thinking of them. "When are you even going to tell me what the Vessel is?"

"You do understand or you wouldn't be here with me now. You were born with the Vessel, how or why will never matter because you are stuck with it and my job is to keep it from Fear so that he doesn't gain any more power. And I have told you what the Vessel is: a weapon. An untapped power that every demon would want to get a hold of, but that will never happen now that the Vessel has taken with you."

"You finally dropped the good Grim act, have ya'?" I yanked his hand from my shoulder and stepped back.

His hand shot right back out. "Careful—be mad all you want, but my hand stays in place or you'll be putty on the floor," he said with a hint of mockery and darn it, my pale cheeks turned rosy. It sucked when you wanted to throw a fit and run away but couldn't or you would turn into a hot mess looking for the other half of this pain in the neck.

Sigh.

"I don't know what I was expecting when I thought we could be friends—or whatever, obviously, we are really different. Go ahead then, protect me or whatever. Let's see if I make it easy. I'll find a way to get back and find Ryan—"

"Just do it, Grim." I looked up to see a pale nightmare gazing down at me. It was Killian and he looked horrible and worn down, but there was still a hint of something dangerous tugging at the tip of his smile as he nodded toward Grim. Grim's chest vibrated with a chuckle and that sent every alarm off in my head. My nerve endings were bouncing all over my skin telling me I should be worried.

"What…" His hand swept over my forehead, and I knew all too well what this familiar sensation was. He was making me sleep. I felt my anger reach a boiling point before it was cut short.

I fell into a cold embrace.

CHAPTER THIRTEEN

I woke confused and disgruntled. I threw the cover on the floor and took in my surroundings. He brought me back to the room he prepared for me. Then I was remembering the events that led to this... he actually put me to sleep instead of listening to me. My ears were on fire along with my face, I was so angry.

I didn't know how long I had been asleep, nor did I have any windows to look outside—not that I would know the difference between day and night here. I hurried out of bed. "He actually made me sleep," I spoke to myself.

The door opened. I lifted my eyes in time to see the feline butler entering. "You're awake," he stated.

"Where's Grim," I snapped. He wasn't the one I was angry with, but he was in my path and that put him in danger of my wrath.

"He's busy," was his answer.

"I don't care. I need to speak with him." I was still in my

nightgown, but I was too upset to care. He brought his hand up in front of me when I tried to walk by.

"He said you would be upset so I brought your breakfast." Did he expect me to forgive him with food? I eyed the table of delicious goodies rolling itself in behind the butler. Bagels, pancakes, waffles, muffins, milk, juice, and five or more different types of syrups and spreads. I licked my lips. I knew this was a trick to make me forget about what happened, but my stomach still grumbled.

Oh, and it smelled so good and… and I was hungry. I sighed, long and hard.

"He said he will talk to you only when you've calmed down," he added, and I shot him another glare. Poor guy—I needed to find out his name—he was getting all of my anger. I stared back at the food.

"He can't ignore me while he has me here," I grumbled, but I knew what I said wasn't true. He could do whatever he wanted and if he chose to never let me see him again, I would never see him again. My stomach churned at the thought.

The butler only looked at me with curious eyes. "I guess I'm stuck here waiting in this prison," I yelled into the room knowing that Grim was probably listening. "Don't think pancakes with blueberries in them will settle anything between us," I added while rolling the table to the bed and flopping down. What? I wasn't going to let this food go to waste.

"You may leave now," I told the butler. I saw the grin on his face as he disappeared from the room.

––––––––––

"Human," Lincoln barged into my room while I was reading. I glared and saved my spot before closing the book.

I took a deep breath and closed my eyes. "Does no one around here—demon or otherwise—know how to say my name or knock for once?" I smiled sweetly.

"Someone's upset." He smiled like he was delighted in my mood. "I heard your little spat with Grim last night."

Anyone in the castle could probably hear us. I didn't care, though. "Woo, you have amazing hearing," I said sarcastically. *And a horse's butt.* I grinned at my own thoughts.

"So, this Ryan…" I already hated where this was going. "He was your lover and died because he was involved with you?" I changed positions on the bed to where my body faced his direction.

"I don't think it's any of your business."

His smile only grew at my reluctance to tell him anything. "I feel for Grim." I arched an eyebrow. "You should have some decency… begging him to save another man." He shook his head.

He was only trying to get a reaction from me, but I felt my anger fizzing. "Mind your own business," I snapped.

"You can't only have feelings for one part of him." His words caught my attention, and I looked back up to him. "They are one and the same, human, you can't have one without the other." I didn't like how everyone automatically assumed I had no feelings for Grim. I knew how I felt, but I didn't think I needed to explain myself to anyone.

"So, you know me, do ya'?

"There's no denying your attraction to Killian."

I moved off the bed and stepped in front of him. "You're the one that told me humans and demons couldn't be together. Why do care what I feel for either of them? Besides, Grim pretty much made it clear, once again, that I was nothing but something that needed his protection."

"You don't understand anything." He looked at me with pity.

"I don't have to listen to a horse-man trying to tell me my own feelings. I'm stuck here for now, but that doesn't mean I won't figure out a way protect my friend and everyone I care about."

His eyes pierced mine. "And just what do you think Grim has been doing? Just who is the one doing the protecting?" I couldn't say anything. "Hmm?" With that, he turned and left the room.

I fanned my face as I flipped to the next page. My whole body was heated as I read, and I would feel embarrassed about what I was reading if it wasn't for the fact that I was so engrossed by it. This wasn't romance; this was demon porn. I was appalled by some of what I had read, but I couldn't stop reading.

I read a lot of erotica, but these books were nothing like anything I had read before. Sure, I was a virgin. But in my case, it was like saying my body was innocent yet my mind was corrupted with filthiness.

I spent the day reading when I should have been causing a ruckus. I tended to get trapped inside a book once I started reading one—especially something fascinating—and couldn't stop until I had it finished. That was definitely the case with this one. My neck was cramped, and I was hungry by the time I finally sat the book down.

I stood up and stretched, deciding I had stayed cooped up in this room long enough. I was hungry and thirsty, and the butler hadn't brought anything since this morning. I grabbed a pair of tennis shoes and put them on. I was sure to look ridiculous wearing this beautiful dress with tennis shoes, but it beat wearing heels. This country girl wasn't used to all the sparkle and beauty these dresses held. Although I had been flattered to get them, I was now realizing they weren't me.

The ballroom was quiet and empty. More like, the whole castle was creepy quiet. I tiptoed—like I was going to get in trouble—toward the double doors that led to the dining room. The kitchen had to be next to it. The doors creaked loudly and I flinched, waiting several long seconds to make sure no one was going to appear and went on in. I was right, the kitchen was the next door in the dining room.

When I realized I was still tiptoeing, I felt foolish and stopped. Why did I need to sneak around? If I was stuck here in the castle, I wasn't going to limit myself to a bedroom.

I gasped. My mom would kill for this kitchen. I missed her and Alex. I prayed time really was different between here and there. I hated to imagine the worry my mom would be feeling if she thought I was missing. I couldn't stay here much longer. I had to make them understand that.

But I shoved those thoughts away for now and focused on the kitchen. It was like it came from one of those catalogs Mom gets in the mail. The floor was wooden or wood-like, I couldn't tell if it was made to look like it or if it actually was. The kitchen felt oddly country—making it seem out of place with the rest of the castle. It didn't have the medieval-dark vibe like everything else.

206

The fridge was built into a stone wall, but the fridge itself had a wooden appearance. There was more than one stove and a beautiful counter set up with all kinds of kitchen appliances.

I went to the fridge and opened it. I grabbed a water and twisted the cap off. The door opened and I froze, hidden behind the fridge door. I wanted to smack myself for getting so wound up over someone coming into the kitchen. I wasn't doing anything wrong. I closed the door. "I was getting something to drink," I said before I looked over to see who it was that entered. "Killian."

His face went from shock to horror as if he was downright terrified to see me. "I shouldn't have come downstairs." His voice was hoarse and he still looked terrible. I stepped closer and he moved back. He turned to leave.

"Wait," I said quickly. He stopped and took a deep breath, but didn't turn around. Now that I told him to wait, I wasn't sure what to say. We were supposed to be avoiding each other. "Uh... how are you feeling?"

He turned his head enough to give me a tight smile. "I'm fine." He swayed and I moved to help him but he steadied himself before I could. "Everything will go back to normal and for you having to stay here, I'm sorry." Something was off. The way he spoke scared me.

"Are you really sick? You're acting weird."

"I will be perfectly fine soon enough." He paused and so did my breathing. "Being like this has made me realize things I couldn't before." It didn't help that I was looking at his back as he spoke. It made me nervous and afraid of things he could say with his back turned. "I was momentarily confused about some things, but I won't be anymore. You don't belong here—I realize that and everything will go back to normal for you in time."

"My life will never be normal," I told him ignoring the pinpricks of fear in my heart.

"We will make it happen." He sounded determined, but he also sounded detached and without emotion. I couldn't tell what he felt.

"Will you look at me when you're talking?" I asked.

"It's already been too long to be around you. It's not safe for you." He opened the door and he stumbled forward. "We can finish our conversation two nights from now." And he left.

I closed my eyes and focused on numbers. On counting, over and over until the tears no longer wanted to fall. My heart twisted like it was being ripped out. Once again, what could have happened between us was coming to end before it was given the chance.

I made the mistake of pushing him away the first time, but it wasn't me this time. I was ready to be honest about my feelings, but I knew exactly what this conversation meant. We couldn't be together. I didn't belong here. Even with the Vessel, I was still human. There was nothing that could change that. Demons and humans really couldn't be?

I never thought to wonder that Grim and Killian might be immortal…

Reality was closing in.

CHAPTER FOURTEEN

Grim stormed into my room that night as I was cramming a cookie in my mouth. I was ignoring my problems by eating and reading demon porn. The bed was covered in candy wrappers, empty plates, and books. I shoved them all to the side of the bed as if that would make the mess look any better.

He was a mass of black so I knew whatever this was about wasn't good. "Do you realize what danger you put yourself in today?" he shouted as he entered the room, shoulders tensed and his black t-shirt heaving in and out with his anger. Did skeletons breathe or was it entirely anger?

"Huh?" The entire cookie I crammed in my mouth was still there and my 'huh' sounded so muffled that even I couldn't understand it. Why did I have to eat when I was stressed? I kicked a wrapper at my foot in a hurry. Good thing I was dumped—rejected before I even got the chance to confess—or else I might have cared that my bed was a pigsty. I needed another cookie, but my stomach was already in protest with everything I had already eaten.

"You met with Killian," he accused. "Do you know what could have happened if you were around him when his powers slipped?" He rubbed his skull in frustration.

"I did not meet him!" I defended myself. "I bumped into him when I went to the kitchen, there's a difference." I gave him a dirty look—determined to shoot him with laser beams… if only I could. But my evil eye had to be impressive regardless.

He just stood there for several seconds. "That's not the point," he argued.

I laughed. "Really? I think it is if I'm going to get yelled at for something that wasn't my fault. I was thirsty, hungry, and bored of this room!" I took a deep breath. "And being seduced is at the bottom of my list of worst things that can happen to me."

He gave me a hard look. "Don't leave this room," he ordered.

"Grim, I am not a prisoner. I won't stay in here," I spoke calmly.

"It's for your protection." I snorted, and he tilted his head like he couldn't believe my attitude. "It's only for one more night after this one," he insisted. I looked down. That was when they planned to merge again, wasn't it?

"Fine." I pretended to be okay with it.

211

He gave me another long look. "That's it?"

"Yeah. Go," I told him.

"Very well." He sighed, suddenly looking reluctant.

I watched him walk out. He snapped his fingers just as he left from the doorway. The mess I made went missing on the bed. All my plates, wrappers, and crumbles—it all disappeared. That only aggravated me more and my cheeks heated. I was about to blow; I just knew it. "I was going to clean it myself," I yelled.

I glared at the door. There was no way I was staying caged in this room.

So, obviously, I wasn't taking Grim or Killian's rejection well because the next morning I woke up extremely angry. I couldn't stand them trying to dictate my life. I didn't want to be a burden to them. I wanted to be someone that mattered but that didn't seem to be the case. Because I *was* a burden.

A burden that didn't listen and would be sure to cause a problem again.

I went on to make things worse. I slipped on another one of the fancy—too gorgeous for me dresses—and some tennis shoes and decided to sneak out. I felt suffocated but then realized that I could just go outside and I would be safe from Killian's sex-oozing fumes. Besides, I had made a friend here. Sky, and I wanted to see her.

212

I stepped out of my room and the secret door faded back into the wall. The castle was void of life, but I still moved around cautiously. Grim might not always be next to me, but there was always that sense that he knew where I was and what I was doing. I ran for the huge double doors that led outside, heartbeat pounding in my ears and throat as the adrenaline and fear of getting caught increased.

I was beyond relieved and excited when I opened one of the doors and slipped out. I closed it back with a smile and took in the fresh air. And once again, I was taken in by the beauty and strangeness of this place. This place was maddening and unreal. It made me wonder if the Underworld was this breathtaking. Somehow, I doubted it. Fear's cave had been nothing like this.

The thunderous roars of the dragons calling to one another above me caught my interest. I looked up as they flew over me. My smile only grew when I noticed Sky with them. Had they accepted her? Rixen was in the front, but his neck snapped toward the back as he let himself slow and fall toward the back of the group where Sky was. When she noticed him approaching, she pinned her wings back and sped downward—away from him.

Sky was avoiding her leader. It made me curious. I was fascinated, so much that I wished I could speak and understand their language. They were getting too far away. I started running to keep up, caught up in the moment watching them.

The sky held no sun in the day, it made me wonder if there was no moon at night? Or did it ever change? I would have to find out. My lungs were burning at this point and I was seriously out of shape. I was reaching the end of the pavement and grew desperate that I would lose sight of them. I brought my hands in the air, waving them around. "Sky!"

Sky turned and spotted me running after her. She swooped back gracefully and I slowed down to wait for her to come to me. She was agile and beautiful as she landed before me, and I had the biggest grin. I bent over to catch my breath. Sweat was dampening my skin and I didn't even run that far. All those sweets I loved to eat were sure to be the problem… and this humid heat.

"Sky," I panted sounding winded.

Her hair was slicked back along with her ears with sweat. Her eyes were gentle as she approached. I brought my hand up to rub along her scales. She gave me a purr in response and shook her entire body at me. "I see you found your place." Of course, she couldn't answer me, but her eyes were filled with knowledge and I knew she listened to every word I said. "I'm only more confused," I admitted to her.

In response, she rubbed her nose into my palm. Rixen flew at a distance, tail swaying as he watched us above. I arched an eyebrow. "Looks like you have problems of your own." Her head

214

turned toward her leader. I felt like it was a lover's quarrel…
almost like Rixen was doing the chasing.

"Is your heart in turmoil too?" She purred in response.

"Melanie!" I recognized Lincoln's voice and turned
around to see him running, all four hooves coming at me fast
pace. He looked afraid and possibly annoyed. Okay, possible—
probably very annoyed.

I swore and looked back to Sky. Her eyes followed the
centaur before she gazed back at me. "A girl can't catch a break."
Sky swiveled around and gave her back to me. She bent down
and I hurried to climb onto her. She brought her tail around to
help push me up and on her. I grabbed a handful of her mane to
hold on to. She wasted no time getting us in the air.

I laughed when I heard my name being called again. I
knew I probably wouldn't get far. Grim was sure to come get
me… but I would relish the moment.

Sky wasted no time. She took us through the sky and
showed me everything. She brought us to a mountain that held
caves all over it. Dragons poured in and out of them. This was
their home. I smiled and rubbed my hand over her neck to let her
know I appreciated what she had just shown me. She took me
over the rainbow-colored trees and finally dived down into them.
All the colors looked unreal in the woods as she flew us through
it. She kept a slow pace to dodge the trees. I wouldn't have

believed such a place existed if I wasn't right here looking at it all, breathing it in.

For a moment, I imagined what it would feel like to be a dragon. Just the thought left me feeling alive and free. Nothing but the roar of the wind in my ears as she picked up speed through the trees. I smiled and brought my hands out to my sides. I wanted to touch everything in these woods—and I would as soon as we landed. The trees looked soft-like, almost like they might feel like cotton candy. Vines trailed up them. The grass glowed like the trees.

She brought us to a stop. I jumped off her and continued my exploration on feet. The air was crisp and clean. I wanted to know everything there was to know about this place. No matter how much I pretended otherwise, something about this place called to me. The same way Grim and Killian did. This was Grim's home, but something about it felt like *mine*. I didn't understand the way I was feeling and might not ever understand it.

Maybe it was only the fantasy of me wanting to be a part of his world that led me to feel this way. But that didn't matter because I wanted to engrave this place in my mind before I had to leave it.

The vines and roots of the trees moved and shifted under my feet as I walked. And I would have freaked out if this had

216

been anywhere other than Grim's home. Nothing would hurt me here. I was still careful though; I didn't want to trip over anything as I went further.

Then I heard the strange noises. Whispers. At first, I thought I might be imagining it, so I would stop and wait a few seconds before I started again, but the whispers grew louder the further I went. I looked back to Sky to make sure she was still following. She reassured me with an encouraging nod. I nodded back and continued forward.

I was starting to understand some of the voices.

"Human."

"Light. Light."

When they suddenly stopped, I stopped walking as well, afraid that maybe I had upset them.

"Finally," their voices said in unison. They spoke in an awed tone.

"We have been waiting for you," a single voice spoke.

Some were still chanting 'light' all around me. I looked around, but I couldn't make out anyone. There was nothing but trees. I knew they had to be talking to me.

Then like magic, tiny lights began to appear all around me, like they just came into existence. One floated toward my face and I brought my hand up to touch it. The light popped and I jerked my hand back. A voice shrieked and I could barely make out the tiny body falling from where the bubble had popped. I reacted quickly and moved my palm out for it to fall into.

I brought my hand up to my face and leaned closer. It was a young man, the size of a firefly. If I looked close enough, I could see that his ears were pointed. He wore a green shirt, brown pants, and shoes. I must have been squinting really hard to see him because he said, "Do you mind?" I moved my hand away from my face quickly. "Thank you, your nostrils are quite scary up close." I wasn't offended. I might have been if he wasn't the size of a nostril himself.

"What are you?" I asked.

"I am Prince Cadence of the elf clan, Melanie." How did he know my name? He placed one foot over the other, bringing one arm out while placing a hand on his chest and bowed. A very princely thing to do, I thought.

"You know me?" I looked at the tiny person in my hand curiously.

"Yes, the land has spoken of you for a very, very long time," he answered. I tilted my head confused.

"The land spoke?" I wasn't aware the land was a 'thing' that could speak.

He smiled at my puzzlement. "We are one with the land, Melanie. It speaks to us as we speak to it." It was hard making out his facial expressions when he was so tiny, but I was sure he was looking at me like I should understand now. I hated to tell him that I still had no clue whatsoever. But I didn't understand the way this world worked.

So, instead of telling him what I didn't understand, I went for something more obvious. "Why would it speak of me?" I shook my head slightly as I spoke.

"You have so many questions, yet we cannot answer." I assumed by 'we' he meant all the other lights buzzing around us. I frowned. "You carry the light within you, I can feel, I can see it." He brought his hand out to point toward my chest before he shook his head. "But I never figured you to be human, I will admit."

"Oh, you mean the Vessel?"

He laughed and shook his head again. "You know yourself not, Melanie. You are not the Vessel, but you have awakened." The lights grew nearer, and more started appearing around us until the whole woods seemed brighter. I studied the Prince in my palm. He gazed down at the ground as if he were listening to something before he turned toward the lights. "Sorry, if they frighten you. We didn't expect to see you here so soon. They are thrilled…" But something about his facial expression seemed off. Almost like he wasn't thrilled, or maybe I was just being

219

paranoid. But still… he looked worried.

"They don't frighten me. I'm just confused," I admitted.

He nodded. "That is to be expected. It's not yet time for you to be here." This little guy was making no sense. His eyes traveled over my chest and stopped on the exposed X. His smile completely vanished. "Heavens, so this is the cause." I brought my free hand up to cover the X.

"Fear marked me as a child."

"He thought you were the Vessel… a mistake that has messed up your order." He sounded completely shook up and it fed my worry. I bit my bottom lip. Did he know something that we didn't? Was I really not the Vessel? My mind was swirling with questions.

Hushed voices fell around me. They seemed to be having their own conversation. One that I couldn't hear. "What is it?" I asked. The Prince closed his eyes and nodded as if he were listening to all of the voices at once. The whispers stopped and the woods fell back silent.

He reopened his eyes. "Your fate has been altered. Even we do not know what will happen because of it," he told me, and it wasn't the answer I was hoping for.

Suddenly, I felt like crying. To come this far, to survive everything I have been through, only to still not have a clue what or who I was. I felt like laughing—it was so ridiculous! "Don't be disheartened, Melanie."

Then I didn't know why I started telling him everything. Maybe the thing about strangers was true… maybe people did find comfort in telling strangers everything. "After Fear marked me as a child, I lived in fear of seeing what others couldn't. That feeling… of seeing ghosts and no one believing me was pathetic and made me feel horrible. I started thinking I really was crazy… I mean, my parents didn't believe me, why should I?" I blinked away the tears and still didn't know what possessed me to spill my heart out. "I spent all those years worrying how my parents and others saw me and if I really looked that crazy to them. Then Grim appeared right when things were spiraling even further out of control." I laughed and shook my head. "And that's what's even crazier… in between the chaos and meeting him, everything finally made sense. Slowly, the fear I've always carried is leaving me. I no longer feel afraid as I used to be. I don't worry about the ghosts. I don't even think much of the demons that are after me… I mean that's weird, right? I should be a lot more afraid… yet I feel…"

"Awakened?" Prince Cadence smiled. "You feel like you for the first time?"

I breathed deeply. "Yeah, I guess you could say that. I feel more alive than ever before. Someone died because of me and I

221

don't even know if he's okay… and I don't know if I will even survive it all, but since meeting Killian and Grim—" I was lost in thought, but my rambling continued in random. "Do you ever get that feeling that maybe you're waiting for something in your life? Something amazing. Something that just felt right? Or waiting for everything to finally make sense? That's what it felt like when he entered my world. I was afraid of him, and everything was crazy when he appeared, but everything also fell into place."

"You know more than you realize." There was a twinkle in his eyes as he spoke.

"No, I don't." My voice fell flat. "You just told me I'm not the Vessel that everyone thinks I am. The only reason he protects me is because of the Vessel. The *very* reason I'm here. The *very* reason I can see him every day and you tell me I'm not what they say?"

"We were never meant to meet today." His expression hardened.

"Why do you say everything in such a cryptic way?" I huffed.

"Because I can't tell you what you need to figure out on your own, but I speak the truth, Melanie. Your fate has changed because of Fear, whether it can be saved lies within the choices you make."

I gave him a frustrated look. "How do I even know you're

not feeding me lies?"

"Then don't listen to me," he snapped. "Stop being afraid and listen to yourself for once. You have awakened—although, it wasn't time, you must now figure out what that means!"

"Will you stop trying to scare me?"

"I thought you said you weren't afraid anymore?" he asked.

"I ain't like I used to be! But the thought of never seeing this place again scares me. He's suddenly pushing me away."

"Your future will be a dark one. You will only experience more grief and loss. You will know heartbreak; you will experience loneliness. The changes have been made and fates already set in motion. It all lies on you now." Way to freak someone out with all this ominous talk. "The choices you choose and what you do with the hand you've been dealt all determine your outcome. Figure out who you are, Melanie Rose and fight for yourself."

I sighed. "Why am I even sitting here listening to a guy that fits into the palm of my hand?"

"We are tiny, but we know truths. We speak to the lands themselves; something that connects to the Underworld and the human one, that is something they all have in common. Land to travel on and to sustain life. It is *everything*, yet nothing to no

223

one. It listens to everything and for those that listen, it will tell you only what it wants you to know."

I opened my mouth, but he brought his hand up. "Whether I speak the truth, is something you must decide. Your choices have already begun, Melanie, choose wisely."

He only managed to confuse me. What the heck could I be if not the Vessel? I had already decided that I best not listen.

After all the time spent hiding from ghosts and getting attacked by demons, you sort of get a sixth sense when something bad was about to happen. And that was the feeling I was getting now as the woods changed—the air felt different and the silence was maddening. That tingle ran along my back right before the elves set off a call—some sort of alert, maybe. There was panic between the lights. I looked down when I felt Prince Cadence running across my palm. "Intruder," he yelled. I could tell he was about to jump from my finger, but he paused and looked up at me. "You're not safe here. Get back to the castle and remember to figure out who you are—" he cut himself off with the shake of his head. "No, find out who you want to be." He jumped and a bubble of light covered his body. The lights scattered and disappeared.

Twigs crunched under someone's weight behind me. I turned. "Sky?" I didn't really expect it to be Sky, but it was a hopeful kind of panic I was experiencing. Vengeance was just as scary as I last saw him. He grinned.

"Vengeance," I hissed.

"It wasn't easy to find you." He stalked forward. "Whatever protection spell he was using to keep you hidden was working until you stepped out of it." He smirked, and I swallowed hard. Grim must have been keeping some sort of barrier up over the castle so that I couldn't be found.

I screwed up.

"You have to know the Vessel can't be taken from me," I warned him, stepping back. "Guess it wants to stick with me."

He laughed and continued forward. I continued taking steps back. "I have heard. That doesn't matter, that's even better. You see, I need a bride and down in the Underworld if I take you as a bride, I can take claim to that power." My stomach fluttered with unease. Fear and Vengeance were both disgusting! "Once we become one, you know how it goes… what's yours is mine and what's mine is mine." His chuckle echoed through the trees. He sounded crazy. He was. My body did a violent tremble.

I heard the wind at her wings and knew she was swooping down over me. "Sky!" I screamed. There was no time to climb on her back. She gripped my shoulders with her talons and lifted us into the air. She took us above the trees. Vengeance's roar carried with the wind and even from this distance—and even over the roaring of the wind in my ears—I could hear him.

I think it was him that whistled—then there was a shriek. I looked above me to see Sky twisting her neck around in panic. I tried to turn myself, but I was locked in her grip. With a lot of work, and me straining my neck and eyes to look back, I saw one of the dragons falling from the sky. Sky decided to throw me up in the air without warning. I screamed, flying high above her. My dress came over my face as I twirled around. I pushed it down in time to see that I was falling back down onto Sky. I had just enough time to brace my legs for the fall against her back.

I took hold of her mane and started searching for the castle. It was a good distance away, but it was in view. I knew we would make it in time, but the dragons were dropping from the sky all around us… I didn't know what was happening, but Sky was whimpering and swaying back and forth as she watched her fellow dragons fall with piercing cries. My heart dropped into my stomach and I wasn't sure what I was supposed to do. I did know that my choices would affect everyone.

"Sky, we need to go get Grim. He's the only one that can help them," I told her. Her blue eyes drifted back to me and nodded. She understood as well as I; we were powerless. We raced toward the castle, but things got worse.

All of the fallen dragons began to rise back up, only they weren't alone. Vengeance's puppets rode their backs as they bucked and panicked before their eyes transfixed like they were spelled. They all started turning in our direction.

"I think they're being forced—or spelled." Adrenaline raced through my veins. I could feel and see the panic in Sky's eyes as she looked at the dragons. I rubbed her head. "Vengeance is controlling them." Still, it wouldn't be a problem for Sky. I knew she could out fly any of them. "We just have to make it to the castle and you are by far the fastest." She went in the direction of the castle. The dragons followed.

There was another roar from the trees. It was Rixen and he rose above the trees at an insane, almost impossible rate. Vengeance was on his back and Rixen bucked and thrashed in the air, flipping and crying out in anger. The anger bubbled in my chest as Vengeance smacked and kicked against Rixen as if he were trying to tame him. Rixen's eyes flickered in and out of the spell. He was fighting it with everything in him. And so far, it was working!

I looked around at all the dragons being controlled. It was a crippling feeling, knowing I was to blame. Rixen continued to fight and hold out from the spell. Sky flew up, jerking her tail away just in time to dodge another dragon's bite. She flipped us upside down over the dragon and I wrapped my arms around her, praying I didn't fall off. She went for the puppet on the dragon's back and tore into its head before yanking it off. The dragon eyes

227

went back to normal and he shook his head, then the rest of his body, like he was getting rid of the spell. The dragon nodded at us before he went for one of the puppets on another dragon.

He was quick and efficient. He managed to free another dragon of the spell. The two now free dragons separated and started helping the others. Another went after Sky and she flew down. I glanced back to Rixen and my eyes widened. Vengeance was beating on him, but Rixen wouldn't let himself go under the spell. Vengeance eyes lit up with evil intent and there was something shiny in his hand. It was a knife.

I looked back at the castle. It was so close… yet my decision was already made. I turned my face away from the castle. There was no safety for myself if I had to continue to let people get hurt because of me. "We gotta help Rixen!" Sky was more than happy to rear back and change directions. Her body glided with purpose and she took out another puppet as we raced toward Rixen and Vengeance. I knew she was flying faster than ever before to get to Rixen in time, but we still weren't quick enough. Vengeance brought the knife into Rixen's side. A sickening wail tore from the dragon as Vengeance took the knife out and stabbed him again.

"No!" I screamed. Blood seeped out of his wounds. Without knowing what she planned, Sky collided into Vengeance. Her talons dug into his shoulders and he roared in anger. She took off with him and I didn't know what possessed me to jump from her, but I did. I lunged for Rixen, but my aim was off. I slammed into his wounded side and he hissed in pain. I felt bad, but I was desperate to get a better grip on him. I couldn't, though, I tried to lift myself onto his back, but my hands were coated with his blood. And I slipped.

I was falling. I screamed. I moved my body around in the air to look around. The trees were approaching. There was no way I could survive this kind of fall. And suddenly I was thinking of all the reasons I couldn't die here.

Then I looked up. Rixen was racing after me. My heart pounded, and I reached out for him. My arms found his chest where I clung to him. He covered me with his wings as we fell. He shielded me with his own body and wings as we hit through the trees and branches. His body thumped against the ground when we landed.

His wings slowly fell open. I scooted out of them and stood up. Rixen lay on his side, breathing hard and uneven. His wound was still bleeding. I bent down to touch him. "You're gonna be okay," I told him. I didn't know if I was lying to him or not. I didn't know how dragons healed and he was pretty banged up. He needed Lincoln or Grim to look at him, but I wasn't sure how I could get to the castle with Vengeance parading around with his puppets. Grim should have already noticed that I was gone. He should have definitely realized something was wrong… where was he? "You need Lincoln to heal you." His eyes were fluttering around like he was having trouble staying awake. His eyes would snap back open and I knew he was fighting the urge to drift asleep with every ounce of strength he had left. "Rixen, I need you to hang in there." He was too weak to respond.

Something that almost sounded like a rattle caught my attention. I stood quickly and strained my ears to listen. I heard it again. I looked around… chains? I didn't see anything close by. I started walking away from Rixen and in the direction of the noise.

I looked up when I heard Sky cry out in pain. Even Rixen, who was barely alive, managed to raise his head up. He whined to her, trying to stand. He had no strength and only crumbled to the ground. I ran trying to reach a clear spot in the trees so that I could see what was happening in the sky. There were too many trees for me to see anything. My mind raced with horrible thoughts. I blinked my eyes. *Please no.* Not Sky.

I should have never left her side.

"Sky!" I yelled, but I could only hear the sound of fighting in the sky.

The chain rattled again and I snapped my head back. I ran a good distance, I realized looking around. The chain moved close and I looked to my left and stumbled forward. "Ryan?" I was both horrified and surprised to see him. He was pacing back and forth in front of a huge tree that he was chained to. Part of the chain was wrapped around the tree and connected to the collar around his neck. It made me sick. He finally stopped pacing and looked in my direction. His face warped, shifting into something close to fear—only worse. "You have to leave right now," he told me quickly.

"How did you get here? And why are you chained up?" I hurried to him. Once I was close, I tried to reach out to him, but he jerked away. That was also when I noticed he was no longer in his hospital gown. His legs were no longer broken and his face wasn't bruised up. He looked completely normal despite the collar around his neck and the fact that he only wore a black pair of shorts.

"I'm sorry, Melanie. Just please go! It's not safe!" He was panicking.

I shook my head. "I can't leave you chained to a tree." I went toward the tree and picked up the chain. Ryan swore behind me. He was scared, I understood that, but I was in just as much danger if I was to leave him and that wasn't an option.

"Melanie, go!" He pulled me by the arm.

"There you are," Vengeance said behind us. I turned around and found myself backing into Ryan.

"Where's Sky?" I glared at him.

"Sky?" His face wrinkled in amusement and he tilted his bald head slightly. "Oh, you mean the pretty white dragon? I'm sure she's lying broken somewhere." My glare morphed into fear.

"Why are you going after the dragons when I'm the one you want?"

"I wouldn't have to if you'd learn to come to me," was his answer. He brought his hand out.

Ryan stepped in front of me. "You're not touching her."

Vengeance took notice of Ryan, his eyebrows shot up and he laughed. "You're a brave one… What are you, a human?" His gaze followed the chain. "Why are you tied to a tree?"

Ryan fell to his knees and gripped his chest. Pain marred his features as he gritted his teeth together. Something was wrong. He turned enough to look up at me. "You have to go!"

I bent down next to him. "Ryan, what is wrong with you?" His face was scrunched up and he could barely focus on me as he howled in pain. "I can't leave you!"

He shoved me away. I fell on my butt. "Leave me and go!" He looked angry, hurt, sad—every emotion seemed to reflect across his face.

"Wait for it," I followed Molly's voice to where she sat on a tree branch dangling her legs. "Things are about to get interesting."

"Molly," Vengeance growled up at her. "I believe I have a score to settle." She stopped swinging her legs and glanced at him. "Lucky we meet again this soon… I don't like being played." They glared at each other.

"You're quite pathetic for such a big, ugly guy. Did you really think Fear would let you take the Vessel?" Molly tossed her head back and laughed. A vein ticked along Vengeance's neck and he jumped at her. She faded and just as he landed on the branch, she reappeared where he once stood.

She smirked. "You're gonna have to try harder than that."

Ryan groaned next to me. I got back on my feet and went to him. Why was he in pain? When I tried to touch him again, he pushed me away. "Don't Melanie. Please, just listen and go while you can."

"Not without you." I grabbed the collar around his neck. "There has to be a way to get this off." I started looking at the collar, but he brought his hands over mine and pulled them into his chest.

I didn't like what I saw in his eyes. "I can't be saved, Melanie." He even tried to smile. It was all wrong and forced.

"You can be, whatever's causing you pain, we can find a way. I'll get Grim—"

Molly laughed at his name. "Don't look for Grim to come

233

save you. He's trapped inside the castle. It has been spelled so that he can't leave. I plan to be long gone before he breaks out." That explained why he wasn't here.

Ryan's face was pale. "I don't want you to see me like this!"

I continued to ignore him. "Ryan, stop trying to make me worse of a friend than I already am!" I snapped at him.

Molly continued jumping around the trees and Vengeance followed. He grew more and more frustrated. Luckily, he had a one-track mind and right now, I was thankful that Molly was distracting him. I ran to the tree and started yanking at the chain. "They are distracted with each other. That gives us a chance."

He grabbed my shoulder and yanked me around to face him. He took hold of my hand and met my eyes. "I don't blame you for any of what's happened to me. You warned me, but I wouldn't listen. I made my choice, Melanie, and I'd make that choice again because I love you." He bent over, clutching his stomach. "But this is where I am sorry…"

I was confused… scared as I watched him. He reached for my hands and gave them both a tight squeeze before he went back to crying out and clutching his stomach. Seeing him like this was scaring me. I didn't know what was wrong.

"Ryan," I cried. "Tell me why you're in pain." He couldn't seem to hear me. He fell to his side, thrashing and crying out in

234

pain.

"I'm… sor…ry…. Run from me," he said, barely able to talk.

Right when I fell to my knees next to him, he became engulfed in flames. I stumbled back in horror and watched as the flames covered his body completely. I was crying—I knew his screams would linger in my nightmares to come.

He thrashed and threw himself around on the ground until the flames died out. Then the realization hit me. I quickly stood up and covered my mouth. Ryan's hair was singed and his body was burned to crisp.

"No… no." I stumbled back as he stood.

Ryan was the charred demon.

CHAPTER FIFTEEN

I started running. I didn't waste time. Ryan was the charred demon... how was that even possible? Fear was intent on destroying everything I cared about. I looked back to see him jerking the chain from his collar. It snapped—fell to the ground at his feet and he came after me. I turned back around. I jumped over a fallen tree just as Molly appeared before me.

"Ah, damn." She smiled "I wanted to see that moment. You know what I'm talking about, the look on your face when you witnessed the human become the very demon that's been trying to kill you." I was yanked back by the hair. I knew I lost my chance at running when Molly stepped in front of me. My head was tilted back, forcing me to look at the charred demon. When I met his eyes, they were Ryan's.

"Ryan," I said and once I did, his eyes faded—becoming solid white. It felt like he waited until the moment I tried to speak to him before he took the last part of himself away. "This isn't you."

He growled in response, showing his teeth. He pulled my hair harder and I hissed. My neck was bent back as far as it could go. "He's turned out to be quite the good demon," Molly said it like he was a pet. I clenched my teeth together as I tried to wiggle free. The charred demon placed his hand on my waist to keep me from escaping with his other hand still holding my hair.

"Saves me the trouble of chasing her myself." Vengeance made his appearance again. My adrenaline spiked and it made my chest hurt. For now, I focused on breathing and ignoring the pain in my neck. Every time I tried to lift my head up to ease the discomfort, the charred demon would twist his hand around in my hair tighter. My neck was on fire—the straining and resistance only made it worse on my part.

"You're still here?" Molly groaned, shaking her head in disappointment.

"That was a nice trick you used on me. Fear has given you a lot of power, I see." He sped forward in Molly's direction. She never moved even as his sword materialized in his hand. She smirked just as he stabbed it through her chest. "Too bad it won't be enough to help you now," he told her and watched as her smile vanished. Blood pooled at the wound. She looked surprised, almost like she hadn't expected it to hurt her. I didn't know ghosts could bleed—I had never seen her bleed before—but Molly wasn't just a ghost. He pulled the sword out. She fell to her knees at his feet.

"You," she hissed, but it didn't sound as threatening when she was injured.

Ryan—the charred demon threw me to the side when Molly was injured and went after Vengeance. He had no weapons, though. Vengeance looked intrigued and lifted his sword—only his grin altered when the charred demon tackled him. Vengeance slung him backward despite his surprise. The charred demon got right back up—went back for more. Vengeance swung his sword out, but the charred demon blocked it with his bare hands. He gripped the sword, bringing it closer to him. He took advantage of the close proximity and kicked Vengeance in the chest.

Vengeance stumbled back a couple steps. Now he was aggravated. He started walking toward the charred demon. The charred demon threw Vengeance's sword down that he still held and ran at him.

I took off running. Molly was on her knees in pain and the other two were distracted. I knew that was Ryan I was leaving back there but in order to help him, I needed him to not to want to kill me. I ran as fast as could—panting and feeling the burn in my lungs. I looked back to see if Molly or one of them had followed and slammed into something solid. "Oaf!" A weird sound escaped my lips. I didn't even want to lift my head up to know that I had been caught.

But I did, and it was Grim. The relief I felt made my knees weak. I pressed my face and body into his bones, wrapping my arms around his skeletal frame. I hugged him—real and honest—with all of the emotions taking me at once. "I'm sorry," I said immediately. I knew he would understand why I said it. I was sorry for not listening. I was sorry for not trusting him enough to know that every action he made—every word he spoke was to protect me. I shouldn't have ventured out of the castle just because I was mad.

His arms wrapped around me instantly. He pulled me close, the essence around him changing to a dark red. I was curious to know what emotion that was for him, but now was not the time to ask. I pulled away from him and met his eyeless gaze. And I started telling him everything, "Rixen is in bad shape and I don't know what Vengeance did to Sky. I haven't seen her..." He placed his finger over my mouth.

"It's okay. I'm here now." And somehow, that was all I needed to hear.

I needed to tell him about Ryan, but two reapers appeared next to us. Both were males and extremely good looking. They gave silent nods and awaited instructions. "Help the dragons." They faded after Grim gave their orders, then he looked back to me. "Stay close... but at a safe distance."

We started walking in the direction I came from. He

stopped—head snapping up just as Vengeance jumped down on us. Grim grabbed him by the shoulders as he got close and threw him in front of us. It didn't matter, though—Vengeance landed on his feet with a cocky grin. He started walking toward Grim. That was when I noticed the huge gash on the side of his head. His skin was peeled back, hanging over his ear. It was disgusting and strange how well demons still functioned with wounds like that. Ryan, the charred demon—I wasn't sure what to call him—must have done that to him.

Just the thought of the charred demon had me scanning the woods for any sign of him. I didn't see anyone, but I knew that meant nothing. Molly and him were still here… they were only waiting for the right moment…

I focused on Grim as his sword materialized in his hand. The scythe morphed into a machete, broad and thick, big enough to hack away at anything—preferably the demon in front of him.

Vengeance lips curled into a snarl. "You have no desire to protect her, so why do something you hate?" His eyes fell on me afterwards. I already knew how he worked. He liked getting inside people's head, exposing the things they were most afraid of. I knew whatever came from his mouth was an attempt to pit me against Grim. It had worked once but never again.

Grim's essence clouded with darkness as Vengeance's puppets appeared behind us, moving in their odd mechanical way as they approached. I took a step back—I didn't want them inside my head again, warping the things I knew and changing them into monsters that ate away at me—my anxieties and fears. I bumped into one as I stepped back—they were all around me. I jerked away, but one was already whispering in my ear.

Grim wants your power.

I smiled. I felt calmer now that I knew the words no longer held any control over me. That must be the glitch in his puppets, they can't hold something against you once you let yourself accept the truth. I grabbed the ear the puppet whispered in and tried stepping around them. There were a lot—dozens. One grabbed my arm and started whispering into my other ear.

You're just the Vessel to him. Nothing more. You don't belong here... with him... Come with us.

The only thing these puppets were doing was freaking me out with their black hollowed-out faces. I pushed one away and went back to holding my ears as I looked for Grim. The puppets were jumping him in a strange way. They were latching onto him, jumping onto each other as they did so. He was completely covered by them—only thing visible was his hand holding the machete. Were they trying to weigh him down? Whatever they attempted had no effect. He started throwing them off. Once enough were off him, he started hacking away at them with the machete. Every time he sliced through one they vaporized into smoke and scattered out before disappearing. But as soon as he got rid of some, more appeared.

"Grim!"

"I don't think you have time to worry about him." Vengeance stepped toward me. Something about the way he spoke—the mockery. He sounded so sure himself. It made me sick.

Grim laughed and something about it was wicked—crazed enough. He was still being jumped by the puppets. It made the hairs on my arms stand. Vengeance's lips curved in disgust. "It's funny how confident you try to be at the face of death." Grim wasn't looking at Vengeance as he spoke. He was still busy with the puppets, but he spoke with such command and power that it was alarming even for me.

I thought I saw worry flash in Vengeance's eyes right as two of his puppets latched onto my arms, preventing me from going anywhere. I wiggled and jerked, but I knew how pointless it was. He smiled as he took another step closer. He didn't get any further. Molly materialized in front of him and stuck a dagger in his neck. She landed on her tiptoes as he stumbled back. She completely recovered from earlier by the looks of her. "You may be powerful, but you're an idiot. You're not the only one here for the Vessel, yet you continuously leave yourself open for someone to attack," Molly said in her child voice, somehow making him

242

look ignorant.

Grim was a giant layer of darkness beside us and the puppets were gone. He turned toward Molly and Vengeance. The charred demon stepped in front of him just as he did, hands clenched together at his sides. He charged at him—the same way he went after everyone he attacked—and Grim braced himself. Once he rammed into Grim—Grim faded and reappeared behind him.

"I think you've interfered enough," Vengeance growled at Molly. I turned to see him pulling the dagger out of his neck. He brought the dagger to his mouth and started mumbling something I couldn't understand, or ever heard before. Then with a smile, he threw it at Molly. She faded and that left the dagger heading in my direction. I felt like throwing up as I watched it get closer. I was held by two puppets and even if I could move, I wouldn't be able to move out of the way in time. Only the dagger disappeared just as Molly did. I stood there a moment, taking a deep breath. That had been too close.

When she reappeared a few feet away, so did the dagger. Her eyes locked on the dagger. She looked annoyed. She faded again, the dagger followed. She swore as she reappeared in a different spot and it was still chasing her. He must have spelled the dagger to follow her. "That should keep her busy." I looked back at Vengeance. He was pleased with himself. Without Molly here, there was no one to keep him busy from coming after me. His eyes traveled over my body—not in a lustful way, more in the desire he had for power—I could see the evil playing out inside his mind.

"Let's go, little human." He came for me.

No.

The voice was back and that same strange sensation started tingling up and down my arms. I wiggled my fingers. The Vessel... could I use it right now? I had a feeling it wanted me to. I had no other options. Vengeance was closing in on me... I tossed my arm back into one of the puppets that held me, placing my other hand in front of the second puppet's face. I didn't really know how to make it happen so I thought of pain. I thought of saving myself and wanting to make them pay. The light felt like static inside my palm as it flew through my fingertips and hit the puppet's hollowed face. It turned the puppet into smoke. I wasted no time doing the same thing to the other. The same thing happened to it.

"It's been said that the Vessel holds limitless power. You honestly think a human can wield that kind of power?" he asked me, stepping closer.

I brought my palm out and held it out like it was some powerful weapon. "I just used it. And I can use it again on you," I warned him. I placed my feet apart, trying to keep the calm

244

composure passing through me, but how tough can I look when I was only holding my palm out?

Still, it was enough to make him hesitant of coming any closer. "That power will most likely kill you using it. A human isn't capable."

I hated this. I hated how crazy my life continued to spiral. All because of demons like him. I felt my palm heat with energy and knew the power was itching to be let out again. I took a calm, reassuring breath and let it go. The light shot out and jumped at Vengeance's chest. He fell to his knees screaming. The light ripped his chest open. Blood flew everywhere and when the light finally faded from his chest, he tipped his head back toward the sky and laughed. Demons were all crazy.

"How interesting." He got back up. His smile sent a chill up my spine. I took a step back. There was a slight pounding in my head. I grabbed the side of my face. "It makes me want it even more."

"I don't understand any of you! You guys are already strong. Why go through all this trouble for more?"

"A human wouldn't understand." He rubbed his fingers over the hole in his chest before glaring at me. "You couldn't understand my need for it, my *thirst* to have more. I don't want to be only powerful. I want to be the strongest being that ever existed. Stronger than Fear, stronger than Grim." He took a step forward. "The Devil himself. Or better yet, maybe I can surpass God."

He was exactly like Fear. No wonder Heaven wanted me safe, this power could be dangerous in the wrong hands. "I won't let you have it and neither will Grim." I started backing away, keeping my eyes on him.

He shook his head at me. "I find it amusing that you stub your nose at me, but you hold Grim on a pedestal." I didn't think that was true. I just knew who to trust. "You do realize without Killian, he's not even a demon, not even made of flesh? He's an entity. All glorified and powerful, but that's it for him. Do you honestly think protecting you or fighting me is anything to a being born without emotions?" I felt my face grow hot with anger. I knew exactly what he was, he didn't have emotions when he came to be—but he had them now. "I can smell your doubt... tastes wonderful." It wasn't doubt. It was anger!

"You have feeling for him when you shouldn't. He can't respond to your emotions when he doesn't have them!" he yelled, and I covered my ears. I didn't want to fall under any of his tricks again. I looked around for Grim. Where was he? The part of me that was weak—scared was slipping out. "It's sad to see something so vulnerable being tricked. I will take you away from here. Come with me and let me have the power. I can take it without harming you, you just have to be *mine*." Something about his words felt hypnotic.

I snapped out of it. "Stop it!"

But he didn't. "Do you think Grim is any different than me? Take a look around." He spread his arms out wide. "This place is an illusion. One that he created in your mind." No, he was lying. "No place is really this beautiful. Let's have you see the truth." He closed his eyes—arms still stretched wide—and everything blackened. It was like a mirage was falling over everything. The trees started wilting and dying—everything turning coal black. The sky was as dark as the night sky I was used to seeing only without stars. I circled around. Everything was dead. I could see for miles through the woods because, without the life of the trees, there was nothing but decay. My head was already pounding and I fell to my knees, gripping my hands together.

He was lying, I knew it. Grim wouldn't lie to me... "Take a good look. This is what Grim's home really looks like." I looked toward the castle. Even from this distance, the castle was no longer the same. The beautiful gray castle was gone and replaced by a terrifying black one. It looked old, rotted, and brittle.

I closed my eyes. "You're messing with my head. Get out!"

"Grim's the one that plays with your mind."

247

"I don't believe what I see. He's nothing like the rest of you." I got up and started running. No one was around. The sky was dark and the woods were dead. All I could hear was the crunch of the twigs breaking underneath my shoes and Vengeance's laughter.

He was suddenly in front of me. I turned around, but he was already there. I moved left; he was there to stop me. He was wanting me to feel trapped. I *was* trapped. I could only face him. "I will never let you have the Vessel." Of course, it was a complete bluff. I didn't know how to prevent anyone from taking it from me. Just because it awakened inside of me… obviously, didn't mean nothing because there always seemed to be another way in the Underworld.

He was angry. "I don't need your permission."

"Your games stop here." Grim's voice drifted through the woods behind Vengeance. He turned to face him.

"Don't you grow tired of doing what you're told?"

"I think you've done enough talking in your lifetime." Grim moved with a dark purpose toward him. "Funny thing, your death has been hanging around me for days... just for this moment." His scythe was in his hand, no longer a machete. "Today's your end." Vengeance looked genuinely afraid this time. I didn't know what had changed, but the huge demon was cowering at Grim's presence.

"I will not die today!" Vengeance sounded like a desperate man.

"Don't act like you don't know. It's predestined. Your death; every death. I know and see them all. The creatures of the Underworld crawl at your feet as we speak." Vengeance looked down at his feet and I did the same. I saw nothing and I didn't think he did either. Whatever Grim saw, we couldn't see. "Death has come for you. There's no escaping me, and you will know true terror in the darkest depths of the Underworld. Satan's Flames."

"No! No!" Vengeance staggered back, and I moved out of the way. The demon was terrified and it was at that moment that I witnessed what it meant to be Death. Grim never took a life until it was their time. That was his truth and Vengeance knew it. The air charged with power that came from Grim. He looked frightening as he stalked toward Vengeance.

"You brought this death upon yourself. Everything led up to this point, to where I take your life. The moment your greed became too much. The very moment you laid eyes on Melanie, it sealed your fate. All I had to do was wait until your death was allowed. That day is today." Vengeance materialized a sword in his hand and attacked Grim.

Grim never held back—he didn't have to anymore. He blocked Vengeance effortlessly and swung the scythe down over

249

his arm. Vengeance cried out as his arm fell to the ground. I had no idea how he was even alive with all the wounds he had on his body. Grim forced him onto his knees.

He spat at Grim. "You think it will end once you kill me?" He grinned. "More demons will come for her when they learn of her existence. How can you protect her from all of the Underworld?"

"I'll protect her," was Grim's answer.

"You know you can't."

"You know nothing." Grim started lifting his scythe. "You shall never see another soul. You shall never seek to harm anyone ever again. Your suffering begins now in the pit of the flames." With his words, he sliced his neck open and blood spewed out. Grim bent down on one knee and with what bit of life Vengeance had left, Grim burrowed his hand into Vengeance's chest and ripped out his heart. The body tumbled to the side and his darkened soul seeped out of his dead corpse.

As he died, the woods went back to normal. His illusion died with him. His soul screamed at Grim. He opened a passage up with his scythe, a mass of flames swirled on the inside. I stumbled away from it—the heat of the place Vengeance was going set my skin on fire. I brought my arms over my face.

Pain… Madness… Anger…. Torment. All of them could be felt from the flames. Sadness… Agony. My heart was racing to a sickening pulse.

Vengeance's soul screamed louder as it was sucked into the passage. The feelings left me as the passage closed, and I sucked in a deep breath. It was only when the passage was gone that I saw what I had done to my neck. I had been clawing at my neck. I still felt the sickness of the passage crawling over my skin even if the feelings weren't felt anymore.

I never wanted to be around when Grim opened it again.

CHAPTER SIXTEEN

Grim stepped beside me, gazing over my body. "Are you okay?" I staggered a bit, the slight pounding in my head was still there and the feeling I got from the passage—Satan's flames, Grim had called it, I thought—left me drained.

Instead of answering him, though; I asked my own question. "Can you not take a life until it's their time to die?"

"I cannot. It goes against my very nature—it's a weakness." It made sense, the Grim Reaper being unable to kill anything unless it was meant to be.

"Do demons know that?"

He sighed. "This is hardly the time, Melanie... but some do, some don't."

I grabbed his shoulders. "The demon with Molly... where is he?" I had to convince Grim that we had to save Ryan. Dread seeped through my bones at the thought that maybe Grim...

"You're asking a lot of questions." He pulled my hands

away from his shoulders and held them. "He's alive. More like, I can't kill him."

"You can't kill him?" I looked to him with horror in my eyes. "Do you know that that demon is Ryan?"

"That's…" Realization startled his voice. "It makes sense. I can't sense Ryan at all and the demon, I sense nothing from him as well." He looked like he was pondering something before saying, "Just what has Fear done to him? I sense no death—no life either, there's nothing." His voice sounded distant—confused even.

"What does that mean for Ryan?"

"I take it Vengeance is dead?" We both turned in the direction of Molly's voice. She looked worn down. "When his dagger stopped chasing me, I figured Grim finally axed him… Good riddance, one less fool I have to worry about." Ryan—still as the charred demon—stepped out from behind a tree and went to her side. She smiled at him. *I made him that way*, I thought.

When he looked over at us, he growled, exposing his teeth. His manners were always the same, animal-like. Every time he attacked, he charged at them and he was always growling. It broke my heart to know that was Ryan. "What has Fear done to him?"

She arched her eyebrows and smiled. "I already told you.

This one's special. Fear used a part of himself to create him. That makes him indestructible. Grim knows, don't you?" Her eyes lit up with darkness. "Sorry, I eavesdropped. There's no death to take, am I right?"

"Even for an entity, creating something… could hardly be easy—or possible," Grim said, gripping his scythe tighter.

"You're not listening." She sighed, placing her hands on her hips. "The boy was already a soul that belonged to Fear. Which meant he was already something—a ghost. He took a part of himself—insert however the hell Fear does his shit—and places it inside the boy. So, it's not that he was created from scratch. Plenty of strong demons could do what Fear did to the boy."

She placed her hand on the charred demon's side. "But you do know why he used the boy, right, Melanie? To remind you of what has become of someone you love… all because of you. Fear really is twisted—wanting to see you fall apart every time your friend over here tried to take your life."

Her words were shrinking—or it was me. I was drifting away from reality. I was falling inside the hole inside my mind. The one that wanted to me to hide from everything. I blinked… blinked… The pit inside me never faded.

"Has he grown afraid now that he knows his death is coming?" Grim asked Molly. She looked confused. "It's

254

approaching and it's making him desperate." Molly almost looked surprised or startled.

Her eyes turned on the charred demon. "Come, dead boy, time to rest." At her words, his burnt skin began to fall rapidly from his body. He fell to his knees at her feet. Naked and himself. He curled up on the ground shaking.

"Ryan!" I called his name, but it was like he couldn't hear me. His eyes were closed and violent tremors were wracking over his body. Molly bent down and picked up his head—pressing it against her chest. She used one hand to hold his head in place and the other to pet him.

"Good boy," she whispered to him.

"Don't treat him like an object!" I gritted my teeth as I yelled. She seemed delighted.

Her gaze drifted back to Ryan. "Foolish boy, even now he clings to his love for you… but for you, there's someone else in your heart." If it was one thing all of them were good at, it was trying to make me feel shame or guilt. I looked down, but this time I didn't feel guilt. I could never change how every part of me felt—my heart. The same way Ryan couldn't change his.

"Let's make a deal—"

"There will be no deals." Grim's voice cut through the air.

"Oh, relax, will ya? Always so temperamental when it

comes to humans." He began to pull in the darkness around him.

"The boy's life returned in exchanged for yours," Molly offered me.

"There is no magic or power that exist to bring back the dead," Grim added.

"The choice is hers. You can tell Fear your answer at the festival." She grinned. She held Ryan tight as she looked down at him. "We will see you guys soon."

Ryan was gone… And I had let him go.

"You're not making any more choices like that again," Grim growled at me. He was quick, pulling me in close before scooping me up in his arms.

"What are you doing?" I mumbled softly. I didn't mind him picking me up. I just didn't know what he planned to do with me next.

"We need to get back to the castle and check on the dragons." I had forgotten about Rixen. I felt my nerves swimming around in my stomach.

"Rixen," I said quickly, worry wrinkling my forehead.

We faded into the darkness—out of time—then the light came next as a signal that we were going back into a time. We stood near the castle where several dragons were. I spotted Sky immediately. She was hunkered down and her white scales were colored with her blood. I ran to her side. She was rubbing her nose against another dragon's head; that dragon was Rixen. "Sky!" She lifted her head, but I didn't like what I saw in her eyes.

I stood next to them. I looked her over for injuries first. There were several gashes and wounds that I could see but none of them looked life threatening. She had gotten away from Vengeance in time… Rixen was a different story. He was barely holding on. Was he even… I couldn't see his chest rising. I waited and waited… there was a slight rise.

But it wasn't good enough.

Lincoln was next to him. Something about his expression left me scared. He drew out a long breath and turned to Grim with another look that made my skin crawl. I dropped to my knees and slid my hand over Rixen's chest. "Why aren't you healing him?"

"I have already tried… he's too far gone. All healing has a limit. I might have been able to save him if I had gotten to him sooner, but—"

"His death is here," Grim spoke behind me. This horrible feeling knotted in my stomach. What had I done this time? "He has no time left, death has already become him."

I looked at the dragon's leader. He was bigger than the others. He was a beautiful, majestic creature—mysteriously enchanting like the others. All the dragons stood close by, saddened and waiting… Why did I keep making mistakes that hurt others?

"NO, he's gonna make it. He's strong. You didn't see him fight Vengeance's control like I did." I shook my head violently. "He won't die after fighting so hard."

"Melanie…" I couldn't handle the way Grim sounded. Like there was truly no hope of saving him.

I moved my body over Rixen's head, wrapping my arms around it. "Please do something. I can't let someone else die because of me…" *Again.*

I could hear him stepping closer. He bent down and placed his hand on my shoulder. "This is not your fault. I should have told you to stay in the castle, that I was keeping your presence hidden inside. My reluctance to tell you is to blame."

Do you want to save the dragon?

I lifted my head up. The voice inside my head was back.

You can save him… at a cost. Little give, little take.

How could I save him? And at what cost? Could the Vessel somehow heal him? Just what kind of power was inside of me? I studied Rixen. Was he even alive? Too many seconds have gone by and I had yet to see his chest rise or fall. Sweat dampened my skin and fear kicked in. No, he couldn't die.

258

Lincoln touched the dragon and he dropped his head sadly.

Time's up. Save him or let him die.

I removed my arms from Rixen's head to scoot myself closer to him. I sat on my knees looking at him. Now, what?

Oh, God. What was I supposed to do?

Think of power! I told myself. *I want to save him! Heal him!*

My body heated instantly and I actually felt like I was going numb. The tingling sensation firing through my arms was different this time. Something about it felt warm, gentle. Powerful, yet... kind. The power spread into my hands. I brought my hands up, palms and fingers facing the dragon leader. The golden lines spiraled out of each of my fingertips, dancing and flowing over Rixen.

Lincoln stumbled back, surprised. Line by line, they wrapped themselves around Rixen. It was beautiful. Bright and golden. They looked to be dancing over and around him. I was mesmerized by my own doing, but my skin grew clammy. Sickness passed over me and I grew faint. I ignored the churn in my stomach.

And despite the way I was feeling, I was still in awe. The lines formed a cocoon around him. The light grew brighter and no part of him could be seen now. The light was almost blinding, but

I concentrated on healing, nothing else. Something was dripping from my nose and I looked down to see blood falling onto my dress.

Grim grabbed my shoulder. "Stop, Melanie! The power is too much for your body." I could hear his fear, but I couldn't stop because I was more afraid of my own fear—the fear of others dying instead of me. The lines stopped flowing out of my fingertips and that was how I knew it was over. I dropped my hands, exhausted, and fell back against Grim.

I fought the need to sleep. I watched as the cocoon began to dim around Rixen. He still glowed from whatever I did. We all waited and I held my breath. Seconds ticked and I was beginning to think that it hadn't worked. But his breath came loud and deep. His eyes fluttered opened slowly. His dark reds gazed into mine and I smiled. I managed to look over at Sky who looked full of life and love.

That was good. I saved him, but I needed to rest now. I tilted my head back to face Grim, but my vision was blurring. "Grim…"

CHAPTER SEVENTEEN

When I woke, I was in dark place. I couldn't see more than a few feet in front of me. I looked down. I was still in my dress and there were blood stains above my knees... I was barefoot, though. I circled around trying to figure out my whereabouts but there was only darkness.

What was this? Was I dead or dreaming? Oddly, I wasn't panicking, but I did feel suffocated surrounded by the darkness. Something moved in the distance. As it moved closer, I saw that it was the silhouette of a woman. She slowly moved through the dark—her white dress was the only thing visible inside the dark void.

I saw her legs, her feet, arms... I could make out everything but her face. It was still shrouded in darkness. She moved no further, staying at the edge of the dark.

"Who are you, and where am I?" I asked her.

"Who are you?" she echoed back at me.

"Am I dead?" I squeaked.

"No, you are not." That was good to know.

"Then I'm dreaming?"

"I suppose you could call it that," she answered. "Have you figured it out?"

I scrunched up my nose. "Figured what out?"

"You awakened a little too soon—but now it's needed."

"Why is it needed? And what is with everyone speaking in tongues?"

"Figure it out. There's a purpose for everything that happens."

"Who are you?" I asked again.

She laughed softly. "You keep asking the wrong questions. The question is... who are you?" She sounded eerily familiar, but I couldn't see her face to know. I blinked, frustrated.

"I already know who I am. I wished people would stop asking me that." First the Prince, now this woman in my dream.

"No."

"You're only confusing me!"

"Be ready, Melanie Rose. You will know soon enough. The truth will reveal itself."

"Just tell me and I'll know."

"Only you can help him now. You can save him."

"Who? Killian? Grim—"

"Do not refer to them as two separate beings." Her voice held anger.

"Right now they are."

"But you know they're the same, don't be foolish. If you hide in your fear for too long, you will risk his life. Don't let Fear ruin any more than he already has." There was a pause. "Find your truth, Melanie. The rest will come naturally."

"What if I can't?"

I didn't think she would answer me. She was quiet for a long time before she finally replied, "Then it's not your life you will destroy."

I woke again—this time for real—staring at the ceiling as I tried to figure out my surroundings. This was the room Grim had prepared for me and I was lying in bed. "You're awake." Killian sat in a chair beside the bed. He still looked rough. I smiled weakly. I must have scared them quite a bit for Killian to be allowed around me.

I raised to a sitting position and Killian jumped up to help.

I was stiff and even sore, but at least I didn't feel nauseous anymore. "Thanks," I told him. "How's Rixen?"

I could tell he was upset with me. His jaw tightened at the mention of the dragon, but he still managed to turn it into a smile. "He's fine, thanks to you." It was impossible not to notice Grim's presence in the room as well. He was leaned against the doorway, whether he was sulking or angry, I couldn't tell. "How are you feeling?" Killian asked me.

"Okay, I guess." I touched my forehead. My head still hurt some and I felt like my body hadn't been moved in the last year… "I don't feel like I did when I passed out, so that's good."

Killian's smile vanished. "Now, care to tell me what the bloody hell you were thinking?"

I groaned. I knew this was coming. "I wanted to save him and *I did*. So what you say doesn't matter, I'd do it all over again if I had to." There was a whole lot of glaring between Killian and I until Grim moved from the doorway. It broke our little feud.

"That's not the problem," Grim added. He crossed his arms and stood at the end of the bed. Now, it was his turn to lecture me.

"What?" I snapped.

"You can't use the Vessel anymore. It's too hard on a human body. It can kill you." I kind of figured that out already

264

when my body felt like it was shutting down after healing Rixen. It wasn't like this was the first time he had told me—Vengeance had mentioned it as well. But it still managed to make me nervous. The thought of dying with this mark on my chest—I shuddered, but then I felt guilty. Because it had happened to Ryan.

"Relax. It's not like I plan on using it again." Neither of them looked like they believed me.

"Melanie," Killian growled. "Don't take what he's saying lightly."

"I can see it in her eyes." Grim was looking at Killian before he turned to me. "You say one thing, but you mean the exact opposite." Killian looked dangerous right now despite being weak. But Grim was right, I was already thinking of how I could use this power to save Ryan.

"I can't even use it when I want," I told them honestly. "But when I'm in danger, I will use it whenever I can." It was making me angry just thinking about it. "I don't understand; why do I have it if it's only going to hurt me if I use it?"

"Because you were never meant to use it. Your body was only meant to hold it, Melanie. Why do you think it's called a Vessel? That's exactly what you are for that power: a Vessel."

I felt my face get hot. I didn't like his answer. Nor would I accept it. What if I really wasn't the Vessel? What if I was something else? Something that was *me?* "What if you're wrong? This power… it's me." I studied my hands and flexed my fingers. I met their eyes. "I don't think I'm the Vessel."

Grim sighed. "Then, what is it? Why did Fear come for you? What about Heaven? Are you saying they got it wrong?" He shook his head. "You can't keep it if you plan to let it kill you."

"I'm keeping it," I made a promise to myself as I said it.

"You've been unconscious for twelve hours because of it!" Killian's concern made me soften some.

"I will be fine, remember, I have Lord Death by my side." I blinked innocently toward Grim trying to butter him up.

Killian was trying hard not to laugh and Grim's essence completely died out for a moment. "Don't ever call me that." He was offended. I smirked. "There's nothing I could do if it took your life. It's not like the times I healed your wounds for you. Every time you use it, it chips away at your life. It shortens it. Do you want to place yourself at Fear's mercy that much sooner?"

"I will only use it when I need to," I promised.

Killian tossed his hands up and groaned. "You're impossible, woman."

"I'm tired of standing still while everyone else is sacrificed."

"We will get Ryan back," Grim added by looking away so that he didn't have to meet my eyes.

I smiled. "But that's not the biggest problem." Killian's tone caught my attention. "Tomorrow night is when we will try the merge again."

"Wait," I paused. "Ain't that a good thing?"

"When we attempt the merge, we will be vulnerable because of two reasons. One: we will be surrounded by hundreds of other demons. Two: we are powerless during our merge; we can't do anything if we were to be attacked because we will be stuck in the process of merging. Let's not forget Fear," Killian said his name distastefully.

I brought my hand to my hair and started raking my fingers through it. One of my nervous habits. "Why will there be so many demons?" I asked.

"The blood moon is also when the Human Festival commences," Grim told me, shifting on his feet.

My skin prickled. "Human Festival? What in the world is that?" It didn't sound good.

"It's exactly as it sounds. The blood moon only comes around once every five hundred years and with it, Satan created a night of free pass for the demons to bring humans to the Underworld. It's nothing but a show—a sport for demons. It's not something I ever wished to show you, but we have no choice. You will be joining us tomorrow night as the human we bring."

My nerves stood on its ends. I looked back and forth between them. Did I even want to know what that meant? "So… I'll be your dates—the plus one?" I sounded ridiculously hopeful.

Killian gave me one of those intense stares that caused me to blush. "Demons and humans don't date."

"So, I've heard." I managed to say and sounded upset in the process. "But, do remind me why you were so desperate for me to understand who you were that night you took me to Deb's?" I can't believe I said something so childish, but I couldn't stop the embarrassing words coming from my mouth. He only grinned.

"What he means," Grim added quickly. "The festival is nothing like a date. It's a night demons can do what they want with humans. Whether to show them off or trade and sell; it's a night of pleasure." Trade and sell humans? That sounded horrifying. "Whatever you're thinking, I assure you it's far worse so mentally prepare yourself."

"You guys actually go to this event?" My voice came out accusing, but I had to know.

"We don't," Killian replied immediately.

"—but our best chance at merging again is being in the

268

Underworld while the festival is going strong; there's the highest potential for power there," Grim added.

"Plus, this year we were invited by Satan himself." My mouth fell open.

Grim nodded. "He must know of Melanie. This is probably his way of taking an interest."

"Why?" I asked. "He won't be there, will he?"

Killian shook his head. "No, but he watches and knows everything that happens." Grim leaned over the bedpost. "He has probably known about Melanie before Fear even found her. We will have to be careful when it comes to him." I was already feeling nervous. Not every day you find out the devil knew you.

"I won't let anyone take your life from you." Grim watched me as he spoke.

Killian took hold of my hand and smiled. "I'd die before I would let anything happen to you." I smiled feeling a bit bashful, but I could tell that his voodoo was slipping again. The scent of him—sex filtered through my skin and senses, caressing me with dirty thoughts. My body turned to goo and my bashfulness turned into me pulling at his hand—wanting him closer. Good thing Grim was around, he walked over to Killian and smacked him in the back of the head. Killian winced, scowling at Grim as he grabbed his head. The scent was leaving the room and I felt like myself again.

"Control yourself," Grim told him.

Killian looked up at him—still rubbing his head. "I can't, I am *literally* dying from being horny. Do you have any idea what that's like?" I knew that his pain was no laughing matter because he was serious, but the giggles tumbled out of my mouth anyway. He brought his finger to his eyes. "Look at these dark circles, this is no laughing matter." Killian glared at me while I was still in a fit of laughter.

I covered my smile with my hand. "I'm sorry, that shouldn't be funny."

"She doesn't look sincere." Grim watched me in the way he always watched me.

"You're the one that keeps stopping him from getting what he needs." I puffed my cheeks out in aggravation.

"Yeah because I don't want to take advantage of you." Killian defended Grim.

I groaned. "I can't wait for you two to be one again! You're always ganging up on me and taking each other's side."

"That's to be expected." Grim crossed his arms over his chest and nodded.

Killian was already nodding with him. "We've been one and the same for three thousand years. It doesn't matter that we're

270

not anymore. Right now, I only feel half of who I am. I'm Killian. I'm Grim."

"I'm Grim," Grim mimicked Killian's exact words. "Just as I am Killian."

I could only stare at them because they were right. In appearance, they were nothing similar, but in their actions, their personalities—everything was the same. Being separated wouldn't change that. "I already know." I found myself smiling.

The room got quiet and I wasn't sure what needed to be said next. "What about Fear?" I asked.

"What about him?" Grim asked.

"He wasn't only after the Vessel, remember? He wanted you too, Grim."

Grim laughed. "Not going to happen. Whatever Fear thinks, he can never merge with two entities. Besides, in order for a merge to work, both the entity and demon have to want it." I sighed in relief. Still, I prayed he was right.

"Don't worry about him. All we have to do is merge again," Killian spoke confidently.

I grinned. "That's good. I'm getting sick of the two of you being separated."

Killian smiled—the kind of smile you don't recover from.

There went my heart in a frenzy, but just as quickly as it came, his smile disappeared. He looked away from me and stood. There it was, I knew this feeling all too well, I was being shut out. "You should get some rest." Grim moved away from the bed. "If this place had a sun, it would be coming up soon and we have a long night ahead of us." Grim left the room right after. Was I just imagining it or were they putting distance between us?

"Why are you guys suddenly leaving? I still want to talk," I mumbled, reaching out for Killian, but he stepped away. A dagger twisted itself into my chest. This was what it felt like to be rejected by these two.

"When I'm able to control myself, Melanie," he whispered softly, almost painfully. "See you tonight." He hurried out of the room.

I took a deep breath. I was okay. I had so much more to worry about. I needed to figure out the dream. I was starting to think I wasn't the Vessel... but what was I? And how could I convince Grim that as well? We had to save Ryan...

My chest hurt... it tightened. Another deep breath... When I stopped what was happening between us the first time, did that change things permanently between us? Did he honestly not feel what was between us anymore?

272

CHAPTER EIGHTEEN

And night came.

I never fell back to sleep. I didn't know how they expected me too. I ate what Ralph—finally asked the butler his name—brought me to eat and paced the floor the entire day. I hadn't seen Killian or Grim.

But that was okay. They were keeping me at a safe distance, but it was no use. I knew how I felt more than ever. I didn't want to hesitate anymore. I wasn't confused or afraid. I knew what I wanted and what I wanted was Grim—Killian. I was drawn to the power in Grim and the demon in Killian. And I wanted—needed for them to be one again.

So I made a decision that day. I would confess my feelings to him the moment they merged. I smiled, feeling my nerves calm. I would save Ryan no matter what. And I needed to figure out who I was—as told by Prince Cadence and the girl in my dreams. I had things to do, so I couldn't get distracted by my own fear.

I wasn't so weak anymore either. I had my own power that let me use it—sometimes. And there was Grim who would always protect me.

Ralph arrived with a wide rectangle box. He placed it in my hands and let me know that Grim would come to get me in another hour. After he left the room, I walked to the bed and sat down with the box and opened it.

It was a dress. I was guessing they wanted me to wear it tonight. I looked around at all of the other dresses going to waste and smirked—he was definitely the type to spoil a girl, I didn't know if he noticed that about himself. I picked up the black material and held it up. Well, it felt very soft... but it was also very small. Skimpy and one shoulder strap. I was not a bold person. I looked at the dress uncertainly.

Melanie, you're supposed to be taking a stand. This was definitely doing something... I thought and sat the box and dress on the bed so I could get out of the one I was wearing. I let the dress I had on fall to the floor and slipped on the black one. It hugged my curves and the strap covered Fear's mark perfectly. Then something weird began to happen. The dress felt like it was moving—I was in the process of tearing out of the thing when I realized what it was doing. The dress was molding itself against me. It started lifting and tightening around my breasts to the point that they were spilling out. A slit formed between them, exposing

274

them even more. I placed my hands on my hips and rolled my eyes. "Men," I muttered as I stared down at my pale cleavage.

Still, I felt the flutters reach my stomach. I was suddenly remembering the fact that Killian's mouth had been hot against my nipple... I pinched my cheeks. "Stop it." Thank God no one could read minds or I would live in constant embarrassment.

Really, though. I took a deep breath. I found a pair of black stiletto boots inside the box. "You gotta be kidding me?" And I really needed to stop talking to myself. I put them on anyway and walked around to see if I could manage wearing them. Not making any promises.

There was also a spray bottle with a note on it that said: Spray me over your head!

I arched my eyebrow. I did as the note instructed and sprayed it over my head. It fell over me like glitter. I could feel my freaking hair moving on my head! I also noticed that my fingernails were now black. Curious of what else it did to me, I hurried over to the mirror.

My hair was up and curled to frame my face. My eyeliner was black and thick, but it only made my blue eyes pop more. I grinned at my reflection. I looked like a biker's chick. I looked kind of wild... I didn't know how else to put it into words. Or a hot mess.

I twirled and watched myself in the mirror. I wore it well. I was actually suited for this look. I grinned foolishly at my next thought. *I look like someone Grim Reaper might date.* But I also annoyed myself. I was once the girl that mocked Tess and her boyfriends with jealous thoughts and now I felt like I was falling into that same deep hole. So, love did make you stupid. I sure felt like I was prancing around like an idiot, but I couldn't find it in me to care.

The door opened and I turned around. Ralph's eyes widened when he saw me before a smile formed on his lips. "Grim awaits," he instructed. I didn't miss the mischievous way his tail sashayed back and forth as he watched me. "You're radiant. Very well suited for Grim's date," he added and I blushed—like I hadn't just been thinking the same thing.

"Thanks." I followed him out the door where they waited for me. Grim stood with his back turned—his cloak completely covering him. Killian was next to him and they were deep in conversation and hadn't noticed me yet.

Killian wore a black tux with a red tie. He still looked pale, but he looked to be concealing some of it. He had his hair styled—well, if a Mohawk counted. He normally left it in a mess—I supposed from his habit of running his hands through his hair. All these emotions put a clamp over my heart; he was so devilishly handsome it hurt to freaking look at him.

Killian was the first to notice me and I loved the way his mouth fell open—and the way his eyes drank me in. As his heated gaze traveled over me, I wanted to look away just because sometimes I couldn't handle the way he looked at me, but I calmed my nerves enough not to. He had this crazy effect over my body that left me with no control and I didn't mean his incubus voodoo. I knew the difference between how I actually reacted to him and the way I reacted toward his seduction. "Melanie… you're beautiful." Killian sounded choked up.

Grim finally turned around, his eyeless gaze swept over me in the same manner Killian's had. His essence pooled around him and I hoped that meant he liked what he saw.

Building up some nerve, I stood straighter—exposing some of that glorious cleavage I wielded at them. I had one of those Cheshire cat grins as I walked toward them. "I'm actually quite suited for this sort of thing… am I not?" I smoothed my palms over my hips. They devoured my every move.

"Definitely," Grim croaked.

"One could even say that I could get used to this lifestyle," I baited. Neither of them seemed to notice what I was implying, so I went on, "With me by your side… I compliment your darkness *perfectly*." Killian realized what I was doing first and tore his gaze away from me. He faked a cough and turned completely around.

Grim did as well, his cloak moving with him as he did. "Let's go," Grim motioned. They ignored what I said. I covered my mouth to keep the grin at bay. They were helping my confidence because I knew they were affected by me the same way I was drawn to them.

I followed behind them. "Where exactly is this festival going to take place?" I asked.

"All of the Underworld is free rein for the Human Festival, but we are headed for the City of the Dead. It's the main attraction and highest potential for power," Grim answered.

Despite telling myself I wouldn't be afraid, I still felt the chill creep over my back. It reminded me there were bigger things to focus on right now. Would everything go as planned? I grabbed my arms and began to rub them, trying to keep the chill of my own dark thoughts at bay. "Are humans taken by force to this festival?" I asked, already having a good idea what the answer would be.

"Yes," Killian confirmed. "But a good lot of them come on their own free will. There is a lot of humans that are obsessed with demons or into Satanism and seek them out on their own. Then you have the ones that are taken by force." Killian's face grew dark, and his fist tightened at his sides. "They are brought to be raped—eaten, tortured until they're broken. Most of them lose their souls to Satan because they are willing to do anything to end the suffering."

I felt sick—nasty that we had to go to the very place where these things happened. "How can that be allowed?" I couldn't even get my throat to swallow—it was blocked off with dread. "Because here in the Underworld, this is Satan's domain. Angels can't enter freely—it takes a lot of willpower to do so. They also risk being tainted," Grim replied. "It's not like they don't try. They manage to save a lot of humans in the human world before they are taken, just not all of them can be saved in time."

"Why do you live so close to the Underworld?" I didn't sound accusing, just curious.

"Where else would I belong?" Grim opened the door and I followed them outside. The sky didn't look much different than it did during the day if this was supposed to be the night sky here. It did seem a bit darker, and there was no moon, but the trees and plants all had a colorful glow to them—like a rainbow and it made it easy to see.

"I will never set foot in Heaven. In order to slay demons, I had to be created from them. And this is home, it doesn't matter how close I am to the Underworld. Not all demons are bad but they are all judged the same. No demon can ascend to Heaven, even if that demon lived a life as a saint," Grim informed me. That didn't seem fair.

Killian studied the look on my face. "I am a demon, Melanie, and the Underworld is my birthplace. When Grim and I merged, that's his burden as well. We are creatures of the dark, not the light."

"It doesn't matter, I am created of demons regardless," Grim spoke to Killian.

"But, that's not fair to the demons that deserve a better afterlife," I spoke too fast, my words become a tangled web of heartbreak. "It's not fair to you."

"I know who I am," Grim told me. "I won't accept the look on your face. Not from you, I thought you finally understood that I am in fact the Grim Reaper."

"That is not what upsets me," I corrected him. "It just doesn't seem fair that you or other good demons can never go to Heaven."

"I'm immortal, Melanie." I looked away from Grim. Killian busied himself with something black in his hand. He used it to open a portal. My worst fear had just been realized. I blinked a few times and tried to sooth my new worries.

"Oh," I whispered.

"Until the world finally ends, I'll keep doing what I do. It's my only purpose." He sounded distant... sad.

"That sounds incredibly lonely," I admitted. Killian

watched us quietly.

"It is."

"Hopefully, this is the last time we go somewhere as two beings," Killian interrupted. It only reminded me of the good that would come out of going to this place.

"Go with Killian through the portal. I'll be waiting for you on the other side." Grim faded.

———————

I entered the Underworld with Killian. Grim was there waiting like he said. We stepped out of the portal and I eyed everything curiously. It was quiet. There weren't any demons around. The place was cleaner than I imagined, and it didn't look like a festival was going on. The ground looked to be black stone. There was no grass, no trees. Everything was a rock surface. I wondered how in the world I was getting oxygen down here.

There were a lot of shops. They all seemed to be made the same way—same build. Simple one story buildings, clean. All gray, black, or dark blues. One shop was called *Love Potion* and the letters were in a hot pink. Another was *Food: Dead or Alive.* Then there was a Demon Clinic. I tried not to let my eyes stay too long on the next one. *Semen Shop*? I shook my head and looked somewhere else. I didn't want to know.

"Where's the festival?" I asked. My stilettos clicked along

the stone pavement.

"We have to cross the gateway," Grim moved beside me.

I scrunched my nose up and gave him a moronic look. A gateway? I thought every place in the Underworld was celebrating the festival? Killian stepped behind me and placed his hand against my back "Look straight ahead," he told me. I couldn't help but notice how nice he smelled as he leaned over my shoulder. I didn't know what I was supposed to be looking for, though.

I sighed. "What? I don't see anything. What am I supposed to be looking for?"

Killian smirked and it was pure chaos for my heart. I crossed my arms in frustration. "You're not paying enough attention, look closer." I tried to pay attention and focus on what I might be missing. "See that, there's a glamour." After he told me what I was looking for, it was easy to spot. The town almost had a faded look to it—like a mirage. It wasn't noticeable and could be overlooked, but every few seconds there was a glitch in the spell and a crack would show. Maybe this was similar to what Vengeance had done to Grim's entire land. Now that I noticed, even the shops looked like a reflection in water.

I smiled, pleased that I could see it. "I see it."

"All we have to do is walk through and we will be at the festival." Killian's hand slid down my back. I felt the

282

goosebumps rise on my skin. He leaned away from me, but I was still responding to him with a slight shiver.

"It'd be best if you ignored everything you're about to see. Block it out if you have to," Grim said, almost sounding desperate to make me understand what he meant. "Don't leave our side." I nodded. I wasn't about to leave their sight in a place filled with demons.

Grim stood at my right; Killian my left, both extending their arm out to me. I grinned and linked my arms into theirs, pulling them close. Grim grunted but otherwise didn't protest. Killian went rigid at my touch. My body pressed against his was only making him worse.

"Shall we?" Killian muttered.

I nodded and we walked through the gateway: into the hidden world that I shouldn't have seen. No amount of self-preparing and time could have prepared me for what I saw. The moment my eyes took everything in, I froze in place, unable to make myself go any further. Demons crowded the streets—monsters, no human would dream existed. My fear took me places my mind didn't want to go, but then I was sure this was the worst of the worst. There weren't enough words of disgust to explain this place. Absolutely horrifying. Sick. Brutal. I didn't think I could actually comprehend the things I was seeing. Now I understood all too well what Grim had meant about blocking everything out.

Demons were having sex *everywhere*. I wished it was that simple. If only I could blink away the sick and twisted things I was seeing. Sex in the air—upside down, at my feet—taking turns, and massive orgies. A girl wrapped in tentacles—legs spread apart as one of them thrust inside her. So many tentacles held her high in the air above the waterfall—whatever the tentacles belonged to had to be somewhere in the water. She writhed and moaned. Another woman was pinned in between two giant demons as they took her at the same time; whether she was crying out in pain or pleasure, I couldn't tell. A beautiful female was sucking on the throat of a male—he looked dazed and confused. When she raised up, blood was dripping from her chin onto her naked chest. *Vampire.* There were no chairs, no beds— nothing. This was on the street that all of this was taking place.

There were all kinds of screaming and moaning, but one caught my attention above the others. I turned around when I never should have. The woman was running naked. "Don't look." Grim tried to steer me in another direction but it was too late. I saw everything. I watched as the demons gathered around the human woman, mocking and laughing at her. Her terrified cries only fueled them more as they tore at her clothes and continued the violation. I would never forget the look and sound of her terror.

I couldn't turn my eyes from any of it because every direction I turned, there was something to see. Sex wasn't the only thing, there were humans being torn apart and eaten; others fighting one another. Human men and women were nothing to these demons. I watched several jerking off as a woman with strap-on screwed a guy from behind while he did the same to the demon beneath him.

Something bumped into us—we had yet to move any further than the entrance. It was a slimy reptilian creature and his snake-like eyes flickered over me in the process. Grim stepped in front of me when his tiny tongue darted out toward me. He kicked it back, but it was Killian that spoke. "Don't even gaze upon her."

This place had managed to suck the life out of my willpower. My resolve to be brave, not weak, completely diminished now that I was here. My skin felt clammy and my body was feeling less of bones and more like strings. I was close to panicking. I tried to take in oxygen but the only thing I sucked in was hot air. I gulped over and over trying to regain composure. It wasn't working, I was losing it. I gasped.

Someone moved me slightly. "She's losing it." Grim was wound up and worried. I no longer felt his arm close by. He bent down and grabbed the back of my neck. "Breathe," he ordered me but I couldn't. I could still hear everything around us. Nothing was fading but me.

Grim swore and turned around as his scythe materialized in his hand. "Stop, Grim. You're only going to make it worse," Killian hissed next to me.

"None of this should be allowed." Grim tightened his grip on the scythe as his essence flared out of his cloak. "They all belong at the tip of my blade," he growled.

Killian sighed. "You know you can't. Just as you know that we can do nothing to any of these demons until it's their time!" Grim looked around once more before he let the scythe disappear.

"I can't," I whimpered. "Please."

"We should probably take her somewhere quiet," Killian said.

I didn't think I could stay here any longer. Grim ran his hand up my back. "Go and calm her down. You don't have much time, I'm sure he will be looking for us." Killian nodded at him, and I gripped my sweaty palms. "I'll make my arrival known," Grim added before looking at me. "I want to see a better look than that when you get back."

Killian grabbed my wrist and began to lead me through the crowd with him. I didn't focus on anything but him. My eyes were burning and so were my lungs—I needed to get a grip on myself. He took us to an empty alley. Well, there was an unfortunate guy getting a blowjob before Killian threw him out

286

with his lady giving us the evil eye.

He caught me off guard next—slamming me against the brick building. He smacked his palm against the building so that it rested by my head. I swallowed down some of my nerves, but Killian gave shaky legs a whole new meaning. "Ow, Killian. What are you doing?" I tried to move, but he pinned me to the wall.

He growled—really growled and Lord help me, it was sending the wrong signals to the place between my legs. I shouldn't have reacted that quickly to him, not after everything I had just witnessed, but nothing could ever waiver what I felt for this demon. Shame heated my face and neck. "You only have a couple of minutes to pull yourself together." Just the thought of going back out of this alley had me feeling sick. "Don't you dare make that face. What happened to your confidence? This world— or yours isn't pretty, you of all people should know that. Hasn't Fear taken enough from you?" he scolded me, and I knew he spoke the truth but it was harsh.

"I didn't expect—"

"Did you not understand the words 'prepare yourself'?" His breath was hot against my neck as was his anger. Intense dark eyes studied me with aggravation.

"Why are you being so cruel right now?" I tried so hard not to make that question come out as a whimper.

287

His features softened, for just a moment, then he was angry again. He punched the wall beside my head and I flinched. He stepped away, took a deep breath while running his fingers through his hair—so much for the styling. I eyed him curiously as he loosened his tie. "Melanie, this place is a nightmare; I'm well aware of that. But don't think humans aren't capable of doing the same things, some are just as twisted as demons," he informed me like I didn't already know that humans were just as ugly. I did know. He was upset, but I could tell he was trying to relax for my sake. "You've never seen anything like that before and you should have never had to, but we have to get through this. Together, okay? I would rather die than let anything happen to you, do you understand?"

I nodded softly. I noticed the change in his eyes—the liquefied blackness that always seemed to take over every time he was about to start slipping out his voodoo on me. "Killian." There was an edge to my voice.

"Melanie, I think…" He grabbed his head, but his movements were quick to change. He stepped forward, pressing himself against me. His hard chest squished me against the rough wall. I tried to wiggle from his grip; we did not have time to deal with his horny personality! His mouth came down over my collarbone and his hot breath lit up every nerve-ending I had. "I'm at my limit," he half admitted, half pleaded in my ear. Oh… we are so screwed because I didn't know how to turn off my own

288

flood between my thighs. First, he needed to stop whispering in my ear. That might save us.

"Do not lose control, Killian," I warned him, leaning away from his dangerous close mouth. His hand cupped my boob and—crap. "If you start letting out those fumes of yours, we are screwed." *Literally.*

I was already going slack against the wall, my body melting for him. "I will if we don't do something. I'm going fucking crazy—please, just help me," he whimpered, and it was the sexiest sound I have ever heard.

"What can I do?" I didn't hesitate to ask.

"Just… let me touch you," he mumbled, voice ragged. Every part of me responded to his words, but I still couldn't see past where we were.

"I don't think I can here." I gripped his shoulders so that he would stop feathering his breath across my skin. "Not in this kind of place."

"Melanie, I just need to touch you…" He faced me—eye to eye, nose touching nose. I was losing myself to him, I knew it, I could feel it. I was reaching a point of no return. "This place reeks of sex and it's only complicating what I've been trying so hard to fight. I can't anymore."

"Go ahead," I said softly, bringing my arm up to hide my

eyes. I wanted him—everything he would give me.

He jerked my arm down that hid my face from him. His eyes no longer flickered black, brown eyes moved over me. "When did I become so pathetic?" He laughed out of pity. "All I need is sex and I wouldn't be in this situation if I could bear the bloody thought of laying with any woman besides you. You're all I can fucking think about anymore. A *human* I met a few weeks ago. You want to know why I was so fucking mean to you when I first met you? Because I was terrified of you. You were a fragile little thing, scared and nervous all the time." He grabbed my hand and placed it against his chest. His heart was pounding. "So why the hell does my heart fucking fall out of my chest every time I see you from the moment I laid eyes on you?" He sounded angry, but it wasn't that, his emotions were spilling out. I felt my own ribs cracking, responding to everything he said in a way that could never be understood. "But then I knew… you're what I've been waiting for… what I've always wanted for so long… for thousands of years…"

Did he realize what he was saying, what he was admitting? Out of all the places this could have happened, why here? I was bursting with happiness and I guessed that was how it went. There was no control over how these moments worked… they just… happened.

It was weird how the feelings of love could make it feel

290

like you could take on anything.

He kissed the place at the bottom of my eye, then my nose. Hurrying, time couldn't be wasted here, his right hand roamed down my side, on down to my hip where he grabbed my butt. I gasped as he hauled me up. My arms fell into place around his neck. His left hand slipped inside my legs, wanting me to spread them. He pressed into me—forcing them open and lessening the gap between us. It caused my dress to ride up, exposing my panties to the bulge in his jeans. My body—mind went into a frenzy.

He cupped my cheek and pulled me in for a kiss. He was rough, but I was always left amazed at how much I responded to all the things I've never done before. Killian's body shook; felt like violent trembles against my skin and he ended the kiss. His took a deep breath and dropped his forehead between my cleavage. "Killian," I panted, worried that he was shaking, but also wanting him to go on.

"It has to be more than this," he mumbled in my chest.

"You're shaking." I touched his arm, finding beauty in his madness.

"It's you, Love, all you." I smiled. "Let me give you something." His voice was raspy—dark.

"What?" I breathed deep. His hands idled at my sides.

"Don't worry, you'll like what I'm about to do, and I can take from your pleasure to sustain myself." His words alone fueled the fire in my stomach. I leaned my head back and nodded. He brought one hand between us, leaning away from me so that his hand could move between us. Was it possible to fall apart under someone's penetrating gaze? Because the way his eyes molded over every part of me as he slid his hand along the inside of my thigh—I tried not to crumble. I closed my eyes. "Melanie." He wasn't going to let me, it seemed. I reopened my eyes and turned my head slightly so that I wasn't looking directly at him. "Don't," he warned. "Look at me." He held me captive with his beautiful dark eyes. His fingers found my panties, grazing across them.

I gasped, letting my head fall against his. He pushed me right back on the wall with his forehead. He smiled and met my panties with his finger. Up, down, his finger moved with precisely the right amount of pressure that my libido increased to insane levels. My body couldn't decide whether it wanted to tense or tingle. My stomach heated—knees weak.

"Beautiful." He leaned in and tickled my ear with his breathing. He pulled at my panties, parting them to the side. I was stuck in between breathing and waiting on him to touch me more. I bucked my hips into his hands before even realizing what I was doing. Once the contact was made, we both moaned. My stomach was in knots and clenched for more.

Killian found my eyes and held me there. He traced my slit until he reached my opening. I was wet and it coated his finger. "Fuck," he muttered softly, breaking our eye contact momentarily. "Just enough for the both of us," he promised. I wasn't sure if he was talking to me or reminding himself. He brought his hand out of my panties and I moaned in protest. He cupped my sex with his hand right after. I fell silent, wondering what he planned to do. His hand heated and it hit me out of nowhere; I unraveled. There was no further build up, no warning; I just exploded into millions of tiny fragments and only existed within the waves of pleasure racking through my body. My sex clenched and unclenched, threading into my stomach. I still felt amazing even after it was over.

When I was able to open my eyes—regaining my senses after the mind-blowing orgasm I just had—Killian admired me in a way that made me fall for him even more. I noticed I was clinging to his shoulder and could only grin. He was noticeably healthier looking now and his face wasn't so pale. I wasn't sure how I helped when he was the one that pleased me, but I was glad. He tried to hide his smile in my cleavage, but I saw it before he hid it. "I didn't know you had power like that," I told him.

He stepped away, dropping my legs down. I felt shaky but good. I adjusted my panties and they were soaked. "Incubi aren't good for much except for orgasms and seduction," he told me, helping me slide down my dress—not that it covered much. "Are you okay now?" Dark eyebrows rose to question me.

I nodded. "What about you?"

There was something in the way his chin lifted—the slight change in his smile that left me alarmed. "All that matters are that we got you up and operating smoothly again," was his answer.

I arched an eyebrow, suddenly feeling suspicious. "But you were the one on the verge of losing control."

He looked out of the alley at the festival raging on. "Yeah… now, come on, we've been here too long as it is." He placed a kiss on my forehead and took my hand. I had a feeling that maybe he wasn't so out of control as he had made it seem… that maybe his purpose was to get me out of the panic attack I was having. And it worked. I gripped his hand as he led us back into the nightmare.

I clung to Killian's hand as he led us through the crowd. Sex was everywhere; a demon was killed in front of us. The demon that killed him gave a victory hoot and Killian shoved him to the side so that we could get through. My body was still in a tingly phase after what Killian had done to me, not that I minded. He could do whatever he wanted to me. And being with Killian in any way—instead of through power—I just knew it would be

294

intense. Those thoughts are what I focused on as my arms smacked into the demons fighting and screwing. Nothing else.

I spotted Grim in an opening that we came to. I studied him, confused. Why was he sitting in a huge, fancy-looking chair? It made him stand out, in a way that felt dangerous. He sat, legs crossed—looking either agitated or bored, could never tell with bones. The space around him was free of demons, opened and a clear view. Two empty seats were next to him. Again, something didn't feel right. I looked to Killian and his expression gave way to my worry. "What's wrong?"

"Time to put on a game face, Love, looks like the Devil's wanting to play with us," he answered me. My heart thudded with unease. "Come on." He pulled me into him, placing his arm around my neck as we walked toward the seats. Grim turned in our direction and I was already squirming, wondering if maybe he knew what we had just been up to. I took the seat in the middle and Killian sat on my other side. I placed my hands in my lap and straightened my back. *Nerves don't fail me now,* I chanted to myself. I didn't want a repeat of earlier.

"Want to tell me the purpose of the chairs?" Killian looked to Grim.

Grim shifted in his seat, bringing his skeletal fingers to rest on his skull. "A gift," he spoke quietly with an unmistakable anger. "From the Devil."

Killian leaned back into his seat, looking ahead with his forehead wrinkled. "I knew it," he spat.

A demon with a potbelly and a pig snout came waddling toward us. He was hideous. I didn't like the way he was looking at me. "What a lovely one you have," he spoke through his nose. He must have been referring to me, I realized. "When shall we see her at her best?" he asked. I wasn't sure what he meant at first, but then my eyes widened—I think I knew now.

"Shall I cut out your tongue?" Grim spoke calmly but there was always something in the way his voice carried when he did. It was terrifying—powerful.

The demon stumbled back, completely frightened—even his movements seemed piggish to me. A snort or a plea came from him. "But Grim… it is said that your human is the main entertainment for the festival." Killian slammed his hands onto his chair's armrests.

"She's *mine*. Mine to look at, mine to touch and do as I please. She's not a spectacle for a lowly creature such as you to even gaze at!" Grim hissed, standing up.

"What if it was Satan that made that choice for you?" I could recognize Fear's sinister voice anywhere—not that he sounded like the evil he was. His voice sounded beautiful—honey dripping even. I looked past the pig demon and saw him standing relaxed and dressed to impress. He must have a thing for wearing

296

kimonos. The one he wore now was silver and black, revealing pale skin underneath. His hair was placed into a ponytail, long and silky-straight. I felt my face heat with anger when I saw Ryan next to him, dressed in chains. Chains that Fear held on to. Ryan wasn't looking toward us; he wasn't looking at anything. He was completely focused on staring at the ground. I felt twisted seeing him so worn down and beaten. He couldn't stay with Fear any longer, I could see the defeat in the way his shoulders were slumped. He wouldn't make it. Molly stood next to him and there it was, that distasteful look on her face like she didn't want to be here. She was a puzzle to me, one that I didn't care if I never solved.

"She's. Not. For. Show." Grim punctuated each word slowly.

"Is that okay for you to decide?" Fear asked Grim, but it was me he was looking at when he spoke. There was something cruel in his eyes before he smiled. "Very well." He turned toward Ryan, yanking at the chain, and Ryan stumbled off balance. My instinct was crawling at me to run and go to him, but I gripped the armrest instead. "He's the human I brought tonight... well, technically he's dead, but I gave him flesh. Wasn't that nice of me?" He looked to Ryan. "I made you something other than a pathetic ghost. Since Grim won't cooperate, I guess you'll be the entertainment for tonight." My heart stopped and his words did something to my very soul. "Think you can handle being used and abused by any demon that wants to have a go at you?" I watched Ryan visibly shake but when he lifted his head to look at Fear, I saw it. The hope I needed as he glared at Fear.

"Don't worry. See, actually, I have other plans for you." Fear clapped his hands together in excitement. "I have another human here tonight." Killian tensed in the seat next to me, and Grim's essence flared to life under his cloak. Fear's tail materialized behind him and it shot forward in my direction. It stretched towards me and I leaned back, automatically protecting my neck because that was what I assumed he was going for but he went for the strap on my dress instead. He ripped it, tearing the fabric to reveal the X. It heated and glowed red against my skin. I winced, hiding it with my palm.

"Let's make them both our show for tonight," he yelled over the crowd. He brought his hands out above his head and circled the demons that waited around with eager excitement. "What do you say?" The demons roared in response. I felt the blood drain from my body.

Ryan held his palm out in front of his face as it burned his skin; the same as mine. He looked at me and all I could see was sadness and defeat. He looked guilty, and that was when I realized that maybe he blamed himself. Because he was Ryan, and Ryan could never see the things he went through because of me. He only thought of what I would have to go through, never himself. Because that was what kind of human he was—honest and loyal, caring and the boy I would somehow save.

"You won't touch her." Grim's essence grew around him, darkening the space around him.

"With that mark, she will always be mine," Fear reminded him. They stood glaring at one another. Killian got up and stood in front of me.

"You're not the one that brought her here, she's mine," Grim snapped.

"She carries Fear's mark," I could hear the voices in the crowd saying. They grew louder until things erupted into chaos. The demons were sure to take Fear's side because of the mark and they wanted a show. I was scared and the idea of losing what hope I did have only made it worse. I leaned forward, enough to reach Killian's hand. I needed that bit of comfort. He turned slightly and gave my hand a gentle squeeze.

"Do you want to ruin the festival and upset Satan?" Fear arched an eyebrow at Grim.

I knew Grim was at a disadvantage. Fear had provoked and moved the demons just as he wanted them. Now we could possibly be at the mercy of Fear's twisted games. "Move," Fear hissed at a demon in his way. The demon was quick to listen. He jerked Ryan by the chain, dragging. Ryan looked at me again, but this time, I was the one that looked away. I was afraid of what might happen to us and ashamed that this was happening to him when it should only be me.

Grim turned around, his eyeless sockets swirled with blackness as he came for me. My stomach filled with dread. I knew what he was coming for. We had to play along. Killian stepped aside. I stood from the chair quickly, placing my shaking hands against my dress to hide them. Before Grim could say anything, I spoke first, "We have to, I know. You wouldn't make me if there was another choice..." He looked down at my hands. I forced a smile on my face—it was a pathetic attempt to make us feel better. I reached for his hands and lifted his head. "Let's get this over with and do what we came here to do," I reminded them, looking back and forth between them. "But, just so that I know, what is going to happen to me?" I knew it would have been better if I hadn't asked. But the feeling I got in the pit of my stomach—the fear—made me want to know.

Instead of answering, he pushed me out into the center of the circle where everyone could see me. I glanced around nervously, taking all the demons in. Grim walked back to his chair—pulled it closer before he sat down. He crossed his legs and leaned back. Killian stood next to him, both were watching me. Their gazes alone could swallow me whole. Grim brought his hand to his skull, almost in a bored like manner. I realized whatever was happening had started.

And I wasn't prepared.

"You want a show. I'll give you one." This time, it was Grim's words that had the demons roaring with excitement.

CHAPTER NINETEEN

"Melanie," Ryan yelled my name. His worry was beautiful—because he always knew how to worry for me, but never himself. I called it beautiful but it was more like a torment for me—the person that continued to destroy his life and afterlife.

"Perfect!" Fear played his part well, adding fuel to the fire. The demons formed a circle around us, cheering and giving me lustful eyes. Some were screwing while they watched eagerly for something to happen. I felt the fear raging inside of my ribcage, but I put a clamp on it. I couldn't afford to fall apart here, not when I had no clue what would happen to me. This time, though, that fear could be valuable, it would keep me alert.

I ignored all the screaming and ugly laughter and put my focus on Grim and Killian, and what might happen to me. Grim's scythe materialized in his hand. My heart pounded so hard, I could see the imprint of it thumping outside my chest. My forehead beaded with desperation. What did he plan to do?

"Step forward," he ordered, and I obeyed. My stilettos clicked on the dark stone as I moved towards him. I was still a good distance away from him—several feet. He brought his scythe out, pointing it at me. It grew and stretched forward. It made me think of the way Fear's tail could do the same. My instinct was clawing at me to step away. The tip of the blade was heading for my chest, and I couldn't handle it anymore so I stumbled back a step. "Don't move," he barked out another order. I froze, his voice alone feeding my fear.

Calm down and Relax, I told myself. I was past the point of comparing Grim to Fear; no matter what, he wasn't Fear. Even now, when I had no clue what he was doing, I trusted him. It was better that he made a show out of me instead of giving Fear the chance. As bad as this was, it could be worse. But I knew my expression was slipping and my fear was put on display. Grim was scary when he wanted to be. Right now, he was, but there was a sweet, dark ache that crept across my skin at the thought of his strength.

The tip of his scythe moved down my dress. Then he started back at the top of my dress—between my breasts—and snagged it with the tip. It started ripping. He moved it down slowly, deliberately, and continued to destroy my dress until it reached the bottom, between my legs. The crowd erupted into cheers. The once tight dress parted, exposing my bra and panties

303

underneath. He didn't stop there. He went on to touch the blade across my leg, pinpricks broke out on my skin wherever the blade went.

When he traveled it across my stomach, the pinpricks spread all over my body. I sucked in my stomach, afraid that I would get cut. But it didn't happen. The blade traveled on up and found my bra. I had a horrible suspicion of what he planned to do next. And it happened. The blade snagged my bra in the middle— *pop*—and you know those horrible cheesy animated pictures of a woman's bra being busted open because her jugs were too huge? That was exactly what I felt like, only my problem wasn't my bust size, but they did hold that bouncing effect as they sprang free. I covered them with my hands immediately. My face, neck, and chest were all on fire from my embarrassment. The crowd was thunderous with their hooting and hollering. "Drop your hands," he said coolly.

Killian's eyes were going insane—flickering in and out of the blackness as they drank me in. Some of my embarrassment faded and I slowly dropped my arms from my breasts. I closed my eyes, taking in a lungful of air. This wasn't how I wanted my first strip to happen in front of Killian—with all these nasty demons. I had always thought he would have taken my clothes off himself, but in a way, he did… I studied Grim, hollowed eyes peered through me.

Let it go...

It was the voice, and it always had a calming effect on me.

I could make things easier if I just focused on something else other than the crowd. On *them.* I started blocking out everything—everyone. I knew Ryan was somewhere behind me, but I even let him fall from my thoughts—I would save him when the time came. I had to focus on getting through this moment, and the only way I could do that was to let myself be here with just them—alone.

So, I started letting myself think of how different it would be if we weren't surrounded by demons. The chaos slowly dimmed around me—there was silence. Grim and Killian were no longer separated in my vision—they were one person again. That thought had my heart wanting to fly from my chest into their arms, and it was another reminder of how deeply my mind, body, and soul fell for him. Which should be weird since I still knew absolutely nothing about him, but that was it, being with him was the one thing that always felt right. Even when I told myself to hate him, fear him.

I wondered if he had those same thoughts when he looked at me. Was he mesmerized with the view I had just given him? Was I the same as every other woman in his eyes or was I different? Would he hold me close and love me gently, or would he be rough and unrestrictive despite my inexperience? What did

305

pleasure look like on him? How did he love? I wanted to know everything because I was foolishly and hopelessly in love with this demon—entity.

I reopened my eyes. Nothing else mattered but them. I smiled, stood straight and held my head high. I wore nothing but my panties and stiletto boots. Grim's dark essence went wild but I spotted the color in his chest. The same beautiful emotion I saw at Fear's cave, shining through his tux and cloak—maybe it was something only I could see. Or maybe I wasn't really seeing it, maybe it was a feeling.

Killian was held captive. His eyes devouring me. He didn't hide it and when he met my eyes, he smiled—and it was both chaotic and beautiful.

Grim's scythe moved through the air, leaving his hand. It changed form as it did so. It floated down onto the floor as a black chain, slithering like a snake toward me. It started up one of my legs, moving between them. I gasped, keeping the roar of the crowd tuned out, and focused ahead. The chain slithered against my panties, rubbing and traveling on to my breasts. Heat flared in my stomach and I was trying hard not to squirm as the chain wrapped around each breast, squeezing and caressing them like the chain was a living being. I lifted my gaze to Grim—the chain was a part of him, the scythe was a connection. My own thoughts drove me wild. The cool touch of the chain suddenly felt gentle against my scorching skin.

Killian stepped forward and the anticipation grew with every step he took closer. None of this should be okay. Getting turned on by a chain—was that even possible? But reality didn't exist here and neither did the Melanie Rose that feared ghosts—life, *everything*.

The chain started to pull me back and I was being lifted off the ground. My head fell back and the chain was all over me now. My feet left the ground and my legs and butt were thrust forward in the air. The chains were parting my legs, and I lifted my head in a hazy state of wonder and anticipation. I was on full display. His eyes held dark intent and I was bound by the other predator, the one that controlled the chain and left me floating in the air. I shuddered, letting my head fall. The styled magic fell from my hair. This whole situation had me feeling strange and weak—maybe it was a coping mechanism. When I felt Killian touch my leg, I forced my head back up to look at him. He was between my legs while I floated. The chain continued its torment against my body.

I must have been blushing. I couldn't tell at this point; my skin was already blistering hot. "You're soaked," he whispered so only I could hear. I already knew that, though. My neck was starting to cramp and I couldn't keep holding it up this way. I brought my head to my arm, trying to put some of the weight there.

"How much longer do we have to do this?" My voice was raspy.

"Don't feel ashamed," he told me softly, tracing his fingers against my inner thigh.

"Please, don't," I begged. "Not here." Despite how much my body reacted and how easily I accepted this role… I knew this place—the actions I made here would haunt me if I let it go any further than this. My entire hope fell on my trust that they would end it soon.

His eyes fell over me gently. "Never," he promised—or denied me, my fried brain couldn't comprehend what that word might mean. He moved his fingers even closer to my panties. The chain moved against me. I arched and whimpered—barely aware I was doing it. "That's why we're not." Hope soared through my chest.

But something came up behind me; the unknown presence had me tensing up until skeletal hands covered my breasts. My head fell against Grim's chest—his touch was a nice reprieve from the burning I felt. "Get ready." I barely managed to figure what he meant before everything happened at once.

Fear's tail shot out in the direction of my chest. The chain—that was wrapped around me—moved to block it, changing into a weapon at one of its ends. I could feel Grim move

308

behind me as the tip of Fear's tail morphed into a giant mouth and came at me again. The chains slid over me—releasing me—and Killian was there to catch me as the chain slid back to Grim. After it moved up his leg and arm, it became a sword. Fear's tail jerked back when Grim stepped in front of us to block the mouth on the tail. His tail backed away and Fear materialized a sword in his hand. Almost an exact replica of Grim's, only it was red—like blood dripping off the blade.

Killian eased me to the ground. Grim took off his cloak, and Fear was ready to attack—I wondered what he was doing until he tossed it to Killian, who then draped it over me. I forgot that I was naked except for my panties and boots. I gripped the cloak and held it close to my body. I could still feel the reminiscence of Grim inside it. It brought reassurance.

I heard Ryan's piercing cry but as I started searching for him, Fear chuckled. The kind of chuckle that lasted all of one second and died off the face of the Earth— or Underworld. "Tonight, both of you will belong to me." I didn't have to guess who he was referring to: Grim and I. Fear lunged for Grim, but he faded and reappeared behind him. Grim kicked him hard—he stumbled forward and hissed in anger, teeth bared and all.

The cloak was almost ripped off me when Killian was caught off guard by Ryan who was currently the charred demon. The impact sent Killian flying—I had expected the charred

309

demon to come after me, but he never even looked my way as he went after Killian. Killian managed to get to his feet in time and avoided the next hit. Punches were thrown back and forth. Killian grunted and the charred demon screamed like an animal. Ryan was human but as the demon, he was evenly matched with Killian. I could see the struggle Killian was having with him. Just how strong did Fear make him? The charred demon only seemed to fight with brute strength alone, though. He threw punches like a madman, never really paying attention to what he did. That proved to be Killian's only advantage. Killian perfectly timed his movement with the demon's recklessness so when the demon brought his arms out swinging—Killian hauled him up by them and threw him to the ground. Killian came down throwing punches repeatedly toward the charred demon.

The crowd was wild. Grim turned and silenced them all with a glare. They all started to scatter. I supposed none of them knew Grim's secret, but Fear could hardly contain his grin. "Funny how they fear you when you can't even hurt them, can you?" Fear used his tail as a weapon—and his sword as he attacked Grim using both back and forth. Grim blocked him every time.

"I can kill them all." Grim lifted his sword to block another attack.

"Oh?" Fear arched an eyebrow as he jumped back to avoid

Grim's blade.

"Sup?" Molly appeared in front of me with her hands on her hips. I jumped at her and it was unexpected for both of us. But forever like a ghost or demon, she faded before I could even get close. I met the ground instead. Splintered pain shot up my palms and knees. She reappeared behind me and shoved me down. My chest smacked the dark stone. I gritted my teeth together to keep from crying out. She pressed her foot into my back, holding me there. "Idiot," she laughed, looking down at me.

My patience was at its end. I looked to Killian and Grim who were both occupied. I lifted myself up and was surprised that she removed her foot. Foolish mistake. I leaned my head back slightly and smiled at her. "Oh, yeah?" I could already feel the power tingling through my arms, shooting down into my fingertips. I lifted one hand up and the golden-colored light hit her. She shrieked as the light engulfed her. Fear noticed and sneered down at me.

"It's true. You can wield the power." Grim shoved Fear back with his sword, earning back his attention.

"Grim!" Killian yelled. Grim and I both looked. He made a gesture with his eyes to the sky. What? I squinted my eyes and looked up. The moon! I never noticed it there before, but—was this the same moon as ours? I didn't have time to wonder. The gray moon was running red, it looked like it was dripping down over the moon. I understood why they called it the blood moon. And every second, it continued to grow in the sky, expanding and taking up more of the sky.

Grim's essence darkened around his feet. Fear was catching on and went for another attack, but the darkness shot out from Grim's feet and attacked him. It wrapped around him—he screamed, but it wasn't because of the pain. He was furious.

Killian shoved Ryan—still the charred demon—toward Molly who was crumbled on the ground still in pain from what I did to her. Killian and Grim both started running toward me. They exchanged a nod before Grim grabbed my hand. I watched Killian pull out something from his pocket, but I saw no further because Grim was taking us into the darkness—the fade out of time. When the light came, we were standing on a rooftop. I could tell we were still in the Underworld. Killian appeared next to us a second later. The festival was still in full swing below us.

"Hurry, or we will lose the chance," Grim said to Killian as they moved next to each other. Killian eyed the blood moon in the sky. It was big, bright, and bleeding.

"There's hardly any time. What if Fear gets here before we can finish?" There was real fear in Killian's eyes. It made me realize that this night wasn't only scary for me but for them as well. This was maybe their last chance. It had to work for them to be one being again. It was like all of our fear met and crossed

312

together on the rooftop. The thought of the person I loved never being whole—it stole my entire breath. My heart felt like a magnetic explosion.

"Let's hurry so that it doesn't happen," Grim told him— out of the two, Grim was confident enough for the both of them— and Killian nodded. They stepped close, extending their hands out and placing them together.

There was nothing that happened at first… but I knew the merge had already started.

Then the sky darkened above them in the same manner Grim's essence did. They stood still—locked in place as the wind picked up on the rooftop. I could only stare, the anticipation, desperation… I felt it all as I waited for something to happen. But nothing had yet, they were still in place. Why weren't they doing anything? Killian's expression was filled with pain but otherwise, they weren't even moving. I wrapped the cloak around me wanting some sort of comfort.

Fear appeared next to them, a dark murderous intent lit up his eyes. He roared and I screamed, "NO!" I was so desperate I was running toward him, but I could only watch as he ripped their hands apart. The mass of power scattered above them—leaving as two.

CHAPTER TWENTY

Kilian was thrown back, landing at the end of the rooftop—almost going over the edge. He wasn't moving. Grim stumbled before bending over, gripping his knees. His eyeless sockets raised to meet Fear. Darkness spiraled out of control around him. I was just as angry. I was so sick of Fear. A terrifying scream erupted from Grim.

And I was so busy watching them, that I never noticed Molly behind me. Not until she kicked the back of my legs, knocking me to my knees. I hissed. Molly was a dead girl—little but strong with the power Fear had given her. That made her hard to deal with, especially since she had already recovered from my attack. I turned quickly and stumbled back onto my feet. I wanted distance in case she wanted to hit me again, but she faded instead and reappeared behind me. She giggled. I turned around to face her just as she started hopping around me in a circle. There was something in her hand… black powder? Whatever it was, she was forming a circle with it around me. I knew it wasn't good for me.

314

I tried to run out of the circle, but I bounced off some invincible barrier. It wouldn't let me pass over. I couldn't mask my worry in time; she saw my fear and grinned.

"Done!" Molly chirped to Fear who was blocking attacks from Grim with his tail.

"Good," he told her, laughing in Grim's face. "Now, kill Killian." I finally noticed the charred demon standing at the edge of the rooftop, awaiting orders. And when Fear finally gave him one, he nodded and stalked toward Killian.

Killian was only now starting to come to. He slowly picked himself up. The charred demon started running. "Ryan!" I yelled, but that wasn't Ryan right now. "Killian!" He lifted his head up and saw the charred demon coming at him. He cursed under his breath and jumped to his feet. Grim appeared in between them, and his sword sliced through the demon's neck. He cried out from the pain, but he was healing just as quickly as he screamed. Fear jumped after Grim and once again the two of them were in the air colliding. Grim split his scythe into two swords and tossed one down to Killian. He caught it just as the charred demon attacked.

Ryan had no weapon, but his claws were dangerous and similar to Fear's. Killian barely moved his head back in time to avoid the claws. Just as he avoided them, he ran the sword into the charred demon's shoulder. The charred demon hissed and it

315

filled my chest with unease. The charred demon was Ryan—I wanted to save him, not hurt him. But nothing seemed to phase the demon, he gripped the sword's blade and pulled it from his shoulder, tossing it to the ground. Killian punched him in the face and threw him to the ground before he got the chance to make a move first.

"Face your future, Grim, the Vessel is in place and Killian will die here tonight," Fear told Grim. The way they bounced back and forth, swords colliding, it was too hard to keep up with.

"You ignorant demon," Grim screamed.

"I will have you, Grim. We will merge." Fear sounded delirious as he spoke.

"What you are trying to do is impossible! You're already merged with an entity," Grim tried to tell him, but there was no reasoning when it came to Fear.

"Why do you think I have the Vessel bound? The spell that has her trapped will channel her power to make sure that the merge happens." Fear was a frightening monster already, but when he spoke of his plans, there was a certain ugliness to him that made my skin crawl. "Too bad for Melanie, though… all that channeling is sure to kill her, but don't worry, when she dies, she will belong to us." His words frightened me and a sudden pit of doom hit my stomach.

"I can't wait to send you into the flames," Grim growled.

316

"What you want will never happen!"

"It already has. Together, you, Fear, and I—along with the Vessel, will have immeasurable power. Even more so than Satan." He wanted to overthrow the Devil? Who after that, God? His eyes were warped with greed and power; his thirst could never be replenished because there would always be something more that he would want. And someone as sick and twisted as him should never be allowed to have any more power.

For some strange reason, I looked over to Molly and there a certain haunted, sadness in her expression as she watched Killian and the charred demon. They were rolling around, throwing punches, and the charred demon was constantly trying to sink his claws into Killian. But whatever that look had been, it faded into a glare when she saw me staring. She placed her arms across her chest and stood outside the circle in front of me. "He's doomed to die here tonight," she told me. I could only glare back at her. "So will you."

I ignored her and put my focus on what was important. The charred demon managed to roll himself on top of Killian. His claws extended and slashed across his face, Killian screamed. I saw the horrible markings that soon covered his face in blood. The charred demon did the same to Killian's chest. I was holding my own chest as Killian gritted his teeth, blood dripping into his mouth. Killian managed to throw a punch and pushed the demon away. He was stumbling to get to his feet, blood covered his eyes and chest. The charred demon moved behind him and sunk his claws into Killian's back. He still tried to stand, but I saw the fade in his eyes; the flicker that scared me. My heart was sinking.

Killian was losing his will to fight. Something was missing in his eyes, that strength and will to go on. He was losing… no, maybe he thought he had already lost when they missed the chance to merge again. "Killian!" I screamed at him but instead of looking at me, his blood covered face dropped in defeat. My stomach dropped—my chest heaved. The tears were unrelenting as my heart screamed at him for giving in.

His shoulders were slumped as he turned toward the charred demon. He threw a punch—very poorly, without any real effort. The kind that lacked any of his true strength. The charred demon gripped him by the throat. I watched the horrible reality play out in slow motion.

"Grim!" I was yelling for a miracle; a miracle I knew wouldn't happen. Grim looked and we both watched as the charred demon stuck his hand into Killian's chest. Killian's eyes were wide and contorted with agony. He dropped to the ground when the demon pulled his hand out.

I didn't even realize I was on my knees. And I wasn't processing my crying or the pain in my chest correctly. I was just thinking that he was going to be okay. I watched him survive an attack like that before. But Grim was caught off guard as well. Fear took the opportunity while he was staring at Killian to slice open his chest. His essence was pouring out, floating around him. Grim landed on the rooftop as Fear followed him down. Grim was looking at Killian and that scared me more than anything. "Now!" Fear yelled to Molly.

Grim snapped his head around to where me and Molly were. A light similar to the one Fear had used to split Grim and Killian surrounded me. And I realized my horror as my body was lifted. We were too late… My hands were forced and bound above me by a force that couldn't be seen. My body felt like it was breaking as it was forced to arch in the middle, leaving me in an awkward position.

I could no longer see anything beyond the light that bound me and soon… I felt the spell pulling at me—trying to reach my power. Something that was *mine.* But I couldn't do anything…

My last few thoughts were crystal clear before my mind was taken in with the spell. I hoped—prayed Fear was wrong and my powers weren't enough to let him merge with Grim. *It won't work, it won't work*, I chanted over and over. I was praying not for my life or Killian's because I was afraid it was already too late for us. The one I was hoping to save was Grim. For if Fear's planned worked… I couldn't even allow myself to think like that. To think of Grim becoming a monster.

319

My eyes turned white and so did my mind... the power began to leave my body.

I was in darkness, but I had been here before. I looked down and saw that I was still wearing Grim's cloak to hide my naked flesh underneath. I crumbled to my knees and brought the cloak to my face and inhaled. It smelled of Grim—Killian. Powerful, enchanting... the scent of the one I loved that could never be whole and now, I couldn't be saved... Ryan couldn't be saved. I cried into the cloak.

Was this me dying? I must be... so, this was what it felt like to die? But this wasn't really death, was it? This was something much worse. What if I was stuck in this darkness forever... always alone. No, I belonged to Fear. When would he come for me? Would he even have any use of me if he already had the power?

He would still torture me. Which had to be okay... because I deserved this much, right? Ryan died and became something terrible because of me. Killian and Grim were broken because of me... now Killian was... Grim was...

I screamed in the darkness. Then she appeared again wearing the same white dress. Her face was still concealed by the darkness. I no longer cried and stood up. "Why are you here?" I sounded angry and I was. She never told me anything.

"Figured it out yet, Melanie Rose?" she asked calmly.

My anger amplified. "No, everything's over. We lost and I'm to blame."

"So, you give up before you even know the truth about yourself?" Her tone was clipped. She crossed her arms. "Killian's life fades to nothing. Grim fights alone, but even an entity will crumble when he thinks a part of himself is dead! And the person he treasures above all else is being drained of her power... her life. What does he have to hold on to? He will fall in despair and within that weakness, he will be forced to merge. Killian: Dead. You: Dead. Grim: No longer himself."

"No!" The word ripped from my chest. I couldn't let that happen, not when the thought alone was breaking me into pieces.

"Only you can save you all."

"How?"

"Think of Humpty Dumpty... he has to be put back together again and only you can do that," she answered. I wasn't feeling very encouraged... the king's horsemen and men couldn't put him back together again, could they? So, how could I help Grim and Killian?

"How do I do that?"

"Who are you?" And wasn't that what she always asked.

"Melanie freaking Rose!" I snapped. "Stop asking."

A bright light shined between us, beautiful and golden, until it engulfed us both. I couldn't open my eyes until the light was gone. Then it made me remember Prince Cadence's words.

"Light," I whispered, echoing my thoughts out loud. "I'm light," I told her.

"Do you know now?" she asked and when I looked up, her face was completely visible and suddenly everything became clear.

I simply looked at her.

Me: My power. My reflection. The me that was kept hidden.

"I know what to do."

Myself nodded and smiled.

CHAPTER TWENTY-ONE

I opened my eyes to see Grim on his knees before Fear. His essence was non-existent. His blue light that flowed around him was completely snuffed out. He no longer cared. He didn't realize the fight wasn't over. I jerked my wrists against the invisible barrier that had me bound. My light was still leaving my body, but I was determined to stop it. I started fighting back—golden lights started pouring out of my entire body, fighting against the light that bound me. Whatever Fear had done to me, I watched it crumble and break around me. Molly's eyes were wide with shock. My feet hit the ground as I glared at Fear.

Grim turned toward me and just like that, his essence pooled back to life around him and through his sockets and bones. "Melanie." His voice was full of hope.

"What the hell is this?" Fear looked completely thrown off, confused.

"Since you don't know or realize." I walked forward,

cooling my expression. "I wanted to let you know I'm not the Vessel."

He shook his head, looking at me like the words I spat out were ludicrous. "You are," he assured me, but he was wrong.

So wrong.

They all had been wrong.

I grinned and tilted my head. "No," I paused. "I'm not." I stopped walking.

He didn't seem afraid, on the contrary, he looked annoyed. "Molly!" He flicked his wrist at me. "Restrain her, I need that power!" he ordered. Grim opened his hand and his sword—the one he gave to Killian and the other that lay beside him—went back together and formed his scythe. He moved it around in his hand before he swung at Fear, but not before Fear jumped away.

Molly ran at me, but I extended my palm out and she stopped. It was good that she knew to be hesitant. The light flew from my fingers and palm to hit her. The light wrapped around her and bound her arms and legs. The only thing she could do was fall to the ground and try to wiggle free.

"A human shouldn't be capable of what you're doing," Fear studied me, suddenly wary. He no longer focused on Grim. His eyes fell over me with rage yet interest.

"I will tell you." There was a fire in my chest. I knew

324

what I needed to do—or more like it was a sixth sense telling me. I brought my hand up and stuck it inside my chest—it went in like I was made of water. I started pulling it back out and in my hand was a golden rod that moved out of my chest. Once it was completely out of me, Fear's mouth fell open.

It was a golden scythe. *My scythe.* Identical to Grim's, only smaller. It shined bright with its golden color. "I'm Light," I told him and lifted my scythe in the air. "Grim's Light." And I said the words with pride.

Grim's cloak I wore began to change colors. The black turned to gold. The hood moved on its own and placed itself onto my head, covering most of my face and hair. It wasn't just the cloak that was glowing, my whole body was. My hair was more like a light instead of color, golden and bright. I knew without a doubt how I must look: regal and *powerful.*

I flashed my teeth before moving at an insane rate toward Fear. He moved into position as I went after him. I let the scythe slip further down my hand as I moved gracefully; something I could never do before. I placed both hands on the scythe—and it hummed against them as I lifted it over my head. I jumped.

Fear barely blocked my attack—he was still thrown off by everything that happened. I landed back on my feet, and Grim stepped in my place. They collided over and over in a matter of seconds. "What are you doing? Attack her!" I realized Fear was yelling at the charred demon. The charred demon was staring at me—he looked bewildered. Something was confusing him. I took it as my chance.

I ran in his direction, pointing my scythe at him. The light flew from the tip and hit him in the chest. He roared, but it slowly became a scream as he shifted back into the Ryan that I knew and loved. He fell on his chest, unconscious, but I still restrained him with the same power I used on Molly.

I turned back to Grim. He was back at full strength so I could focus on Killian. I needed to make sure he was okay, but he was lying in a puddle of his own blood. "Killian!"

"I'll kill you!" Fear screamed, stepping in front of me. I jumped back as Grim blocked the attack from hitting me. I moved to the side and went after Fear. He already knew to block my attack, but I swung my body around and kicked him hard. He staggered backward. My mind was telling me to hurry. Killian's life was on the line. He lay at death's doors.

But Fear must have sensed that as well because his eyes roamed to Killian. He faded, but we knew where he was headed. Grim was already standing over Killian when Fear attacked. He pushed him back. "Killian, get up!" I was desperate. His eyes fluttered, there was life rising and falling in his chest. That was all I needed to see.

My impatience with Fear grew. I needed him gone. I had

my own Humpty Dumpty to put back together. I gritted my teeth, and I went after him. "Grim!" He looked at me, but I was already throwing my scythe in the air. Somehow, he knew, the same way I did because he tossed his in the air with mine. They sought out Fear. He panicked and jumped, avoiding mine, but he had no time to avoid Grim's. It struck him in the chest. Grim was already in front of him, pushing the blade in deeper.

Fear roared in agony as Grim dug the scythe into his flesh deeper, but there was anger in his eyes. "You can't," he tested Grim. Grim ignored him and that was when I saw the fear fall over his face. "You dare!"

"Your death is upon you," Grim went into Reaper mode as he spoke. "Soon, but not tonight." He pulled the scythe out. And that was the cruelest thing, that we had no choice but to let him live. Blood oozed from Fear's chest. He tipped his top lip up into a snarl before he faded and reappeared next to Molly. He broke the bind I had over her. She stood quickly. He turned toward Ryan next, but I stepped in to block his way. "No," I warned him, guarding Ryan who lay unconscious behind me. And then Grim was in front of me, blocking him as well. Fear snarled but it quickly became a smile.

"I worry not. The boy will come to me on his own." And with words that left me afraid, he faded with Molly.

As soon as he left, I hurried to Killian. I fell on my knees

327

and picked up his head to place it in my lap. I smacked his face. "Killian!" Nothing. I pressed my hand into his chest. He was alive. His chest moved with his breathing and his heartbeat but barely. "Killian, you have to get up!" Grim was a statue next to me, too afraid to move. I saw movement underneath his eyelids. "You don't have much time, hurry and get up so we can finish the merge," I ordered him. His eyes finally fluttered opened.

I was covered in his blood and so was he. His eyes even had blood in them. "It's too late," he muttered, coughing as he spoke. "Missed... our chance."

I took a deep breath, telling myself to stay calm despite the panic I was feeling. "You're wrong," I said gently. "I can put you guys together again."

He looked at me. "So..rry." His eyes closed back. I smacked him on the shoulder. I held tears back.

"Don't you dare," I warned him. "Not after all of this. You need to freaking stop getting hurt like this, it's starting to piss me off!" Instead of crying, I fueled my anger.

"Love, I think yelling at him isn't going to work." Grim placed his hand on my shoulder. I looked up at him. He had never called me that before, only Killian had.

Now I couldn't hold the tears anymore. "Please, I haven't even had a chance to tell you anything!" I was sobbing loud and ugly. "Killian, if you care for me at all—if you want to be with me then you have to get up and do the merge," I told him again.

He reopened his eyes and looked to Grim. Grim extended his hand down to him and said, "Time to stop milking it... Besides, if you die, I'll never be whole."

I wiped my eyes and smiled when Killian started to lift his head. "I was only resting," he grunted in pain. It took him a minute to raise up. He winced in the process and bit his lip to fight the pain.

"Yeah, yeah," Grim muttered. He finally took Grim's hand and helped him to his feet. My scythe started to brighten on the ground next to me before it flew in the air above them. Grim's scythe wiggled in his hand until he finally let it go so that it could join mine. They latched together in the air—becoming one.

Darkness spread from our scythes and fell over Killian and Grim. I stepped back as the darkness engulfed them. The wind was crazy. I held my breath and waited. I couldn't see anything so I had no idea what was happening in the darkness until it slowly faded...

Killian was alone, smiling. And I knew what that meant. They were one again. I ran to him. The cloak I wore turned back to normal as I collided with his chest. He laughed—deep and husky as he scooped me up in his arms. His laugh vibrated against my cheek as I melted into his chest. Our scythes disappeared in the air as he spun me around. He had me laughing.

329

I felt happy and alive. He planted my feet back on the rooftop and grinned, cupping my cheeks with his palm. "What are you?" He looked star-struck as he gazed into my eyes, and there was something beyond precious about him when he didn't hold himself back in front of me.

I placed my hands over his while they were still on my face and leaned up. "I'm yours." And I was slightly embarrassed when I said it so I stole his lips to hide it. I poured my heart and soul into that one kiss. So did he. He brought me to life with every small touch, like fireworks along my skin every time he touched me. His caress was gentle, sweet against my mouth. We finally parted our lips and I was still smiling. "My very existence was made for you—to be with you. I am Light, *your* light."

Only his face wasn't full of happiness like mine. "That's not possible." His voice was a whisper.

My smile faded. "Is it," I assured him. "You're my eternity, and I am yours."

He moved away from me, even turning around. I touched his back, afraid. "I'm telling you that's not possible."

"It's the truth," I told him. "You saw it yourself." I tugged at his arm.

He turned back around, grief covered his handsome face. "I didn't have to see what I've already known from the moment I first saw you. I have always been taken in by you, Melanie Rose.

Light or not. Fate, destiny, or none—I would have still fallen in love with you." His confession had a sweet, warmth spreading throughout my chest. I moved into him. When he hugged me, I wrapped my arms around him.

But I wasn't an idiot. I knew something was wrong. "I love you." He placed a kiss on the top of my head and squeezed me tighter, inhaling, taking every part of me in.

I let go of him and met his haunted expression. "Melanie, I see your death in the future. I've seen it since the first time I saw you. That's why I know there is no eternity for us." My thoughts of forever. My life with Grim completely shattered. I felt my lip tremble and eyes water but forced myself not to cry.

"I see." So much emotion in two words.

"You live as a human… and you die as one." I hated the truth he kept telling me.

"Then you won't love me despite that?"

He grabbed my hands, took them to his mouth, and kissed them. He met my eyes. "I will love you no matter what," he promised.

I blinked and the tears finally spilled. That was enough. "Even though I can't give you an eternity?"

He pulled me closer—but we were as close as close could get. "You gave me something I never dreamed I would experience. Love. You will be my eternity regardless," he whispered softly. "I will cherish you over and over again, whether it be by spirit or body."

His words send a shiver of pure unmasked love over my skin. "Then, 'til death do us part?"

"And my eternity after." He smashed his mouth down over mine. In that moment, I was lost to him, and maybe it will always be that way.

And that was perfectly okay.

In his arms, I would hide from my troubles because once our kiss ended, reality would come rushing back.

I couldn't be this happy when Ryan was unconscious, bound by my own power. I would protect him from Fear.

No, I would save him, and I would save myself.

… and Killian would protect us all.

CHAPTER TWENTY-TWO

__Angel Sanctuary__

Faye rested her head on the side of the seeing glass as she watched the happenings of the human world. She closed her eyes and sighed. Guilt was a horrible thing for an angel to feel— actually, they never experienced that emotion because they didn't do things they weren't supposed to like Faye had.

Gabriel's footsteps were silent, but she knew he was behind her. She lifted her head up and turned around. "Do you understand what it is you've done now?" His words were meant to scold her, remind her of the mistake she had made. One mistake that she had thought had been a no biggie when she had done it. But it was a big deal.

Faye had altered the fate of three people nine years ago. Now one was dead and the other two met before they were supposed to. How did it happen?

Fear had mistaken Melanie Rose for something that didn't

333

even exist. The Vessel was a lie created by angels one night to lead demons on a desperate search for something that never even existed. Of course, most demons lost interest over time and a lot of them even forgot about it… or maybe they were smart enough to know it never existed in the first place, but some were too eager, too desperate for power.

Fear was one of them. And because he was an entity— immortal and already more powerful than any demon, that made him dangerous. But he was chasing after something that didn't exist.

Until he found something else.

Something so much more valuable.

And Faye had been gazing into the seeing glass—like she had just been doing—when Fear found Melanie and marked her. She was outraged at first—she raised from her chair and ran to the door then she stopped. And that was when Faye made the wrong choice.

She turned around and watched as Ryan Jones—the boy that was now dead—reach out and touch the mark. Two marks by Fear. Two people she could have saved. Instead, she reached into the pool of water and plucked out the memory of it happening. No one would know what happened to Melanie. From then on, she made sure she was the one that kept watch over her so that no other angel would notice what was happening to her.

It was horrible, she knew. The things Melanie went through—none of it should have happened. But Faye wasn't a bad angel. She was just desperate for Melanie and Grim to meet, even if that meant they met before it was the right time.

So, she waited nine years before she finally sent the message to Grim. Melanie would be safe until her eighteenth birthday. Fear couldn't take her to the Underworld until then. And obviously, Faye didn't want him meeting her when she was still a child, it would mess up the entire purpose!

But little did she know things would turn out so disastrous.

Melanie had awakened too soon, not even knowing exactly what she was, and as she was, her body wouldn't last if she continued to use the power. And now that Melanie is known by the Underworld, it was too dangerous.

Grim hadn't even figured out what she was. All that work to get the two of them together was a mistake. She knew that now. And the mistake was made all because she wanted to see the entity happier sooner. She had watched over Grim for a long time. She knew the lonely soul long before he merged with Killian. He didn't know her—he had met her before but didn't even know her name. When she heard of God's plans for him, she had gone to tell him.

But the wait for Melanie to come into this world would be

a long one. And after all the time spent—all the centuries waiting, Faye made the wrong choice.

Now all that was left to do was fix what could be. "I understand," Faye replied to him.

He tilted his head at her—the heartbreak was there in his eyes as well, but he concealed it when he spoke again, "Everything must go back to the way it was—as much as it can be." Faye turned back toward the seeing glass. Melanie and Grim had yet to come back to the human world.

She knew that she would be seeing them in time, though, but it wasn't the way she had hoped. She wouldn't be bringing the words they wanted to hear.

MICHELLE GROSS

'TIL

DEATH

WE MEET AGAIN

Available Now!

AUTHOR'S NOTE

I hoped you enjoyed the second book in the series! If you would leave a review on Amazon and Goodreads it would be extremely helpful. I love reading what y'all think!

You can find me on Facebook:

https://www.facebook.com/michellegrossauthor/

Twitter: @AuthorMichelleG

Instagram: michellegrossmg

Join my Mailing List here:

http://eepurl.com/cRXrUX

Made in United States
Troutdale, OR
08/13/2023

12032028R00189